NADIA'S SWEET TEA

OF 2 GIRLS, 2 CATS

By Laura Beth

Many Happy Adventures!

L. Beth

ISBN: 10-1499539878
ISBN-13: 978-1499539875

First printing

This book is dedicated to my three lovely nieces: Natalie, Julee and Leah.
They are my inspiration behind this fun, fictional, family saga.

Don't forget to read Laura Beth's previous books...

"2 Girls, 2 Cats: A Magical Mystery"

"LACEY And Her Tigers"

"JILLIE And Her Sassy Cat"

"Graduation Summer"

As Laura Beth says, "The Magic and The Mystery Never End!"

Laura Beth would love for you to visit her website @ www.2girls2cats.com

First and foremost, I want to thank God and my family and my friends.

And, I want to say thank-you to my READERS for giving my books their time.

Table of Contents

Preface

When twenty-year-old Lacey moves into her grandparents' home, she notices lights in her great-grandparents' old farmhouse going on and off during the wee hours of the night. Lacey invites her thirteen-year-old cousin, Jillie, to visit and help her check out the old house that is supposedly empty.

What Lacey and Jillie discover changes their lives forever. The cousins discover a beautiful mother cat and two unique kittens that are magical and are there to protect them. Felines, Miss Virginia, Tye and Tess are all apart of this land's magical and mysterious destiny. These beautiful cats become the most ferocious beasts when anyone or anything threatens their Lacey or Jillie. As Lacey and Jillie explore, they find hidden stairs that take them down to underground tunnels. These tunnels lead them under their great-grandfather's barn and down into the pasture to a very old and large oak tree. At this oak tree are two time portals. One takes them three hundred years into the past and one takes them three hundred years into the future.

The most amazing discovery the two girls make is finding their Uncle Jake, who has been missing for ten years. Meeting their uncle, and so many others from the past, the present and in the future, they all realize how intricately woven the web of this magical and mysterious land is and how it continues to weave its promise for the people chosen to live and thrive.

As these two girls grow together, discovering more than they want to handle, they find out it's the birth of their tiny cousin, Nadia, that initiated their magical and mysterious destiny determined many centuries before their time. Lacey's destiny leads her to achieve an environmental law degree and endure many trying encounters. Lacey also adopts one of the kittens that she and Jillie named Tye. An adorable, grey feline with a white star on his forehead, Tye is there to protect Lacey. When Lacey discovers he can change to a ferocious tiger, she realizes she holds so much responsibility and now she has to hide her beast. When she meets a handsome warrior, Tame Tiger, three hundred years before her time, Lacey's life becomes complicated. She not only has to convince her sweetheart, Blake, that this man is just a farmhand, but she also realizes she has another beast to control. Lacey is thrown many unexpected surprises. And through it all, she finds the most unusual pull to the people who walked this land many centuries ago, her great-grandfather's farm and her one true love sent by destiny.

Jillie jumps at the chance to hang out with her cool, older cousin to return to the farm. Jillie had spent many hours with her grandparents and great-aunt on the farm during her toddler and younger years. As Lacey adopts Tye, Jillie adopts the fluffy, white kitten with the grey tipped tail. Tess, as her brother Tye, is not only a cute, cuddly kitten; she becomes a ferocious black panther whenever Jillie is in harm's way. Having a very sassy and protective cat causes Jillie to have more hurdles to clear than the average teenager going through high school. Jillie's path also crosses with many others that are all a part of this woven destiny, including Miguel, her future love. Jillie's high school years are full of magic and mystery that lead her to fulfill her destiny, as a great healer, determined many years in the past.

Once Lacey graduates from college and Jillie graduates from high school, the two cousins spend the summer on the farm. Lacey, has now secured the farm from being sold off and is determined to bring life back to this special land. Jillie just wants to help her older cousin any way she can. The adventures cause them to engage their brothers and cousins to learn the unbelievable secrets of their great-grandparents' land. They all work together to get the farm in operation once again. With more surprising encounters from the past and the future, the destiny's web continues to be woven. They meet Sir Edward Miller, who secures the land that will one day be sold to the girls' great-grandfather.

Their little cousin, Nadia, grows up coming to the farm for many family events. The magical mother cat and her kittens love Nadia and Nadia loves them. Everyone notices the command this toddler has over these felines. When Nadia is blessed with her own protector, at such a young age, Lacey and Jillie soon realize the mother cat knew Nadia would be facing a life threatening illness.

As Nadia battles her illness, Lacey and Jillie meet young Lope, who comes from the future. He takes them to his home, three hundred years in the future, for one tiny pill that he knows will cure this little girl who is an important link to his own life. On this brief visit to the future, what Lacey and Jillie see guides them to accept their destiny and their ever surprising lives.

Nadia is blessed with a wonderful family and a very intellectual mind. Unlike her two older cousins, she welcomes her destiny that brings her the most joy and the most unique friends into her life.

CHARACTER WHO'S WHO

- **Anna Grace** – Jillie's and Miguel's first daughter
- ***Aunt Daisy*** – Daughter of ***Tess and Tye*** **-** older sister of ***Teresa*** **-** She is in a nursing home with Ted and Teresa and suffers from dementia. She explored the secrets of the land, but never told anyone. She is the great-aunt to ***Lacey, Jillie and Nadia***.
- **Beautiful Butterfly** – Betrothed to Tame Tiger until she was captured by the English soldiers and shipped back to England.
- **Beautiful Light** – Spouse of Jake - mother to Son of Jake 1 and Son of Jake 2 aka Oneson and Twoson
- **Betsy, Cindy and Debbie** – Middle school bullies
- **Blake** – Long time boyfriend of Lacey - He was captured alongside of Beautiful Butterfly and shipped to England.
- **Blake Fierce** – Second son of Lacey and Will
- **Brad** – A school bully, who becomes one of Jillie's best friends and Courtney's sweetheart.
- **Brave Wolf** aka Skip Swiftbare – Miguel's father
- **Calm Water aka Smitty** – Medicine man in the Appalachian Mountains - He taught Jillie her skills of the natural healing from Mother Earth.
- **Challenging Wolf** – Spouse of Fierce Tiger - mother of Tame Tiger
- **Courtney** – Jillie's best friend - sweetheart to Brad
- **Crazy Horse** – Best friend of Tame Tiger
- **Dan** – TV reporter Jillie befriended and knows her secret
- **Ellie Sondeerun** – Older rider of Nadia's riding troop - grandmother of Miguel Lope Letour
- **Fierce Tiger** – Chief of the tribe Jake befriends three hundred years in the past
- **Frederick Barron** – spouse of Lope's cousin, Anna
- **Ginger** – Spouse of Wayne - mother of ***Lacey and Gregory***.
- **Gloria Morning** – Nadia's sixth grade homeroom teacher
- ***Gregory, Aiken, Andrew, Chase, Adam and Luke*** – grandchildren of Ted and ***Teresa*** **-** brothers and/or cousins to ***Lacey, Jillie and Nadia***
- **Hank** – Lucy's spouse
- **Healing Heart** – Medicine Man for Chief Fierce Tiger
- **Jake Sondeerun** – Grandfather of Miguel Lope Letour - descendant of Son of Running Deer and Running Antelope
- ***Jeremy*** – Son of Ted and ***Teresa*** **-** spouse of Stacey - father of ***Adam, Luke and Nadia***
- ***Jillie*** – Lacey's cousin, who is seven years younger - She is a granddaughter of Ted and **Teresa** and daughter of ***Karla*** and Kent. She is destined to save this farmland.
- **Kai** – Black/white cat aka Black Wolf

- ***Karla*** – Daughter of Ted and ***Teresa*** - spouse of Kent - mother of ***Aiken*** and ***Jillie***
- **Kent** – Spouse of Karla - father to Aiken and ***Jillie***
- ***Lacey*** – Great-granddaughter of ***Tye and Tess***, who moves into her grandparents' home place that is on the farm of her great-grandparents. She is a granddaughter of Ted and **Teresa** and daughter of **Wayne** and Ginger. She is destined to save this farmland. Secretly marries Tame Tiger aka Will Hayes.
- **Lexi Wheatmore** – Jillie's college roommate and fellow vet.
- **Lope** – Descendent of Nadia three hundred years in the future (Don't get confused with Running Antelope or Miguel Lope.)
- **Lucky Lad** – Lucy's adopted, search and rescue dog.
- ***Lucy*** – Daughter of Ted and ***Teresa*** - aunt to **Lacey, Jillie and Nadia** - mother to ***Andrew*** – She is the dear friend of Brave Wolf and Dancing Star and Mrs. Leigh.
- **Miguel Lope Letour** – Grandson to Mr. and Mrs. Sondeerun.
- **Miguel Swiftbare** – Son of Brave Wolf and Dancing Star. ***Jillie***'s sweetheart.
- **Miss Flint** – Nadia's third grade teacher.
- **Mrs. Ellie Sondeerun** – Grandmother of Miguel Lope Letour.
- **Mrs. Joann Darling** – Admin. Assistant
- **Mrs. Petree** – Nadia's fourth grade teacher.
- **Mrs. Swiftbare** aka Dancing Star – Miguel's mother - instructor at ASU
- ***Nadia*** – Lacey's youngest cousin, who is twenty years younger. Granddaughter of Ted and ***Teresa*** - daughter of ***Jeremy*** and Stacey. She is destined to save this farmland.
- ***Running Antelope aka Lope*** aka Chief Running Antelope's Wolf– Son of Son of Running Deer, who becomes ***Jillie***'s best friend and sweetheart. He runs away when his village is captured and is thought to be dead. He first returns to guide his people to the mountains and returns one last time after he is named chief.
- **Running Wolf** – Chief of the Appalachian Wolf Tribe in the late 1700's and Running Antelope's father-in-law.
- **Sally** – Daughter of Ted and ***Teresa*** - aunt to **Lacey, Jillie and Nadia** - mother to ***Chase.***
- **Shadow of the Night** aka Shadow - Tame Tiger's horse
- **Shining Star** – Susan's horse
- **Shining Star** - Chief Running Antelope Wolf's wife
- **Sir Edward Miller** – English soldier from three hundred years ago - It is one of his descendants who sells some of the land to Tye and Tess.
- **Son of Running Deer** – Uncle Jake's best friend he met as a child when he discovered the time portal
- **Stacey** – Spouse of Jeremy - mother to ***Adam, Luke and Nadia***
- **Steve** – Sally's Spouse; father of Stevie and ***Chase***
- **Storm Cloud** – A grey stallion gifted to Blake by Tame Tiger (Will) and the sire of Little Girl and Baby Boy.
- **Susan Scout** – Nadia's best friend beginning 6th grade - daughter of Lucille and Earl Scout.

- ***Tame Tiger aka Will*** **–** Son of Fierce Tiger - At one time, he was betrothed to Beautiful Butterfly. But now, he and ***Lacey*** are secretly married.
- **Tea** – An important part of Nadia's life that you will get to know in this book.
- **Ted** – Spouse of ***Teresa*** **-** He is in a nursing home with his wife and sister-in-law.
- ***Teresa*** – Daughter of ***Tye and Tess -*** sister to ***Daisy*** and ***Nash*** - grandmother to **Lacey, Jillie and Nadia** - She is in a nursing home.
- **Tess** – Virginia's female, fluffy white kitten with a grey tipped tail, born at the time of Nadia's birth. She is Jillie's protector and she turns into a ferocious black panther whenever she feels Jillie is threatened.
- **Tom Goodheart** – Veterinarian hired to run the barn and take care of the horses.
- **Tye** – Virginia's male grey kitten with white star on his forehead, born at the time of Nadia's birth, which will help protect the girls' destiny to save this farmland. He is Lacey's protector and he turns into a ferocious white tiger whenever Lacey is in danger.
- **TYE & TESS** – Great-grandparents to Lacey, Jillie and Nadia – parents to Daisy, Teresa and Nash
- ***Uncle Jake*** – **Lacey's, Jillie's and Nadia's uncle**, who has been missing for many years and living on this farmland three hundred years in the past. He discovered a time portal when he was only five-years-old. Even to his surprise, he is the 'gatekeeper' that linked the farm's families together. He is the son of Ted and ***Teresa*** and the twin of ***Jeremy***.
- **Vance Service** – Long time friend of family who lives in NYC and owns a famous jewelry boutique.
- **Veronica Flowers** – An eighth grade student
- **Virginia aka Miss Virginia** – A mysterious, female cat that is an important part of this farm's destiny. She lives on the farm in the past, in the present and in the future. She turns into a ferocious lioness whenever danger threatens her people.
- **Warrior Girl -** A dapple grey mare that belongs to Lacey. She is the dam of Little Girl, Baby Boy and Whispering Willow.
- ***Wayne*** – Son of Ted and ***Teresa*** - spouse of Ginger - father of ***Lacey and Gregory***
- ***Wayne Jake*** **–** Lacey's and Will's first son
- **Whispering Willow** – Offspring of Warrior Girl and Wolfriend gifted to Nadia.
- **Wise Owl** – Holy Man of the Appalachian mountain tribe in present time
- **Wolfriend** – Miguel's stallion
- **Walter Tripp** – documentary explorer and historian
- **Mr. Yellman** – Nadia's fifth grade teacher

Chapter 1: A Destiny Is Born

"Hey everyone, we have our new little one safe and snuggled with her mommy," Jeremy wrote in a group text to his brothers, sisters, nephews and nieces. "She was born at 12 noon and she is just a quiet, little mouse. She seems like a wise, old soul. Oh and BTW, we're calling her Nadia."

Within seconds texts were coming back from everyone with congratulations and well wishes. And in another time and in a special place, something truly wonderful had also begun the second that Nadia was born.

***

Jake was pacing near the portal opening waiting for something special to happen. If it was truly going to happen, then all the things he had been told were actually true. His best friend, Son of Running Deer, paced right behind him and kept on walking on the back of Jake's heels.

"Look!" Son of Running Deer screamed in his native tongue.

Jake stopped and watched as the mystical portal window wavered in a wonderful pattern with all the colors of the rainbow shining through radiating beams of light into the night. A ferocious lion leapt from the portal entrance, as she magically appeared.

"Miss Virginia, it's happened, it's happened. The little one has arrived and our time has just begun. I have to go back over and see what all is happening. Lacey should be all settled into my parents' home by now. It's about time for you to have your little ones too, isn't it?" Jake said, as he patted this gentle giant's head and before his eyes she turned back into a beautiful, fluffy grey and white cat.

"I am going to run back to the village and let everyone know, she is here. Our land will be safe now and the destiny has come true," Son of Running Deer quickly said, as he rubbed Miss Virginia's head and smiled as she loudly purred. "I am off Jake, my brother."

Jake grinned and they gave one another a big bear hug. "I'm heading through the portal. I have to see what is going on over there." Jake looked around for Miss Virginia, who jumped in his arms and they were off to another time.

When Jake arrived at the big oak tree, he quickly opened the earthen, trap door. He let Miss Virginia jump down and then he followed behind her into the open room and headed through the tunnels that he traveled so often to check on the family he had left behind years ago. He was almost skipping because he was so excited. As he thought about his third niece being born, he felt sad for not being able to be apart of his brother's excitement. But, he knew he was where he was supposed to be and he loved his life and his family. He was going to hang out around the old farmhouse and help Miss Virginia find a wonderful place for her little ones to come into this world.

It was daytime, so he needed to use the tunnels to go all the way to the house. He decided he should send Miss Virginia ahead of him to make sure the coast was clear for him to enter the house through the hidden stairs.

"Okay Miss Virginia, go check the house out for me. I don't want to run into anyone who might be visiting the place today. You know how my uncle likes to come over and just hang out," Jake whispered, as if he could be heard from under the house.

Miss Virginia disappeared and Jake hung out in the open cellar-like area and peered over towards his old home place. He didn't see Lacey's car, so he figured she was out and about or at school. Miss Virginia returned and startled him out of his trance, as he stared at his parents' home.

Miss Virginia thought out that it was fine and she had already found the perfect spot for her little ones to hide and play. Off they went up the hidden stairs that led to the bedroom closet and then on up to the unfinished attic room.

When they emerged from the stairs, Miss Virginia scampered off and jumped up onto the corner, where she wanted to make their bed. She looked at Jake and meowed.

"Oh, great place Miss Virginia," Jake whispered. Jake went to work finding some old clothes and materials to fluff up a nice and comfortable bed for these special little felines.

"Okay Miss Virginia, here you go. Now, you just do your thing when you feel the time is right. I am going to walk through the house and see if there is some cat food left here from Aunt Daisy. We'll bring some of your favorite mush of course. Just in case, we should have some regular food around for your little ones." Jake left the unfinished room and headed through the large upstairs room and down the stairs to the main level of the old farmhouse.

Miss Virginia stayed back and went to work the magic she was so happy to do. She loved this land and would make sure it was safe for dear old Tye and his wonderful wife, Tess, who had loved her dearly.

As Jake quietly made his way through the house, he heard voices coming from the outside. Before he opened the large kitchen door which led to the outside porch, he stopped and listened for a moment. He realized that they were coming inside. He quickly left the kitchen and made his way back to the front of the house. He went into the front bedroom and then into the closet to the hidden stairs. He slowly and quietly made his way back up to the unfinished attic room, where he found Miss Virginia laying quietly in the bed he had put together just moments ago. Jake couldn't believe his eyes. There lay two tiny creatures hooked to their mother and suckling her milk. He slowly and ever so quietly walked over and smiled down upon his special feline friend and rubbed her head. Miss Virginia looked up and stared into Jake's eyes.

"It is time," she thought out and looked upon her newborn kittens.

Jake admired the tiny grey kitten and then saw the fluffy, white one with a grey tipped tail. "Beautiful." Jake whispered and touched each one with his right index finger, which was almost as big as these tiny creatures. "Okay, I guess this means you will be staying here for a bit?" Jake softly whispered to Miss Virginia.

Miss Virginia quietly meowed back to Jake, as she was aware she must keep her little ones a secret for now.

"I'll make sure to come back and forth to help you get your nourishment, so these two little ones grow big and strong."

Once Jake had enough time to admire these two new additions, he turned his attention to what was happening downstairs and moved back towards the hidden stairs. He turned to face Miss Virginia and smiled. "I'll be back later to check on you, when it is dark. I better get out of here for now."

Miss Virginia stared back, let Jake know she understood and that she would be just fine.

Jake smiled and quietly descended down the stairs

closing the hatch behind him. He made his way back to the downstairs closet and decided to go into the bedroom and see if he could tell who was in the house. He also didn't want anyone to cause any damage or steal something from his family's beloved home. He quietly walked over to the door and leaned up against it to listen for the voices. He heard them faintly, so he cracked the door and waited to hear them again.

"I am telling you dad, I see lights on over here at night sometimes. I just think it's weird," Lacey said to her dad, Jake's older brother.

"Well, I'll take a look around, but nothing looks out of place so far. I'll go check out the front bedroom and you go upstairs," Wayne said.

Jake moved quickly back to the closet and pulled the door closed and descended down the hidden stairs. He heard his brother come into the bedroom and then over to the closet. He heard his brother open the closet door for a brief second and then Jake heard the closet door shut.

"Nothing in this room here," Wayne yelled out, as he closed the bedroom door behind him and headed to the stairs that led to the big room and the unfinished attic room.

"Lace, you find anything?" Wayne yelled up to his daughter feeling too lazy to climb the steep steps.

"No, but I am not going into the attic room. It's spooky to me," Lacey yelled down and came to the top of the stairway. "Do you want to come up and look in there dad?"

"No, not really; there is no one here. I bet Uncle Nash has a light on a timer. Try and remember where you see the light and I bet we'll find a timer," Wayne said, as he walked around the front room looking at the lights and their plugs.

"It is not the same room dad," Lacey answered, as she came out of the staircase and locked up the door.

"That is why I think someone is here sometimes dad. I see different lights on or a flashlight moving through the house at night."

"Well, are you scared? Do you want to forget living next door?" Wayne asked.

"No, I am not scared. I'll keep an eye out and you can just drive over one night," Lacey replied and gave her dad the 'evil eye' look.

"Don't give me that look. If you say you see something, I believe you. I just don't see anything right now," Wayne said. "Let' go. I need to get home and help your mom with the yard."

"Have fun dad. Wish I could help, but I got my own yard now," Lacey said and smiled at her dad.

"Yeah you do. Get to work," Wayne said and hugged his daughter.

"I'll lock up here dad. I want to mess around and just have some fun looking this old stuff.

"Okay, just be sure and lock it up. I don't want Uncle Nash to get upset, but I know he loves you being next door to keep an eye on the place," Wayne said, as he headed back through the house to leave.

Lacey sat down and looked around the front room and then heard something.

"It's just me Lace," Wayne said, as he came back to see his daughter. "You know you should go visit your new little cousin, Nadia, one of these days,"

"Oh, I am. I'll go this weekend," Lacey replied and smiled at her dad, as he waved good-bye and left again.

Lacey sat back and scanned her great-grandparents' front living room. She wondered what was going to happen to this old place. She closed her eyes and tried to imagine what it was like to grow up here, but she was jolted out of her thoughts by a noise. She got up and hurried herself out of the house, locked the door and practically ran back to her home.

"I know, I'll go call Jillie and see if she wants to have some adventure with me," Lacey muttered to herself, as she hurried back into her house and went straight for the phone.

Jake watched Lacey as she ran into his parent's home and smiled. "One day, we'll meet I am sure," Jake whispered to himself and went back through the tunnels to his time to fetch some mush for Miss Virginia and her kittens. He would return tonight with his best friend. He needed to make sure this farm was kept in the family.

Chapter 2: The Magic Of Nadia

"Did you see that Stacey?" Jeremy asked. "Nadia just gave me the peace sign. I swear she did!"

"Oh Jeremy, she is just an infant. It was probably just a coincidence," Stacy replied, as she hurried around the kitchen making food for everyone. "You could help me you know. We have some hungry people here."

Jeremy couldn't take his eyes off of his little girl. He felt something extra special about her, but he could not put his hands on it. He held out his hand over to his new little bundle. Sure enough, she grabbed his finger and squeezed with all her might.

"Well, she sure is strong for such a tiny thing," Jeremy said, as he laughed and gently tugged on his finger with his daughter's death grip on it. "I think she is meant for great things."

"Well, of course, she is your daughter Jeremy. Every father thinks their daughters are meant for great things. She is probably some princess, switched at birth, to allow her to have a normal life," Stacey said, as she laughed looking at her husband smiling so proud.

"Well, if you're right, where is our daughter?" Jeremy asked alarmed.

"Jeremy, it's a joke. I was just joking. She is our daughter and she is a princess in our eyes," Stacey said, as she rolled her eyes and circled her finger around the side of her head.

"Oh okay. Yeah, I get it," Jeremy said, as he studied his daughter very carefully.

"I know you're something very special little girl, but only time will tell. Just please be a good little girl for daddy, okay? I cannot take a little devil child."

Nadia's little eyes twinkled, as she squirmed in her little bouncy seat. Jeremy studied his tiny daughter. Stacey smiled to herself, as she rushed around the kitchen preparing a Saturday lunch.

"Okay, what are my chores today?" Jeremy asked, as he continued to stare at his daughter.

"Well, you read my mind. I already made a list of things for you. The main thing is to take care of Luke of course. Adam has already gone off to practice with friends. You and Luke may want to go take a ride and pick Adam up from practice. That will give Luke something to do, so I can take care of Nadia's demands," Stacey replied, as she sat food down on the table for Luke, Jeremy and herself. She would feed Nadia in a bit since she seemed very content watching her dad as he was watching her.

Lunch was uninterrupted, as little Nadia was content hearing the sounds of her family talking over their lunch. Whenever she would hear Luke's voice, she would squirm, which Stacey and Jeremy both noticed.

The afternoon was more peaceful than it had been in many months. It seemed that once Nadia had arrived, everyone in the house fell into sync with one another and things were just easy going.

The next few years passed by with ease for Jeremy and his family. The boys were great big brothers and Jeremy found a way to work more from home. Nadia barely fussed and seemed to love her food. She never turned anything away and even loved eating from her grandfather's plate at the nursing home. Everyone noticed how she took to animals. When Lacey and Jillie came upon their mother cat, Miss Virginia and her kittens, everyone noticed how attached Nadia seemed to all three of them. Everyone knew where to find Nadia or the cats. When you found one, you found them all. Whatever Nadia would say, whether baby jibber jabber or her first words, the cats seemed to react to her voice. Jeremy constantly took pictures of his little girl surrounded by the three adoring cats at their family functions. One particular Thanksgiving, held at Lacey's, he even caught her pointing, as she talked with Miss Virginia, Tye and Tess. They seemed to be looking in the same direction she was pointing, as she pointed towards the pasture with her mitten covered hand.

"Nadia, what are you pointing for the kitty cats to see?" Jeremy asked his daughter.

Nadia was four-years-old and was talking up a storm, but sometimes she didn't make sense to anyone but the cats.

"Peoples down there daddy. See dem? The kitties see dem", Nadia answered, as she pointed into the pasture towards the old oak tree.

"Lacey, Lacey, come over here," Jeremy hollered for his niece, who was trying to put together a game of football with all the men of the family. She was doing this for Tame Tiger, who everyone knew as Will in this time.

Lacey came running and chuckled to see how bundled up little Nadia was with her tiny mittens that looked like little cats.

"What's up Uncle Jeremy?" Lacey asked, as she picked up Nadia and hugged her tight.

The cats all circled around them and meowed trying to tell Lacey that Uncle Jake, Lope and Son of Running Deer had come over to visit.

"Nadia keeps pointing towards the pasture and the cats all seem very interested and it's making me think she really sees something or someone," Jeremy said.

Lacey looked around hoping that she wouldn't see anyone and knew that Uncle Jake and some others must have appeared at the tree and Nadia had noticed, but it was so far away for anyone to really see. Lacey looked at Nadia, who was looking at her and her right eye twinkled, as she smiled up at her big cousin. Lacey smiled back and gave her a big hug.

"Oh Uncle Jeremy, she is just playing and imagining as all little kids do. She's just having fun. Sometimes, I think I see something run around the pasture too and it's just my imagination playing tricks on me," Lacey said, as she quickly thought of something to say.

"Yeah, I guess," Jeremy answered, as he stared out across the pasture.

"Come on; let's get this holiday game going before it gets too cold. Everyone is waiting. That will keep little Nadia occupied," Lacey said. "Here take your cute little bundle back." Lacey walked away rolling her eyes and thinking how careless of Uncle Jake and his troop. "I am going to tell Uncle Jake, he needs to be more careful," Lacey thought to herself and went to find Jillie and Will to tell them how Nadia is becoming very in tuned to their lives.

Nadia squirmed in her father's arms and wanted down to be near the cats. Jeremy placed her down and she took off with the three cats in tow behind her. Jeremy laughed and shook his head.

"My daughter is magical, I just know it," Jeremy said out loud to himself, which was overheard by his older brother, Wayne.

"I heard that. So, you think there is something magical or better I say strange about your daughter and those cats?" Wayne questioned.

"Yeah, there is something very odd, but it's a good odd," Jeremy replied.

"I feel it too with my own daughter, but she just tells me I am being ridiculous or she avoids my questions," Wayne added.

The two brothers exchanged stories how they

thought things with their daughters and the cats were strange, but so cute.

Kent listened from afar and finally moved over to his two brother-in-laws. He listened more to their stories and then interrupted Wayne.

"Excuse me, but can I interject something here?" Kent asked with a serious look on his face.

Wayne and Jeremy both looked at Kent waiting for him to blast them with a lecture or something.

"Jillie acts just as weird. And that cat of hers has my hunting dogs scared to death. She shows up in the yard and you have never seen two dogs cower down, but usually they go running for cover. It's disgusting. The better part of this story is that pretty, little cat comes up to me and wraps me around her little paw, just like my pretty, little daughter does to me. I swear that cat is more than just a cat."

"I hear ya," Jeremy answered.

"That is how I feel," Wayne added, as he scratched his head and looked around for his daughter, who was organizing the family football game.

Calls from the line up interrupted the three men's conversation. They dropped the subject and ran onto the playing field. The game did keep the cats and little Nadia occupied. Every so often, Nadia would run across the field and pounce on her dad when he was down. Of course, the cats followed right behind her and they all pounced all over Jeremy and anyone else who had been taken down mainly by Will. Everyone would stop and laugh at this new family ritual that would last for years to come.

Will caught everyone by surprise. He and Gregory made a great team. Gregory's cousins were knocked down or thrown around by Will. Little did they know, but they were playing with a very strong warrior from the past. Will was one of the best athletes of his time and this football game proved it. The women hollered and chuckled from the sidelines, as their men were thrown down or just fell down for safety. Ted and Teresa sat in their wheel chairs and loved seeing their children and grandchildren have so much fun. Teresa looked off in the distance and held back her tears of sadness. Her sister, Daisy, noticed and grabbed her hand.

"What are you doing that for, you old lady?" Teresa said, as she took her hand back.

"I see your sadness Teresa and I feel the same way. We'll never know what happened to him, but maybe he will return to us one day," Daisy said.

Teresa looked at her sister and started to yell at her. She was going to remind her that they had seen him. But she decided not to go there. She realized her sister had already forgotten, as they were sure they both would do. But, she had not. She knew her son was still very alive, but living many years before their time. She would have never believed it, but her wonderful granddaughters had taken her back in time. Daisy had been there many times herself, but now she didn't even remember her travels. Teresa kept her son's secret to keep him and their people safe.

Lacey happened to notice her grandmother's tears and came running over to her.

"Grandma, you okay?" Lacey asked, as she knelt down and rubbed her arm.

Teresa looked at her granddaughter and smiled, as tears rolled down her cheek. "I'm okay," she whispered. "Thank you for letting me know the truth Lacey. These are tears of joy knowing he is alive."

Lacey squeezed her grandmother's arm, hugged her tight and whispered into her ear opposite of her Great-Aunt Daisy. "He's watching from the farmhouse grandma. He and his friend are looking from the upstairs window. I'll turn you a bit and you just look up there and wave to him. He'll see you too." Lacey held back her own tears.

Teresa looked at Lacey and smiled. "Thank you," she mouthed, as Lacey turned her grandmother just enough so that she could look at the farmhouse.

For just a quick second, Jake opened the window and blew his mother a kiss. Teresa lifted her hand and did the same back to her son. That was all she needed and she asked Lacey to leave her this way. As Lacey was about to walk away, little Nadia ran up and jumped up in her grandmother's lap. She looked at her grandmother and asked her why she was crying. Teresa was shocked that this little thing noticed her quiet tears.

"Kitties, come here, come here. Grandma T is sad," Nadia yelled for the cats.

In seconds the cats were all there. All three cats began circling Teresa and Daisy rubbing up against their legs. Nadia hugged her grandmother and then turned around and sat back to watch the silly game. She giggled and this made Teresa laugh too. Daisy laughed too and both women turned all of their attention to Nadia. The cats took turns jumping into Daisy's lap, which made her so happy. She was an animal lover and the cats knew it.

Lacey got Jillie's attention and they both laughed at the scene. Lacey quickly told Jillie that their grandmother had been able to see Jake. Jillie smiled too and they both turned towards their Uncle Jake for a second and held up their hands to acknowledge him.

Kent noticed this and looked at the farmhouse, but Jake could not be seen now. He and Son of Running Deer were hiding back away from the window. Kent turned his attention back to the game in time for his son to knock him down.

"Boy, you are going to get it from me now," Kent yelled, as he got up and held his son down under his foot.

Karla yelled from the sidelines, "Kent, don't you hurt my boy!"

"Did you see what your boy just did to me?" Kent yelled back.

"You can take it," Karla yelled back and laughed.

Jeremy noticed his daughter with his mother and smiled. Then he noticed the cats all around his daughter, his mother and his aunt. He shook his head and ran over to Wayne and pointed. "See, look at that. Now look at those cats. It is as if they are guarding the three of them." Jeremy also got his wife to look over at their daughter. She just smiled back and kept on talking with her sister-in-laws.

"I know. I see how they act around all three girls, especially little Nadia. They watch her like tigers," Wayne said. "Hey Jeremy, you want to test something out?"

"What do you mean? What are we going to test?" Jeremy asked.

"Wait a minute, we're about to get hit," Wayne said and they both fell to the ground before Adam and Andrew could tackle them.

"Chickens," Adam yelled out and the boys jumped over them and went after Will together.

The brothers laughed and looked at their wives, who were pointing and laughing at their wimpy husbands.

"We're the smart ones. Why not fall, before getting knocked down," Wayne yelled back.

"You're so smart sweetheart," Ginger yelled from the sidelines. "You need to work in the yard this week, so it's okay with me."

Wayne rolled his eyes. "That is all you're worried about?"

Ginger laughed and blew her husband a kiss.

"Okay, let's run over and grab up your little one and see what those cats do," Wayne said. "I'll do the grabbing."

"Okay, but don't hurt her," Jeremy said.

Wayne gave his brother a look of disgust and shook his head. He took off running towards his mother and little Nadia.

"Nadia, Uncle Wayne is going to get you and eat you up," Wayne said, as he ran up to his mother and picked Nadia up in his arms holding her up in the air.

The cats all stopped instantly and watched as Wayne tossed Nadia into the air. Miss Virginia was at Wayne's feet immediately. She sat down and intently watched Nadia being tossed into the air. Tye and Tess came running over too. All three cats patiently watched Wayne toss Nadia into the air and catch her.

Nadia screamed with delight. As soon as her uncle stood her back down on the ground all three cats surrounded her. Nadia screamed again. All three cats circled around her and rubbed her as they continued to circle. Nadia babbled to the cats and they meowed in unison as if answering to her.

"Look at them," Jeremy said. "It is as if they know what she is saying. I am telling you there is something very strange with these cats. As long as they don't want to hurt my little girl I am good."

"Why would they hurt her?" Wayne questioned, as he rolled his eyes again at his younger brother. "Stop over analyzing so much Jeremy. I think it is kind of cool."

Jeremy snubbed his older brother and whisked his daughter into his arms. He carried her off to the safety of her mother's arms.

"Here, you keep an eye on her while I go and put some hurting on those younger boys," Jeremy boasted, as he ran back onto the field.

The men and the boys had fun being silly, but Will and Gregory won the game. They were unstoppable. The older dudes just let them take it all the way, as they stood or fell around, except for Jeremy. He tried to actually run, but his nephews tackled him every time and tried to convince him he wasn't going to get down the field.

The feast had been wonderful and the family football game had been a blast for everyone. Even Jake, Son of Running Deer and Lope had fun watching, laughing and wishing they could run onto the field. They all noticed the little one and the felines' attentiveness. Jake beamed as he knew it was this niece who was the most important link to the families' existence. The stories were handed down and he was witnessing the legend come to life. There was much more mystery to unfold and only the magic of time would tell.

Chapter 3: Nadia's Kitties

For the next six months, Nadia's four-year-old life seemed to be as any little girl's. She loved being a princess. She loved playing with her dolls. But, she loved playing with stuffed animals, especially the stuffed kitten that Lacey and Jillie had given her for her fourth birthday. She called it Kitty. Kitty was usually with Nadia at all times. Bath time was the worst time of the day, because Kitty wasn't allowed to take baths and Nadia wanted her kitten to be clean too. Stacy would have to secretly wash the stuffed animal at night, because it was the only time that Nadia wasn't aware of her toy. She or Jeremy made sure Kitty was clean and dry by morning and placed back next to their daughter or the mornings were gruesome. Only once had Kitty been forgotten wet in the washer. Stacey and Jeremy were not about to explain to their four-year-old that they had ran it through the washing machine. So, the story was that Kitty must have gone on a hunt for food and they all looked and called for Kitty to come home. The only saving grace was that Nadia didn't miss pre-school for anything but sickness. She loved school, her teachers and her friends. Kitty was dried while Nadia attended school that day. Kitty road in the family's SUV and greeted Nadia at pick up. It was a picture perfect moment when Nadia saw her cat sitting in her car seat. Stacey even got teary eyed, as she watched her daughter cry, hug and kiss the stuffed animal. She quickly grabbed her phone and put it to video mode to capture a memorable moment to share with Jeremy.

"And, don't you ever go on a hunt without telling me," Nadia scolded her beloved pet between hugs and kisses. Not until a certain magical day did Kitty take second place to any other toy or pet.

"Hey Stace, come here and see what I am seeing in our back yard," Jeremy yelled to his wife.

Stacey came running, as she thought something really scary might be in their yard. "Jeremy, it's a cat."

"Yeah, but it's just sitting there and I swear I saw it yesterday too," Jeremy replied staring out the window.

"Just please don't feed it. We have enough on our plate and besides Kitty might be really upset if we take in another cat." Stacey laughed at herself and Jeremy laughed too. "Better yet, our daughter might just have to have a real cat. Don't show it to her. Promise me Jeremy."

"Don't worry, I'm not that stupid. I know our daughter and she'll scoop that thing up and we'll have a litter on our hands." Jeremy continued watching the cat sit and stare in his direction. "Spooky, but she kind of looks like that cat at Lacey's house."

"Lots of cats look alike Jeremy. Listen, I have to get the boys out this morning. You have Nadia detail. So don't be running off to the office. She's still sleeping and I'm going to get out the door before she gets up and decides she is going to play football with her brother's team."

"I hear ya and Kitty has to help her. Kitty gets so nasty dirty," Jeremy added, as he chuckled to himself and walked away from the window. "I'm going to get some breakfast or better yet, lunch ready for her. I think I'll make my famous 'Charlotte Dog'. Have you fed the boys?"

"Yep, they ate and we are heading out the door," Stacey yelled back, as she went to call the boys. "Let's go boys. I'm in the car."

Adam and Luke came running through the house. They waved at their dad and took off out the door.

Jeremy smiled and continued gathering cabbage and all beef hotdogs from the refrigerator. Before he started cooking, he decided to go over to the window again. This time, there were three cats and a small kitten. "Oh my gosh, they do look like Lacey's and Jillie's cats, but that little one is new," Jeremy said out loud to himself.

Nadia called out that she wanted someone to come and help her get dressed. Jeremy left the window shaking his head with disbelief. "On my way Nadia," Jeremy yelled back and placed the food down on the counter.

Nadia had her closet open trying to pull an outfit down. Of course, it was a Snow White dress.

Jeremy took the outfit down and handed it to her. "You sure you want to be Snow White today? I think you might want to put a t-shirt and sweats on this morning. You and daddy might go outside and get all dirty. I have to work on your tree house and you have to hand me some tools."

Nadia looked at her dress, as she was in deep thought. "Okay daddy; I'll dress in my dirty clothes," Nadia said giggling. "It's fun to get dirty."

"I like to get dirty too Princess," Jeremy said, as he pulled the 'dirty clothes' outfit from Nadia's chest of drawers and handed them to her. "You can get them on right?"

Nadia giggled. "Daddy, I am a big girl now."

Jeremy nodded his head back and smiled. "Of course you are and daddy is so proud of you. After you get dressed, go potty and brush your 'teefers' too."

"Daddy, they are not 'teefers," Nadia stated with

her hands on her hips. "They are teeth."

"You see Nadia, you are smarter than daddy already. Get going and meet me downstairs for breakfast in five young lady."

"Yes sir," Nadia replied saluting her dad.

Jeremy shook his head in disbelief. "Now where did she learn that?" Jeremy mumbled to himself, as he headed back downstairs to the kitchen. He headed back over to the window and there they were – all four of them. "I've got to call Lacey."

Jeremy picked up his phone and dialed his niece. "Lacey, it's your Uncle Jeremy. Just what does your cat and your cousin's cat look like?"

"Tye is all grey with a cute white star on his forehead. Tess is all white with a grey tipped tail. Why do you ask?" Lacey replied back to her uncle, with a puzzled voice.

Jillie, who was with Lacey, turned down the music and turned her attention to her cousin's conversation, as Lacey listened to someone.

"Well, Stacey and I have noticed a grey and white cat hanging around our house and it kind of looks like that cat's picture you girls have shown us at the farmhouse. And now, I swear I just saw your two cats with her and they have another little kitten with them," Jeremy went on, until Lacey interrupted.

"What? You think our cats are over at your house with Miss Virginia and another kitten?" Lacey almost yelled out, with excitement and surprise.

Jillie was all ears. "Put him on speaker phone Lacey," Jillie whispered.

"Oh yeah," Lacey whispered and did as Jillie requested.

"Well, it's just too odd Lacey. Where are you? Can you come over here? I know it's a little bit of a hike," Jeremy ended. "We're not scared or anything, but we're just confused why all the cats would be here and it's a little unbelievable that they would be Miss Virginia, Tye and Tess all the way over here. I know it may be a bit of a hike."

"No, it's okay. Jillie and I are on our way right now," Lacey said, looking at Jillie shrugging her shoulders

"Jillie?" Jeremy asked. "I thought she was off to Pennsylvania, Paris or something with a P."

"She got kind of sick this morning and opted out of going and called her big cousin to save her. I think her mom and dad are out of town or something," Lacey replied, making it up as she went along. She knew that their Uncle Jeremy was too busy to even really think about it all.

"Oh, sounds good. I'll see you here in about forty-five," Jeremy said and hung up before Lacey could say good-bye.

Nadia bounded into the kitchen just as Jeremy hung up the phone.

"Guess who is stopping by to see us in just a little bit?" Jeremy asked.

"Who daddy, who daddy?" Nadia yelled, as she danced around her dad. "I love company."

"Your two big cousins, Lacey and Jillie, will be here soon. So, let's get you something to eat."

Nadia screamed and ran back to her room where she looked for Kitty. Once she found her, she kissed the stuffed animal and placed it back in her bed. "Now, stay here Kitty. I'm having company and you need to rest." Nadia quickly ran back downstairs to find her dad heating sausage and liver mush. "Mmmm, my favorites."

Jeremy kept getting side tracked talking with Nadia, keeping an eye on the backyard and wishing the girls would hurry up. He was so busy looking out of the window that he never fed Nadia her Charlotte dog he had made earlier. Now, he was also making sausage and liver mush. Nadia didn't seem to mind either. She was so excited to see her cousins.

When the girls finally arrived, Jeremy picked up Nadia and headed outside. "Hey girls; come on in the house. I was just about to feed this little gal. You know how she loves her food and I need to feed her before she eats me."

The girls both laughed and they both blew out their cheeks. Their little cousin loved her food and everyone else's too. Jillie held out her arms for her little cousin to come to her. Nadia didn't hesitate and practically jumped into Jillie's arms.

"How is my little monster eating machine?" Jillie asked giggling, as Nadia grabbed a hand full of Jillie's long, blond hair.

Jeremy led the way and the girls followed him into the kitchen. Jillie placed her little cousin in her booster seat. Nadia was eager for her food. Lacey looked around and didn't see any sign of cats. She walked over to the kitchen window and looked outside. There they were all lined up: Tye, Tess, little grey and white kitten and Miss Virginia sitting close to the edge of her uncle's yard near the woods.

"Jillie, come here," Lacey commanded.

Jillie walked over, looked out and looked back at her cousin with big eyes, as if saying "what do we do now".

Their uncle was beside Nadia gently talking with her as she ate her liver pudding that Nadia loved to call liver mush. Jeremy had also reheated her Charlotte Dog just in case.

"Where is Aunt Stacey?" Lacey asked.

"Oh she and the boys are out and about. Adam had football practice and Luke loves to watch and get all dirty. I chose to watch Nadia and make sure those cats don't do anything weird."

"Oh Uncle Jake, Miss Virginia is a wonderful cat. I think she wants to bring her new kitten to you or little

Nadia. Remember at Thanksgiving every year, how the cats just love Nadia. I think she wants little Nadia to have her own cat," Lacey explained.

"I don't know about that," Jeremy answered back, as he continued to give Nadia more food to devour.

"Come on Jillie, let's go out and see if we can actually get close to the new kitten," Lacey said.

Lacey and Jillie headed out the door and walked slowly toward their cats, Miss Virginia and the new, little, adorable kitten sitting there so sweetly poised. Its eyes were so different looking than Tye's or Tess's. They were big, round, golden eyes for such a small little kitten.

Miss Virginia got up first and meowed at her kittens. All three obeyed. They all got up and started walking toward the girls. Tess and Tye guarded their new little brother or sister. The kitten seemed totally calm.

Lacey went down on her knees. Jillie followed her older cousin's lead and kneeled down too. Miss Virginia quickly moved towards the girls and rubbed all around them. The girls both sat down and held out their hands to Miss Virginia. Tye and Tess hurried to get to the girls. The little kitten gracefully moved behind them and waited its turn.

Lacey held out her hand towards the little kitten. It slowly moved up to her and sniffed, but didn't go any further. Jillie watched and held out her hand. The kitten moved to sniff Jillie's hand and quietly sat down.

"Uncle Jeremy," Lacey hollered towards the back door. "Bring Nadia out here."

A few minutes later, Jeremy came out holding Nadia's hand. When Nadia saw the cats, she pulled lose from her dad's hand and ran as fast as she could to reach the cats. Miss Virginia, Tess and Tye all quietly sat back and watched. Lacey and Jillie quietly sat and smiled, as their little cousin met her protector. Jeremy held his breath not knowing all there was to know.

Nadia scooped up the tiny grey and white kitten with the big, yellow eyes and hugged it tight. Everyone could hear the kitten purring, as it snuggled its little face into Nadia's neck. Jeremy whipped out his phone, put it on camera mode and snapped this unbelievable picture. Lacey and Jillie looked at one another and exchanged winks.

"Well now, if that isn't something," Jeremy commented and stooped down to join everyone else on the ground.

Miss Virginia made her way over to Jeremy. She softly meowed and rubbed up against him. Jeremy smiled and sat down. As soon as he did, Miss Virginia crawled upon his lap.

"Wow, this cat seems like she knows me or something," Jeremy said, as he smiled and rubbed the cat. "Oh yeah, she is the cat that everyone thinks is a descendant of my Grandmother Tess' cat. Maybe she does know me. I used to tease that cat whenever it was sitting in the bathroom window. I would come up to the screen, from the outside, and put my face into the screen and just stare at her. She would push back and we would have a contest to see who could push the hardest."

"Well they say that cats have nine lives Uncle Jeremy," Jillie said.

"Yeah and she seems like she really loves Nadia. I mean, she came all the way over here to bring her a kitten," Lacey said, wondering if their uncle would start thinking too much now.

"Yes, it's kind of strange, but 'what-the-hey', my daughter loves that little kitten and that kitten loves my daughter. That is enough for me to be 'in'," Jeremy said, as he smiled looking at this daughter and continued to rub Miss Virginia.

"So, you're going to let her keep it?" Lacey asked. "What is it anyway; a boy or a girl? What do you think you should name her?"

To all of their amazement, Nadia answered the question. "She is my cat Tea."

"You mean kitty Nadia," Jeremy said, as he thought about her stuffed animal.

"No, my cat Tea," Nadia said again.

"That is cute. You can call her catty," Jeremy said.

Nadia put her little fur ball down and stood up. She placed her small hands on her hips and looked straight at her dad.

"No daddy, she is Tea."

Jillie figured it out. "Uncle Jeremy, Nadia wants to name her cat Tea."

Nadia jumped up and down. "Tea; my cat is my sweet Tea!"

As Nadia jumped up and down, her tiny necklace caught her cousins' eyes.

"Hey, what is that necklace you're wearing little Nadia?" Lacey asked moving towards her little cousin.

"My 'toof', I mean tooth rock necklace," Nadia said, as she held out a small, black shark's tooth wrapped with a thin, leather rope.

"Oh that is something I found in Jake's things when we were young and he let me hold onto it. He told me not to lose it. Nadia found it in my bedside table drawer and wanted it. She wears it all the time."

The two older girls both glanced at one another. Lacey sat back and just smiled.

The kitten jumped up into her arms and Nadia responded immediately. She caught the kitten perfectly in her arms.

"Wow, my daughter is a smart little thing. Don't you think girls?" Jeremy asked, as he looked towards his nieces and smiled.

The three adults all laughed, but Nadia sat back down looking and talking with her kitten. Tess and Tye joined Nadia and the kitten. They all seemed to have their own private conversation. Lacey and Jillie noticed, but Jeremy only thought his daughter was too cute. Nadia's older cousins sensed a power stronger than either one had even known. Seeing their little cousin surrounded by these three cats made them see a very strong bond. Nadia looked up and smiled at her older cousins with a look of much knowledge. The girls glanced at one another and then at their uncle, who was just sitting back watching his daughter looking cute.

"So girls, what do we do? Do you think we're supposed to keep this little furry thing? Do you think Miss Virginia here wants to leave Tea with Nadia?" Jeremy asked, holding up the mother and rubbing his nose to hers. "Maybe we'll just keep Miss Virginia here too and make sure we know what to do with this little thing." Jeremy placed Miss Virginia down and her right eye gave that magical sparkle.

Although Jeremy didn't notice the sparkle, Lacey and Jillie saw the magical sparkle come from Miss Virginia's eye. Yes, Nadia had her protector and nothing would separate them now. Nothing would separate these three cousins from joining together for the rest of their lives. It was truly a magical mystery that keeps bringing surprises and adventures their way.

Lacey and Jillie hung out with their uncle and little cousin for another hour. The girls wanted to ask their uncle about his other brother, but didn't want to bring up the sadness. So, they talked about all the things they were going to work on at the farm and invited their uncle to bring little Nadia over as often as it worked for him and Stacey.

"Uncle Jeremy, I would be happy to baby sit little Nadia some this summer. I think she would love coming over to the farm too," Jillie said.

"We'll see if Stacey is okay with it. I hope she is okay with this catty. I know Luke and Adam will be okay with it, but they will probably want their own catties," Jeremy said.

"Mine," Nadia said looking at her dad.

Lacey and Jillie laughed. Lacey looked at her younger cousin and tapped her wrist to let her know it was time for them to leave. Jillie nodded at her in agreement.

"Oh, I better get some cat food," Jeremy said. "Come on little girl. You and daddy are going to take a ride to the pet store for some kitten and cat food. I'll just ask the pet store staff for the best food for these two."

Nadia placed her little kitten down beside its mother and was ready to go without any further explanation.

The girls walked with their uncle and little cousin to Lacey's car. Jeremy and little Nadia said their good-byes to the girls, Tess and Tye. Lacey backed out of her uncle's driveway, as Jeremy put Nadia in her car seat. Lacey beeped her horn and took off.

Miss Virginia and her little one, Tea, sat on the front porch waiting for Jeremy's and Nadia's return.

Chapter 4: Tea Time

"What were you thinking Jeremy?" Stacey yelled. "We said we were not going to get any animals for at least a couple of years!"

"Stacey, you have to see our daughter with this kitten. You will melt. I am sure of it," Jeremy replied.

"What if the other two want their own pets now?" Stacey sternly asked. "Are you prepared to say 'yes' to them too? You probably already said yes to Nadia."

Virginia quietly sat outside with her kitten by her side listening to the arguing between Stacey and Jeremy. She looked down at her kitten and meowed explaining that they were going to have to help Jeremy out a bit. So, a bit of magic might have to be thrown into the situation.

"Mom! Dad!" Luke called out from his room. "I just saw a mouse run across my room!" Luke yelled, as he came bounding down the stairs to the kitchen.

"What?" Jeremy yelled. "We don't have mice or rats in this house."

"Just come and check my room out with me," Luke begged and he grabbed his dad's hand.

"Come on Stace," Jeremy called out for his wife. "You're going too. I'm not good with rodents."

As Luke and his parents ran upstairs, Nadia opened the door and motioned for Virginia and Tea to come inside. She picked her kitten up and took off upstairs. Stacey glanced at her daughter with this kitten and rolled her eyes.

"I think it's over there under my toy chest," Luke said, as he pointed from just inside his bedroom door.

Nadia bounded into the room and placed her Tea on the floor. "Help us out Tea," Nadia lovingly said in her tiny voice.

Tea went into a tracking mode. She slinked down and quietly crawled over to the toy chest. Everyone watched in total amazement as the kitten circled around and around the toy chest until she stopped near a corner. She lowered her body and began scratching at the bottom of the chest.

"That cat is going to scratch Luke's chest," Stacey said.

Jeremy held his hand up for everyone to be quiet. Sure enough a tiny, field mouse bounded out from the opposite corner. Within seconds, the tiny kitten pounced upon the mouse and captured it. She held it down with her front paws until she got its tail in her mouth and rushed out of the room. Jeremy, Stacey, Luke and Nadia followed the kitten out of the room. The kitten was waiting at the back door for someone to open it. As soon as Jeremy opened up the door, the kitten leaped out of the house and into the backyard. She ran to the end of the yard and let the little creature free into the woods. Seconds later, she was back in the arms of Nadia.

"See that Stacey?" Jeremy excitedly asked. "See that?"

"Okay, okay, you win," Stacey replies, as she turned to her daughter. "You are responsible for that kitten young lady."

"Mommy, I will, I will," Nadia yelled, as she hugged Tea in tight and stooped down to rub Virginia. "I'm going to take Tea outside." Nadia took off running out the door with her kitten in tow.

Jeremy bent down and rubbed the mother cat. "Your little one will have a good home here. I hope you're going to stay here for at least a week." The mother cat leaned in for Jeremy to rub her head. "Sounds good to you? Me too," Jeremy said, as he scooped the cat up in his arms and walked her down the stairs. "Stace, Virginia is staying for a while too."

"Whatever," Stacey replied, as she continued towards the laundry room. "You're responsible for her and Nadia is responsible for the little one."

Jeremy smiled. "Let's round up Nadia and Tea and go work on the tree house." Jeremy headed out the door with Virginia in his arms. Virginia jumped out of Jeremy's arms and ran off to catch up with Nadia and Tea. Jeremy laughed and watched Nadia running around the backyard with Tea close to her heels. Virginia ran behind her kitten, as if she was guarding them both.

Jeremy grabbed his tool box and headed out to begin putting the tree house together. He had already placed the boards around the trees that he had planned on using as the main wall studs. He had also rented sturdy, platform ladders to help him with the framing of the house.

Nadia ran over to her dad with the cats close behind. "Can I help daddy?"

"Not right now Naddie Girl. I don't want to drop a board on you. You take the cats and play over there, but you keep an eye on me in case I need you to get mommy to help me out."

"Okay daddy," Nadia said and ran off as quickly as she had run up to him. The kitten took off, but Virginia sat down to watch over Jeremy. Little did he know, but she was guarding his safety.

Stacey soon came out and yelled that she was leaving with Luke for the football fields. Jeremy blew his wife a kiss and pointed at the cats. Stacey threw her hands up in the air and then pointed at her husband letting him know they were all his responsibility.

Shortly after Jeremy began putting together his expensive ladder, his older brother, Wayne, arrived to bring him some stuffed cabbage. "Hey," Wayne yelled from the driveway. "You are doing that all by yourself?"

Jeremy stood up and saw his older brother. "No, you promised you were going to help me," Jeremy yelled back with a big smile.

"I never said that. I didn't even know you were building a tree house," Wayne replied, as he held up the big container of stuffed cabbage. "Hey, your sister made this and she instructed me to deliver a container to you. So, here it is. I am going to put it in your outside 'frig'."

"Okay and then come down here," Jeremy yelled back.

Wayne did as his younger brother requested and headed down into his brother's backyard. Nadia came running up to her uncle.

"Hey little Nadia," Wayne said, as he picked her up and flung her around. "I see you have a new kitten."

"Put me down Uncle Wayne. I want to show you my cat Tea."

Wayne placed his niece down beside the kitten, which immediately jumped into Nadia's arms so naturally.

"That was cool Naddie. Did you teach her that?"

"No, she just does it and I catch her," Nadia replied with a big smile. "This is my sweet Tea."

"Sweet Tea; that is an unusual cat name, but it's your cat," Wayne said and smiled.

"Her name is Tea, but she is sweet Uncle Wayne," Nadia replied with disgust in her voice. "Her mommy is here too. She's over there with daddy."

Wayne looked towards Jeremy and saw Virginia. "Oh, that cat looks like Miss Virginia."

"It is Uncle Jeremy. Come on, let's go see daddy."

Wayne walked along side of his niece holding her kitten. He thought it was weird how Nadia thought Virginia was Tea's mommy.

"Hey man," Jeremy said, as he was positioning his ladder. "You busy for a while or can you help me?"

"I'll help you for a bit, but don't think I am staying here all day. I only came because Lucy made me bring stuffed cabbage for her little brother. She said she was too busy to drive over and you love it. Hey, Nadia said this is her kitten's mother and it's Virginia?"

"Yeah, it is," Jeremy said, as he wiped his forehead and looked at the mother cat. "She showed up here. Not only did she have this one with her, but she had Lacey's and Jillie's cats with her too. It was so freaky that I called your daughter and she came over with Jillie not too long ago. I told you, things are weird about these cats. But the girls all love these cats and they seem to love them back."

Wayne scratched his head. Virginia walked over and rubbed up against Wayne's leg. "I see, you want me to rub you don't you," Wayne said, as he bent down and ran his hand along Virginia's back. "Okay, what do you want me to do here Jeremy?"

Jeremy looked at his older brother with a big smile. "Help me build this tree house or at least help me get the main studs in place."

"Okay, I'll help you get the foundation together and then you should be able to handle it by yourself," Wayne answered, as he stood up and rolled up his sleeves.

"Naddie Girl, Jeremy said, "you need to take the cats and play away from this area. I don't want you to get hit with a board."

"Okay daddy," Nadia replied. "Come on Miss Virginia and my sweet cat, Tea. Let's go play."

Nadia took off with the cats right behind her. Nadia happily screamed all the way around the yard.

The two brothers worked hand in hand, telling jokes, cutting up and occasionally arguing as they built an amazing tree house foundation. They would both look around and make sure they saw Nadia within eye sight. She seemed quite occupied and happy with her cats.

"Something else, isn't it?" Jeremy asked his brother.

"Yeah, I don't get it either. Those cats are just so mysterious to me, but in another way almost magical. But, I think we are just reading too much into it all the time. At least that is what Lacey keeps telling me when I ask her."

"We probably are, but as long as they don't harm my little girl," Jeremy said. "Hey, I think I can take it from here big bro. I really appreciate the food and the help."

"Yeah, I think you should be able to handle the rest. It's going to look good. Send me a picture when you get it finished. I think I'll head home after I say bye to Nadia and her felines. I guess Stacey and the boys aren't here."

"Yeah, Adam left for sports hours ago and Stacey left with Luke just before you got here. Hey man, thanks again," Jeremy said, as he gripped his brother's hand tight.

Wayne hit his brother on the right shoulder and walked away to say good-bye to his niece, who was sitting down with the kitten in her lap and Virginia snuggled close to her right side.

"Bye Naddie Girl," Wayne said, as he walked up and bent down beside her. "Can Uncle Wayne take a picture?"

Nadia put Tea on the ground and jumped up. She did a one legged pose with her arms up in the air. Virginia and Tea stood under Nadia's bent left leg. "Okay," Nadia said with a big smile on her face.

Wayne stood up laughing, stepped backward as he pulled his phone out of his pocket. He put it on camera mode and snapped an adorable picture. He immediately sent it to his daughter and Jeremy. "Okay Naddie, I am leaving now. Take good care of your kitten and Virginia."

"I am," Nadia replied and went back to talking to the cats as if they knew everything she was saying.

Wayne smiled as he shook his head and returned to his car. When he got into his car, he beeped and pulled out of the driveway. Jeremy waved to his brother and looked over at his daughter chatting away to the cats. He watched as Nadia got up, placed her kitten on the ground beside its mother and told them to follow her. The cats did just that. They followed directly behind his daughter.

When Stacey and the boys returned, they walked down to the tree house that Jeremy was now over halfway done. Adam, who already knew the wonderful secret, joined in helping his dad, while Luke ran off to catch up with Nadia and the cats. Stacey chatted for a moment and headed into the house.

When Luke approached his sister, he reached to pick up the kitten. Nadia yelled, "NO! She is my cat!"

"I want to hold her Naddie," Luke said and bent down to pick up the kitten. But, it didn't happen, because the kitten gave Luke a low growl that made him retreat backwards. "She just growled at me."

"I know, because I told her to," Nadia replied, as she picked up her kitten. "She only wants me to hold her."

"You don't know that!" Luke yelled and ran off to his dad.

Miss Virginia took off after Luke and caught up with him. Luke slowed down and the mother cat purred and circled around his legs. Luke went down on his knees and Virginia allowed him to rub her.

"You want to play with me?" Luke asked the cat.

To Luke's surprise, Virginia stood up and got into a playful, pouncing position. She meowed at Luke and took off running. Luke jumped up and ran after her. The cat ran all around the backyard until Luke tuckered out.

Virginia knew that she had to keep peace within the household to allow Nadia and Tea time to get to know one another. The boys were a part of Nadia's life and everyone would have to live in harmony. Next, she would work on Stacey too. She knew she could recruit Adam if needed.

Chapter 5: Nadia's Future Blessings

For the next year, Virginia made sure Nadia and Tea grew together. She knew Nadia would need her. She entertained Luke and warmed up to Stacey and Jeremy more and more. She spent time with Adam going back and forth to the farm, tending to the horses and helping Lacey, Will and their Uncle Jake. Pre-school was only half a day, but when real Kindergarten began life for Nadia was not like all the other children her age. The summer before Nadia was to start Kindergarten, Nadia was diagnosed with a blood cancer known as Leukemia. So, Nadia's school days began in the hospital and at home. Jeremy and Stacey hired in-home tutors, who Lacey helped them find. Lacey and Jillie knew that they had to do something and they found their way to 'The Leukemia & Lymphoma Society', an organization that works towards the cure of blood cancers. Through all the information they gathered, Nadia had a good chance of survival. They began raising money to further the efforts of this organization's mission and they formed a 'Light the Night' team. Even though Nadia was sick some of the time after her treatments, she quickly rebounded and wanted to do her studies. She seemed to be as happy as she had always been and Tea made sure of that. Tea was with her every second that she was home. Jeremy, Stacy, Lacey and Jillie noticed how attentive Tea was to Nadia's every move. No one wanted to talk about Nadia's fate. But her fate was to live and the magic of her destiny took control.

As quickly as she became sick with this blood cancer, she was miraculously cured. The magic of the time portal had brought back Lope, one of her very own descendants, who brought back a cure; a cure that would not be discovered for years to come. A tiny pill was secretly given to Nadia by Lacey without anyone's knowledge. Lacey had taken a huge chance. Knowing that her cousin would live, she took a huge chance with no going back.

Doctors wanted to do tests after tests on Nadia when they realized her blood cancer was no longer evident. Jeremy and Stacey declined having their daughter used as a guinea pig. They thought she had been misdiagnosed and decided they would only take her back for quarterly check-ups until they felt confident that it was in her past. They also felt like home schooling for the rest of her Kindergarten days was the right thing to do. Nadia learned at an accelerated rate, because she had so many people teaching her. She was either with a professional tutor, her parents, her brother or Lacey. Even Jillie made trips home on some weekends to help Nadia with her schooling. And, each and every night she had Tea curled up beside her. Nadia loved being home, but she wanted to go to school and be a big girl too. First grade couldn't come soon enough for Nadia.

Lacey and Jillie mourned the loss of Uncle Jake and their huge family that had fled to safety in the mountains of North Carolina. While Jillie was busy with her studies that would bring great healing to the farm animals and more, Lacey was busy with the farm. She was getting to know her true love, Will, and spending quality time with Nadia.

The week before school was to start, Lacey picked Nadia and Tea up and took them back to the farm. Tea ran around with Tye and Tess while Lacey and Nadia enjoyed time with the horses. A car horn sounded and Lacey went outside of the barn to see who was honking.

Lacey saw a UPS truck in her driveway. "Nadia, you stay right here and I'll be right back."

"Okay," Nadia replied and continued petting Warrior Girl. But, Nadia didn't stand still for more than five seconds. She walked back further into the barn. When she turned the corner, there was an older boy peeking up from the hidden, underground tunnel. Nadia smiled and he smiled back.

"Who are you?" The boy asked.

"Nadia," Nadia quickly answered. "Who are you?"

"OMG; I am Lope! I'm your…" Lope realized that this was his distant great-grandmother that he helped save. "How are you?" Lope smiled at this little girl.

Nadia smiled. "Good."

"Are you here all by yourself?" Lope asked.

"Lacey had to run up to the house," Nadia answered. "Why were you in the ground? You look funny."

Lope didn't exactly know what to say. He wasn't supposed to be here, but he continued to come back and explore. "Don't tell Lacey I was here okay Nadia?"

"Why?" Nadia innocently asked.

"If you promise not to tell her, I'll be your best friend."

Nadia giggled. "Okay."

Lope lowered himself back into the underground tunnel. Before he pulled the door closed, he looked at his very young distant great-grandmother one more time. "I'm glad to have met you Nadia. I have to go. I'll be back. I promise and we'll go somewhere that you will love seeing one day."

"Okay bye," Nadia replied.

"Nadia, Nadia," Lacey called.

Nadia ran back around to the front of the barn and found Lacey looking for her.

"Why did you go back there?" Lacey asked. "I

was worried."

"Back there talking with my friend," Nadia truthfully answered.

Lacey looked at Nadia and quickly walked back to the back of the barn and looked around. She didn't see anyone. "Okay, I guess you have an imaginary friend?"

"I have a best friend," Nadia replied.

Lacey smiled. "Okay, you'll have to introduce me sometime."

"He's my friend," Nadia said with a frown on her face.

"Okay, okay," Lacey said. "He can be your friend."

It didn't even cross Lacey's mind that someone might have really been there, especially someone so connected to Nadia as Lope. Lacey saddled up Warrior Girl and placed Nadia onto the saddle. Then she pulled herself up and sat right behind Nadia. Warrior Girl took them on a nice ride down into the pasture. As they rode past the big, oak tree, Lacey didn't notice Lope sitting on the limb high up in the tree. Nadia saw him, but never said a word.

Chapter 6: The Tea 'n Teacher

Nadia's first day of first grade arrived. She was so excited to go to school all day. Unlike her brother Luke, she loved school and loved being around her friends. Nadia was up all on her own with Tea by her side. Virginia was still around and mainly hung out with Luke to keep him from being jealous. Jeremy and Stacey had gotten so used to having Virginia around, that they just assumed she would remain with them forever. She and Tea seemed to keep Luke and Nadia so busy and occupied that Jeremy and Stacey realized how wonderful pets can be to have around. Adam was now off to college and rarely home. And, when he was home, he was on the farm. He was studying Horticulture and Forestry that made his Uncle Jake so proud.

"Wake up, wake up," Nadia yelled into her daddy's ear. "I'm ready for school!"

Jeremy and Stacey opened their eyes to their six-year-old already dressed and ready to go. "Okay, you still have to eat some breakfast," Jeremy said. "Is your brother up yet?"

"Daddy, NO. You know Luke doesn't like school. I'll go run and get him up," Nadia said, as she and Tea raced out of the bedroom.

Jeremy and Stacey laughed. "I'll get breakfast Stace and you make sure Luke is up," Jeremy said, as he slowly dragged himself out of bed.

Stacey sat up and stretched. "You took the easy job."

Virginia was snuggled next to Luke and lazily looked up as Nadia and Tea bounded into the room. "Get up Luke! It's the first day of school!"

Luke turned away and ignored his sister, but Tea didn't allow him any rest. Before Virginia could stop Tea, the cat pounced onto Luke's side and pulled the covers off of him. Nadia jumped up onto the bed and kissed her big brother. "Good morning sleepy head."

Before Luke could retaliate and do something he would regret, Stacey walked in and saved them all. "I'll take it from here Naddie Girl. You, Tea and Virginia get downstairs and have some breakfast. Don't forget to feed your cats and give them fresh water. You and your dad are still responsible for the cats. I love them, but you will have to keep up your end of the deal."

Nadia backed off of Luke's bed and smiled up at her mom. "No problem mom, I love my cats. Let's go Miss Virginia and my sweet Tea." Off they went.

Stacey shook her head in amazement, smiled and turned her attention to her son.

Nadia, Tea and Virginia ran through the kitchen towards the laundry room. "Daddy, I'm going to feed the cats."

"Okay, try and keep it neat for your mom," Jeremy yelled smiling. "That's my girl, ready for school and taking care of the animals."

Nadia ate her breakfast and was ready to go in no time. "Daddy, may I be excused now. I need to talk with Tea and Virginia about being good while I am gone today."

Jeremy looked at Stacey and smiled. "Of course, be sure and tell them to be really good or mommy will have to put them in time out."

"Oh no, she won't!" Nadia commanded. "They are very smart and they know how to behave." Nadia looked at Tea and Virginia. "Come on with me and we'll go over the rules again." Nadia stared down her mom and left with Tea and Virginia in tow.

Luke rolled his eyes and yawned. "Like they really know what she's saying."

"Maybe you should be talking to Virginia. She seems to be quite taken with you Luke," Jeremy remarked."Naaah, I'll let Nadia think she's talking with them. I think she is crazy dad and that cat of hers. Well, she looks at me like she wants to attack me sometimes. I like having Virginia on my side if you know what I mean."

"I hope you're not being mean to Tea," Stacey added.

"Oh heck no mom; she is mean and I am not stupid."

"Tea is not mean," Jeremy commented. "Maybe you give off a bad vibe or something."

"The only thing I do is give Nadia a hard time and that cat gets in between us and glares at me. And, I swear she roars at me like a tiger whenever I mess with Nadia."

Jeremy chuckled a bit. "I guess you cannot mess with your little sister and you better not."

"Don't worry, I am not going to try and see if that little beast of Nadia's does attack. I have better things to do anyway, like sports. I'm ready mom, can we go now?" Luke got up from the table waiting for his mom's reply.

"No problem, let's hit the road," Stacey said. "Nadia, let's go."

"Coming mom," Nadia yelled back and turned her attention to the two cats. "Now, be good and enjoy your day. I love you. I'll see you after school." Nadia hugged the cats and they followed her back through the house to the garage door where her dad was waiting to say good-bye.

"Bye Naddie Girl. Make me proud."

"Okay daddy; you make me proud too."

Jeremy laughed, bent down and picked up both of the cats. "We'll be fine and I think I am staying home today to work. I'll make sure the cats are good."

Nadia smiled, rubbed each cat's head and raced to the car. She waved as they pulled out from the garage. Both cats meowed. Jeremy looked down at them. "She'll be back." He gave them each a quick head rub and returned to the kitchen to clean up from breakfast. The cats went to the front windows to watch the car until it was out of sight.

***

Nadia didn't need Stacey to walk her to her class. She wanted to be a big kid and walk in with her friends from Pre K. Nadia gave her mom a kiss and off she went. Stacey waited and watched her daughter greet her little girlfriends with hugs.

The day started off great and Nadia was so excited to be in school until nap time came. She didn't want to take a nap. Naps were for babies."

"Nadia please put your head down on you mat. It's nap time."

"Can I draw or something?" Nadia asked. "I don't take naps.

"I am sorry Nadia. Everyone needs a little rest time."

"My mommy and daddy tell me to draw or read when they say its quiet time. Why can't the ones of us that don't take naps do something quiet while the others nap?"

"Nadia, I am the teacher and I make the rules!"

Nadia was upset and she wanted to cry, but she didn't want to be a baby. She put her head down and quietly sobbed into her arm. Little did she know, Virginia and Tea were watching from outside. Tea was mad, but Virginia wouldn't allow her to make a move and thought out to her own child how hard it can be for a teacher to allow different rules for everyone. Nadia had to learn to respect the teacher. And minutes after nap time was over, Nadia was smiling again. The teacher complimented Nadia on her listening and following direction skills. Tea learned a valuable lesson too. She had to make sure Nadia was in true danger before she took any action. She and Nadia were both in school. Tea had to make sure she would be a good teacher for Nadia in her years to come.

First grade went wonderful for Nadia and Tea. They both grew and learned each day. Every month, several students were allowed to have their parent bring in their family pet for show and tell. When it was Nadia's turn to have Tea brought in, the teacher was totally in awe of Tea. Tea did everything Nadia commanded. When Nadia introduced her cat to her teacher, Tea held up her paw for the teacher to hold. Even Jeremy was amazed, as he had not paid attention to how his daughter had trained her sweet cat.

Towards the end of Nadia's first grade year, Virginia began leaving for long periods of time during the day when Luke and Nadia were at school. Jeremy and Stacey assumed she was out prowling the neighborhood. Little did they know, she was back on the farm with Lacey, Tye, Tess and Will, all who were working hard while Nadia grew up.

The summer after first grade went by so slow for Nadia. She loved school and she loved being smart. Her illness seemed to be totally behind her and she spent most of her time with her cat and a book. Jeremy and Stacey loved it when Nadia wanted to go to the farm, because they were so worried about how she didn't want to play with other children. She seemed too mature and she hated playing dolls or dress up. She wanted to play with her best friend and that was Tea. She called Lacey and asked if she could come spend the night. Lacey of course was excited to have her little cousin.

"Mom said she will drop me over after dinner and I can stay all day tomorrow," Nadia told Lacey over the phone.

"Okay, we will all see you later. We'll have some homemade ice cream," Lacey answered.

"Yeah!" Nadia yelled. "I want banana and pineapple."

"You got it," Lacey replied. "See you later, gater."

Nadia laughed. "In a while, crocodile."

Stacey arrived on the farm just after seven. Lacey and Will were making the ice cream. "Want to stay for some homemade banana and pineapple Aunt Stacey?" Lacey asked.

"I'll have a taste, but I want to hit a store that is out this way. Just one big spoonful please."

Lacey handed a tablespoon full of ice cream to her Aunt Stacey.

"Mmm good," Stacey said, as she handed her spoon back to Lacey. "Thank you for keeping our little girl here."

"She helps keep the animals in check and they listen to her better than they do to me," Lacey replied smiling.

"Nadia loves those animals. She definitely has so much compassion. I wonder if it's because of how life's challenges made her a better person at such a young age."

Lacey looked over at Nadia, piling ice cream onto the sugar cone. "I think she was born with a special gift."

Stacey looked at her daughter. "She's a keeper. I better get going. Jeremy or I will pick her up just before dinner tomorrow."

Lacey stood up and gave her aunt a hug. "We'll be here."

Will came out of the house just as Stacey pulled out of the driveway. He gave Nadia a big hug and twirled her in the air. "How's my third favorite girl?"

Nadia looked at Lacey and then at Will. "I'm you're second favorite."

Lacey thought of Beautiful Butterfly, but didn't say anything.

Will laughed. "My mom would be crushed if she wasn't my number two."

Nadia rolled her eyes. "She's your mom. She cannot marry you."

Lacey looked at Will and then at Nadia with big eyes. "So, you want to marry my man. That might be fighting words little girl."

Nadia held up her fists. "If he cannot be mine, then I'll have to have someone just like him."

Lacey looked at Will and she knew he was thinking the same thing. "I just bet you will meet someone even more special," Will replied and winked at Lacey.

They all enjoyed the homemade ice cream.

"I'm full of ice cream," Nadia said. "I'm going to go see my horses."

Will bowed and held his right arm out motioning that she was free to go. "I've fed and watered them. Just give them a carrot and a peppermint."

Nadia went skipping off with the cats right behind her. She looked down at the cats and smiled. "Maybe Lope will be there." When Nadia reached the main barn, the horses all greeted her. She made her rounds and treated each one with hugs and treats. The cats were off climbing into the hay loft.

Once Nadia was finished rubbing and talking with the horses, she headed to the hidden earth door. She tried to pick it up, but it was too heavy for her. She stood there thinking how she could pry it open. But, she didn't have to think long. The door magically started opening. Lope was coming up into the barn.

Nadia was standing behind Lope, as he quietly

peered around. He jumped when he saw Nadia standing there staring at him.

"Whoa mama, it's just you," Lope said, as he pushed the door further open and came out of the tunnel opening. "What are you doing here?"

"Hanging out and I'm not your mama," Nadia answered. "What are you doing here?"

"Hanging out and it's just an expression," Lope replied. "I come at least once a week after Will has been down here. I come on the mornings I have free time for first period."

"It's summer," Nadia responded.

"Not for me. We go all year around with quarterly breaks. Schools and businesses do this so that families can be together and parents don't have to worry about finding something for their children to do and someone to watch over them."

Nadia smiled as she thought a moment. "It makes such good sense to me. I'm glad things change for the good."

Lope looks at this young girl. "How old are you? You seem much older than you look."

Nadia stood up tall. I'm seven and I read a lot. Some kids my age don't really like me, because they think I'm a nerd. I'm really not, but I do love reading and learning. How old are you?"

"I'm almost thirteen," Lope replied. "Don't worry about what other people think or say. Just be yourself. I think you're a really cool kid."

Nadia smiled at this boy. "I think you're cool too."

"Hey listen," Lope said. "I gotta get going. Are you going to be here tomorrow? I'll come back and we'll do something really fun."

"I am; I am going to be here until about six!" Nadia excitedly said, as she jumped up and down. "What time are you coming?"

"Well, you have to meet me at the big oak tree," Lope answered. Can you be there about ten am?"

"I'll be there five minutes before," Nadia excitedly answered. "How should I dress?"

"Something casual and comfortable," Lope answered and smiled. "And no high heels."

"Got that right," Nadia replied. "See you tomorrow. Don't be late."

"I am never late, because it's rude and disrespectful," Lope answered and gave Nadia a wink.

Nadia gave the horses one last hug and skipped all the way back to the old farmhouse. She couldn't wait for tomorrow and she was going to 'hit the hay' early, take care of her farm chores and be off. She had to come up with some excuse to go down to the oak tree, but she couldn't say where she was going. She ran into the house and found Lacey all by herself. Will had gone next door.

"Hey Lacey; I'm really tired. Do you mind if I go to bed early tonight. I want to get up super early and go down to the barn."

"Of course I don't mind," Lacey replied, as she looked at Nadia a little worried. "Are you feeling okay?"

"Oh yeah Lacey; I just have a lot I want to do tomorrow and enjoy the farm. Oh, do you mind if I explore some. I want to gather some leaves and make my own fact book. Something I would like to do for show and tell when school starts."

"Knock yourself out," Lacey said and smiled. "Just don't wander too far down into the pasture. Don't go too far past the oak tree okay?"

"I won't; I promise," Nadia said. "Want to watch a little TV?"

"Let's watch for about an hour and call it a day," Lacey replied.

Lacey and Nadia watched "The Big Bang Theory", laughed together and they both went to their beds by ten. Nadia's alarm sounded by five and she was dressed in minutes. Tea lifted her head, but didn't budge from her space on the bed. Nadia gave her a quick kiss and quietly hurried downstairs and through the kitchen to the bathroom. She grabbed a flashlight and headed down to the barn. She was going to do everything she could now and not be missed when she went on her little adventure. When she made her presence known, the horses all began neighing and butting the stall gates. Nadia unlatched each stall gate and let the horses trot all around her as she put fresh water, hay and feed into the large troughs. Will walked into the barn soon after Nadia began cleaning the first stall.

"Hey little woman; you have a lot of energy this morning."

Nadia pushed her pitchfork into the ground and looked back at Will. "Thought you would be happy to have some of this done early and I want to work on a project in the pasture today."

"Project?" Will asked. "You're not in school."

Nadia put her free, left hand on her hip. "I want to do a project for me. I'm collecting leaves and I'm going to wax paper them with crayons. It's something I learned at school."

"Sounds nice little one," Will commented. "You will have to show me when you're finished."

"Maybe, if you're lucky," Nadia cleverly answered. "Now, let me get my chores done."

Will laughed and helped her out for a while, but left her to the horses while he went to repair some fencing. When Nadia finished up around eight, she headed to the house for some food. Lacey had a wonderful spread all ready to eat. Nadia fed the cats and then let them go outside to explore. She talked her leaf project up to make sure her cover was set. After she helped with the dishes, she went upstairs to change for her adventure with her cool, best friend.

"Leaving Lacey," Nadia yelled, as she waved to

Lacey and Will. They were working in the garden next to the barn.

Lacey waved and Will held up his palm. Nadia returned the gesture and laughed. She made sure she walked around some trees and plucked off some leaves. She casually looked back to see if she was still in view of Lacey and Will. When she knew they couldn't see her any longer, she took off running like the wind. When she reached the big oak tree, Lope was sitting at the base of the tree.

"Hey Lope," Nadia said.

"Well hello there little woman," Lope answered back.

Nadia laughed. "That's what Will just called me this morning."

"You are a little woman. I probably shouldn't be doing this, but I just wanted to show you something that I hope you will appreciate someday."

"What are we doing?" Nadia asked.

"Have you ever time traveled?" Lope asked.

"Will takes me back in time to check on his family's village. We're waiting for many people to return from the safety of the mountains?"

"I'm from the future and I am a descendant of this family," Lope said, but he didn't want to tell her that she was his great-grandmother many times removed. He just wanted to show her the world she helps shape and thank his great-grandmother for a wonderful family and farm.

Nadia looked deep into his eyes. His name was so familiar to her and Running Antelope just didn't cross her mind at the moment. But Lope knew that one day when she met the man of her dreams, she would know him just a little more. Today was not the day for all of that. She was just a young girl.

"How do you make this thing go to the future?" Nadia asked.

"Easy, just follow me," Lope said, as he climbed

up the tree to the lowest branch and then held his hand down to Nadia. “Grab hold and I’ll pull you up.”

Nadia reached up and barely could get her fingers into his hand. Lope held on to a strong branch with his right hand as he pulled her along with his left. She was smart enough to use her feet to walk up the tree to the branch. “I made it.”

“Okay,” Lope said, “follow me. I think the branches are close enough for you to make it now.”

When Lope reached the one branch that dangled into the portal door, the wavering portal door appeared. “Get right behind me Nadia and move as I move. The worm hole will grab you and thrust you forward, but we’ll remain on the tree limb. Just grab a small branch and hold tight.”

Nadia inched her way right up to Lope’s shoes and moved in sync with him. Lope vanished with Nadia right behind him.

***

When they landed, still in a crawling position, it was dark. They were on a much larger and longer tree limb.

“You okay?” Lope asked, as he looked back. “Now, you have to back up and start your way down. Much bigger tree, huh?”

“I think it is, but it’s kind of dark.”

Lope held up his arm and his cube glowed for Nadia to see. “This should help. I’m so used to doing this; I hardly need to see. I move all by memory.”

“I’m a bit scared Lope,” Nadia said and that was all it took. Seconds later, three fierce beasts landed on the tree limb and leapt down to the ground.

“Oh no,” Nadia said. “I caused the cats to come watch over me.”

Lope knew them well. “Its fine, we should have

brought them along in the first place."

"You know them?" Nadia said, as she slowly shimmied her way down.

"I've met them before now. And well, we have their descendants amongst us now."

Nadia jumped the rest of the way down with three large beasts waiting for her. Nadia laughed as she rubbed her three huge protectors. "Okay, you can be cats. You know Lope I understand them."

The beasts became three playful cats and they also lit up the area a bit for Nadia to see. Lope jumped down and pulled up the hidden door that Jake had shown him a few years earlier.

"Recognize this?" Lope asked.

"Yeah; is that the way we're going?" Nadia questioned.

"I think its best. No one will see us and I want to show you the barn. Lacey and Jillie were here not too long ago."

"You know Lacey and Jillie too?" Nadia asked.

Lope thought for a moment. "Yes, I met them when you were just a little girl. I accidentally fell through the time portal to your time. That's how I know about the hidden door too. Your Uncle Jake showed me. Well, I kind of semi-promised them I wouldn't return, but I love those horses and the barn. It's my history you know."

"I think it's kind of cool Lope and I'm not going to tell anyone if you aren't." Nadia replied. "You go down first and help me okay?"

"But of course my little lady," Lope answered making Nadia giggle.

"I like you Lope. You're fun and I love we have a secret."

Lope jumped down into the hidden tunnel and turned up the brightness of his cube for Nadia to see the steps. Nadia climbed down and called for the cats to follow her. The three cats magically appeared in the tunnel without going down the steps. Lope and Nadia both greeted them.

"Come on Nadia; I want to show you your barn as it is today." Lope said, as he held his hand out for his distant great-grandmother.

Nadia talked it up the entire way there telling Lope all about her life. Lope contently listened to this young, little girl, who would one day be a wonderful, grown-up woman. He hoped he would see her again and again. But, if this was the only time, he would be content. He wanted to show his great-grandmother just how wonderful the farm had become. He knew that one day she would realize that she had met her great-grandson many times removed and she would have peace in her heart that her love lived way into the future. This was his gift to her.

Nadia was in awe as Lope showed her all around the barn. She felt like she was in a dream and never wanted to wake up. "I cannot believe I am three hundred years in the future. Now I have seen the farm three hundred years in the past and now I'm in the future."

"Nadia," Lope began, "you cannot tell the family I brought you here. They would be so upset. You're so young and you were so sick."

Nadia looked at Lope. "How did you know I was sick?"

Lope didn't know what to say and he couldn't say anything about what he did for his own great-grandmother. "I think you said something about it in our first meeting."

Nadia thought back and couldn't remember. "Maybe I mentioned it. And yes I was very sick. I will be in trouble if I don't get back to the farm in my time."

A voice came from out of nowhere. "Lope; is that you?"

Lope's mother was in the barn. Lope grabbed

Nadia and threw her inside a stall. The three cats dashed inside to be with Nadia and they all stayed quiet as little mice.

"Back here mom," Lope answered.

"What are you up to tonight? Teresa asked her son. "I have been paging your cube."

"Sorry mom; I'm just exploring as always. I did my chores today you know."

"Don't stay out too late; we're heading for an early horse ride to check all the fencing."

"No worries mom," Lope said with relief. "You know how I love to check the fences."

"Midnight, I'll expect to see you walk through the door," Teresa said and smiled at her roaming child.

"Got it," Lope said waiting for his mom to leave. "Love you mom."

"Love you too son," Euzelia said, as she slowly walked back through the barn admiring all the history of her family.

Lope waited for his mom to close the door behind her. "We better get you back or we'll both be in trouble. Sorry I had to throw you down little girl."

Nadia smiled. "I got to see another descendant; your mom. She's so pretty."

Lope smiled. "She looks like her ancestors for sure."

"I wonder which of us she is related to," Nadia said, as she thought about Lacey and Will and Jillie and Miguel. She was way too young for all that boyfriend stuff.

"Let's go," Lope said. "I'm feeling a bit uneasy about bringing you here."

"Don't worry Lope," Nadia said, as she put her little hand in his. "I promise; I won't tell a soul and I'll make sure the cats don't tell either." Nadia looked at Tye, Tess and Tea directly in their eyes. "Our little secret."

The cats all meowed and circled their Nadia. She was theirs to protect. Nadia giggled and walked with Lope back to the underground tunnel. Lope felt a bit uneasy and wanted to get Nadia and the cats back. He didn't say much and Nadia did all the talking. She was in her glory. She had a secret.

***

Lacey decided that she was uncomfortable with Nadia wandering around the pasture lands all by herself. She went and told Will that she was going to check on Nadia. She saddled up Warrior Girl for a nice ride. The other horses were a bit upset, so she released them to go along for some exercise. "Nadia would be doing this if she hadn't wanted to go look for leaves," Lacey thought to herself.

Lacey blew Will a kiss and slowly headed out for a nice stroll. As Lacey reached the point where she could see all around the pasture and the oak tree, she didn't see Nadia. It was at this moment that she realized the cats were nowhere to be seen either. Something didn't seem right. Lacey whipped Warrior Girl around and gave the command to 'high tail it' back to find Will. Will saw Warrior Girl, with Lacey on her back, flying back towards him and he ran out to meet them.

"What's wrong?! Will demanded.

"I think something has happened to Nadia and the cats are nowhere to be found! Why wouldn't Tye come to me when I thought out for him?"

Will turned around and whistled for his stallion to come. In less than a minute, the black stallion was there. Will jumped upon Shadow's back. "Let's go!"

Warrior Girl and Shadow took off with barely a nudge from their riders. They raced down into the pasture. Will and Lacey raced past the old oak. Neither one of them ever thought that Nadia would dare time travel without Uncle Jake or one of them.

Moments after Lacey and Will flew down the hill to search near the creek or beyond, the portal door wavered. Nadia, Lope and the cats appeared back on the limb. The cats immediately sensed Lacey's fear. Tye took off down into the pasture. Tess and Tea stayed back to guard Nadia. Miss Virginia appeared out of nowhere. Nadia was surprised and excited to see the mother cat. Lope felt like something was wrong and he wasn't sure exactly what he should do.

"You better get back Lope, before its noon here and midnight there. Your mom gave you+ strict instructions."

"I feel like I should stay here in case something is truly wrong," Lope replied.

"Can I get in touch with you if I should ever need you?" Nadia asked, as if she was so grown up.

"Send Virginia to get me if you ever should need me Nadia," Lope said, as he bent down to pet this mother cat. She knows me well."

"Okay," Nadia replied. "Now get going. I'm fine and thanks so much for hanging out with me."

Lope smiled and ruffled Nadia's hair. "It's my pleasure little woman."

Lope helped Nadia down the tree and then he crawled out on the limb back to his time. Nadia looked down the pasture to see if she could see why Tye left so fast. It was only seconds later that she saw Lacey and Will riding hard and fast back towards her. Lacey jumped off of Warrior Girl before the horse really stopped.

"WHERE HAVE YOU BEEN?" Lacey cried out

Nadia stood up stiff as a board with her eyes opened wide in fear. "Uh, uh," Nadia began, "just running around down here."

"WHERE?" Lacey demanded. "Tell me you didn't go back in time to see if Uncle Jake has returned!"

Nadia relaxed a bit. She wasn't going to have to tell her secret. "Of course not Lacey; I was just exploring between here and the barn as I promised." Nadia thought how she wasn't exactly lying to Lacey. She just left out the time element.

Nadia held out her hand with some leaves she had actually picked three hundred years in the future. Lacey touched the leaves in Nadia's hand.

"Okay; we're sorry. We just got to thinking we shouldn't have let you go down here all alone and we decided to join you. When I didn't see you, I panicked. I guess I brought Miss Virginia back to help didn't I?" Lacey bent down and picked up Miss Virginia and hugged her in tight. "You'll help me watch after this little one right? Have you been to the mountains?"

Virginia meowed and all three of her kittens joined in to let her know they would all watch over her.

Will, who never got off of Shadow, clapped his hands together. "Jump up little woman; let's get you back up to the barn with these two horses. What about us taking the other three out for a ride?"

Nadia smiled as she thought about the other person who called her 'little woman'. She ran over to Will's extended hand and grabbed a hold of it. Will swung Nadia up and behind him to sit on Shadow's behind. Lacey remounted Warrior Girl. The four cats took off leaving the horses to catch up.

Lacey looked over at Nadia. "Just don't want anything or anyone to hurt you. Your parents would have my head on a plate."

Nadia laughed. "Not your head, but maybe your hide!"

Will and Lacey laughed at the smarts of this young girl. They went back and saddled Storm Cloud, Baby Boy and Little Girl for a quick ride. The four cats ran all around the horses mainly to make sure Nadia was safe.

The summer slowly went by for Nadia whenever she wasn't at the farm. She couldn't wait for school to begin and just be around other children her age. She dreamed of having at least one good friend.

When second grade came, she was ecstatic. Tea was just a pet that waited for Nadia to come home. Virginia was no longer needed, as Luke was no longer jealous of Nadia's Tea. He was too wrapped up in his sports and his own friends. Nadia was not only excited about second grade, she was also excited about the summer after second grade. Lacey and Will were going to be married and she was going to be in the wedding. She and her big cousin, Jillie, were both in Lacey's wedding.

Chapter 7: Nadia's Little Secrets

Second grade was wonderful for Nadia. She began reading on her own and before her parents knew it, she was reading two grade levels above her age. She loved going to the public library and checking out as many books as her parents would allow. She loved reading historical books. She loved reading all about the first Thanksgiving between the Pilgrims and the American Indians.

Finally, an exciting weekend came for Nadia. She was going shopping with her cousins, Lacey and Jillie, for bridesmaid dresses and lunch. Nadia woke up earlier than her normal early time. As always, she got herself ready and even fixed her own cereal. She usually beat everyone up. Today, she was so excited. She loved being with her older cousins. Tea sat in the chair beside her and listened to Nadia read her new book about Pocahontas. Jeremy and Stacey got up and found their daughter as they did many mornings. She was sitting at the kitchen table with her nose in a book, eating her cereal and reading out loud to Tea.

Lacey and Jillie arrived almost to the second they had promised Nadia. She was very tuned in to time. Everyone in the families had realized that Nadia was not only very smart, but she was also very grown up. She did not like being late for anything and she did not like people who were not punctual. Jeremy and Stacey felt like her illness had forced their little one to grow up so fast. The schedule she was on during her illness made a huge mark on her life.

Tea heard Lacey's car drive up and practically flew off the chair to the back door. Nadia was close behind and opened up the door for her two cousins. She greeted them with a big smile and a hug for each of them. Tea circled all around Lacey's and Jillie's legs expressing her love. Lacey bent down, picked up the cat and hugged her in tight. Jillie took Nadia's left hand and they all went back to the kitchen where they found Jeremy and Stacey having coffee.

"Hey girls," Jeremy said.

"Would you like something for breakfast?" Stacey asked, as she shared her chair with Nadia.

"I'll have a cup of coffee," Lacey replied, as she pulled out a chair and sat down with Tea.

"Nothing for me," Jillie said. "I am saving my appetite for lunch. Lacey's buying."

"Oh no, it's on me," Jeremy said, as he handed Lacey a folded up fifty dollar bill.

"Thanks," Lacey said. "We'll have some fun with this."

"Me too," Nadia said. "I want to have fun."

"Don't worry," Lacey replied. "You are going to be our princess today and we are your servants."

Jillie made a funny face. "I'm not your servant little girl. I am your queen."

Nadia giggled and wiggled off the chair. "You're too young to be a queen silly Jillie."

Everyone laughed. Lacey got up and placed Tea on the floor. "Come on girls, we have some wedding dresses to find."

"YEAH!" Nadia yelled and ran to the door. Tea ran after her. "No Tea, you have to stay here."

Tea stopped and sat down. Lacey poked Jillie as they noticed how quickly Tea responded to Nadia. Jillie smiled and shook her head. They knew their little cousin was someone very special and they felt like her guards.

"Okay, let's hit the road," Lacey said, as she looked back at her uncle and aunt and waved.

"See you later girls," Stacey called out. "Nadia, behave yourself."

Nadia looked up at her cousins and smiled. "I always behave myself."

Jillie tussled Nadia's hair. "You're amazing little cousin and you're going to make your parents so proud one day." Jillie said and grabbed a car booster seat from one of the cars and she helped Nadia get strapped into Lacey's tiny back seat.

On the ride to the shopping mall, the girls asked Nadia all about school and she excitedly talked about what she was learning. Jillie poked Lacey this time. Lacey smiled and quickly glanced over to her cousin.

When they reached the mall, Nadia waited patiently for Jillie to help her out of the car. "Hold our hands Nadia," Jillie directed her young cousin and Nadia put her left hand in Jillie's right and her right hand in Lacey's left.

"Let's just go into each store until we find what each of us like," Lacey said.

The girls walked into the big department store and headed towards Nadia's section first.

"Okay Miss Nadia, let's see what you think you would like to wear in the wedding," Lacey said, as she pulled the girls towards the little girls' dressy section.

Nadia took off running to a rack of beautiful dresses. "This one, this one!"

Lacey hurried to the dress, took it off the rack and held it up. "We better make sure one is your size."

Nadia took it from her hands and twirled around. "I think it's my size."

"Wait a minute little girl," Jillie said and she eased the dress from Nadia's clutches. "It's a size 6 and I bet it is your size. Let's go try it on." Jillie took Nadia's hand. "Lacey, you wait here and our model will be out in a moment."

"Okay, I'll be waiting right in this chair and I expect a grand walk down the runway," Lacey smiled, held up her left hand and admired her beautiful ring Will had bought from their friend, Vance Service. "Who knew this famous jeweler would end up being a true friend," Lacey thought to herself and chuckled as she remembered their first meeting in New York.

"Okay," Jillie called from the dressing rooms, "I would like to introduce Miss Nadia."

Nadia floated out of the dressing rooms with a big smile on her face. She held out her dress and twirled around for Lacey to admire her and her beautiful dress. Jillie came out from the dressing rooms and watched her little cousin 'ham it up'.

"Bravo," Lacey said, as she clapped for Nadia. "Twirl your way over here and let me see the detail of the dress."

Nadia danced her way over to her big cousin and even curtsied making Lacey and Jillie both break out in laughter.

"What a ham you are," Lacey said, as she admired the dress. "OMG, look Jillie, the dress has beautiful kittens embroidered all over the front. And, they are in cream like my dress has!"

Lacey's dress was made in London by a special dress maker. She didn't even know, but Beautiful Butterfly had made this dress that had been sent over to America centuries ago. It somehow magically ended up in the attic of the old farmhouse for someone to find. It just happened to be found by Lacey.

Jillie walked over and they looked at one another and then at the dress. The dress was white with cream colored embroidered cats that looked so delicate and sweet. The dress was a stunning satin with embroidered organza overlay with the front of the skirt embroidered with the delicate cream colored kittens. It also had a matching organza cape.

"I love it Lacy," Nadia squealed. "I want this one please."

"I think it's a match little girl. Let's not get any shoes just yet, because I am afraid you will grow out of them. Let's go look and just get an idea of what you would like. We'll come back just before the wedding and buy them."

The girls found several pair of white shoes they all liked and the sales clerk assured them they would have plenty of these in many sizes. Lacey bought the dress and asked for the clerk to leave it hanging.

"Okay, let's go get some lunch," Lacey said. "That was fun, but I think we need to fuel our minds to find Jillie her dress.

"Sounds good to me," Jillie added.

"Can we go to the food court?" Nadia asked.

"Nothing finer than food court food," Jillie said laughing. "It's my favorite too and we can each have what we like."

"Food court, here we come," Lacey said, as she reached for Nadia to take hold of her hand. "You know you have to stay with me or Jillie and no running off by yourself young lady."

"I know, I know Lacey," Nadia replied. "My daddy and mommy told me that most people are nice, but there are some bad people out there acting nice. My daddy told me to always let him know if a stranger tries to talk to me anywhere, anytime and he'll make sure they are nice."

"That is great advice Nadia," Jillie said. "And, if mommy or daddy is not around always go to an adult you know or a police officer."

"Yep, that is what mommy and daddy tell me."

"Okay, we're good to go," Lacey said.

Jillie offered her hand for Nadia to hold and the three cousins headed to the food court. Once they all had their food choices, Lacey and Jillie ate while they listened to their little cousin tell them more history that she was reading and learning. She told them about 'Lewis and Clark' and 'King Arthur and the Round Table'. She even said, "as Merlin said, books are as important as gold". Lacey and Jillie wanted to laugh, but they both saw that their young cousin was extremely serious and very thoughtful when she spoke.

"Lacey," Nadia said, "you know our cats are really special.

Lacey choked on her bite of food and Jillie placed her fork full of food back down. The two older cousins looked at each other. They were in shock and didn't know what to say back to Nadia. Lacey took a deep breath. "What exactly do you mean?"

"Do I really need to tell you both?" Nadia asked with disgust in her voice. "They all talk to me. Don't they talk to you?"

"Okay, okay little smarty," Jillie said. "You cannot talk about this with anyone but us."

Nadia looked at Jillie, put her hands on her hips and glared at her older cousin. Jillie stared back and then looked at Lacey for help. Lacey cleared her throat. "Nadia, tell us more about your conversations with which cats."

"They all talk to me and have been since I was a baby," Nadia started. Virginia explained to me that I am a very special person and she made me promise that I would never share our talks with anyone but you and Jillie. I have never been around you alone long enough to tell you. And, Virginia told me that I didn't have to tell you."

"Okay," Lacey calmly responded. "We definitely didn't know that, but thank you so much for telling us. You are very special and I don't know how much you know, but I hope it doesn't scare you."

"Scare me," Nadia spit out. "I love being important to our cats, Uncle Jake and Will."

Lacey and Jillie were so taken back finding out their little cousin was aware of so much. They sat in silence for a few moments, but Nadia continued eating her lunch like it was 'no big thing'. Lacey decided to eat and think in silence and Jillie did the same. Again, it was as if they were all in sync and didn't need to further discuss anything. Lacey wanted to concentrate on her wedding and Jillie just wanted to have a normal college career.

"I'm done," Nadia said with a big smile. "Jillie, are you ready to 'shop 'til we drop'?"

Jillie and Lacey burst into laughter. Lacey tussled Nadia's hair. "You are way beyond your years little girl."

Nadia smiled and nodded her head in agreement, which made Lacey and Jillie laugh even more.

"Let's get out of here before you tell us you're going to be the next President of the United States," Lacey said, as she pushed her chair back. "I'll carry your dress, so Jillie can find her dress now."

"I want to help you Jillie," Nadia yelled like a six-year-old. "I don't want to be President. I am going to be a history professor, a famous equestrian and an animal whisperer. Will said I am an unbelievable rider."

"Animal whisperer?" Lacey asked. "Where do you go to get that degree?"

"It's something very special and Miss Virginia tells me that I am one."

Lacey and Jillie didn't laugh, but they both smiled at their little cousin. "I think that's great," Lacey replied. "But, I think you should finish grade school first."

"I didn't really know you were riding so much," Jillie commented.

"Oh yes," Lacey replied. "But, I have to admit, I

don't know how really good she's getting. Will or Adam is usually watching her. I'm so busy managing the farm."

"I can show you after we find Jillie's dress," Nadia said and she pulled Jillie along.

"Sounds good to me," Jillie said. "I need to get this dress selection done fast."

Jillie guided them to one of her favorite stores, where she had found formal gowns. Now that she knew what Lacey's and Nadia's looked like, she was ready to find hers. "I think I want something light yellow if that's okay with you Lacey."

"I think it's great for a summer wedding and I think we'll stick with yellow, white and very pale green," Lacey commented, as she was keeping her eye on Nadia, who was pulling out dresses and inspecting them.

"What do you think of this one?" Jillie asked, as she pulled an elegant light yellow gown with an empire waist with a square neckline. "This is my size and it's simple, but elegant. And, it has a cute shawl."

"Go for it," Lacey said.

"Yeah, go for it Jillie," Nadia mimicked.

Jillie looked at Nadia. "You're something else."

"Yes, I have been told that," Nadia replied. "Can I go back with you?"

"Sure, why not," Jillie answered and she held her hand out for Nadia to take. "Be right back."

"I'm excited to see it," Lacey commented, as she leaned up against a column in the middle of the department

A few minutes later, Nadia appeared. "I would like to announce Miss Jillie in her beautiful, yellow gown."

Jillie strolled out with her arms out and she twirled around for her cousins. "I think this is meant to be like Nadia's. It's the first one I saw and it fits like a glove. I think this is destiny as we know it."

Lacey nodded and smiled in agreement. "It looks

wonderful on you and I think it was definitely made with you in mind."

"We're done," Jillie said. "Let's get it and get back to the farm for some horseback riding."

"YEAH!" Nadia yelled, as she jumped up and down.

"You go get changed, but give me the tag and we'll go pay for it," Lacey said.

When Jillie came out, Lacey had already paid for the dress. The cousins rushed back to the car and headed to the farm. They were going to take the horses for a stroll around the farmland.

***

Lacey pulled into her driveway. Will, along with Tye and Tess, were outside heading to the barn. He stopped and waited for the girls to get out. Lacey showed him the dresses they picked out for Jillie and Nadia.

As usual, the cats were all around Nadia. She was chatting up a storm to them and they answered her back. Will, Lacey and Jillie all smiled at this normal, but always awesome sight.

"Beautiful," Will said, "I cannot wait to see your dress."

Lacey smiled and reached up to give him a quick kiss. "I'm going to run these inside. Someone is about to die if she doesn't get to ride the horses. If you go, we can take them all, but Shadow, for some nice exercise." Lacey hurried to the house with the dresses.

"Please Will, please Will!" Nadia begged, as she jumped up and down in front of him. "Just let Shadow come along and run beside us."

"Well, I guess we're going riding. Shadow can run beside us for sure. But afterward, we all clean out the stalls that I was about to do." Will walked over and hugged Jillie. "Have you talked with Miguel lately?"

"He's busy in the mountains doing whatever he does," Jillie answered. "He'll be here a couple of days before your big day to help us. He's going to take care of things so you and Lacey can concentrate on all the things you're trying to pull off. Lacey told me some special people are coming to the wedding and you have to get them all dressed up. I cannot wait to see them all, but it'll be hard to act like we don't know one another very much. When you two get back from your honeymoon, I'm going to join him in the mountains and we're going to learn more about being a veterinarian from the old dudes."

Jillie and Will laughed together thinking about some of Will's people coming three hundred years into the future for his and Lacey's wedding.

"Here comes Lacey," Nadia yelled and ran to grab her hand. "Let's go."

Lacey whistled for the horses and in seconds they saw them running. Nadia ran to meet them. All five horses stopped to nudge their little Nadia. Tye and Tess were right in the thick of it all.

"Don't worry Shadow; I'll take you for a ride in just a bit if you want to go again." The horse nudged Nadia.

"Look at that," Jillie said.

"Oh, that's nothing," Will replied. "She has total command of all five horses and they love her so much."

"Let's get some saddles on them" Will called out to Nadia, who guided them straight into the barn and talked to them all the way. The two cats and the five horses made all kinds of noises back to Nadia. This was all normal to Nadia.

Lacey placed blankets on each horse and Will came behind her with a saddle for each horse. Jillie took Baby Boy and finished with his bridle, while Nadia took care of Little Girl. Lacey took care of Warrior Girl and Will was in charge of Storm Cloud. Will checked behind each girl to make sure the horses were all properly saddled up. “Let’s go for a ride,” Will directed and then he whistled for Shadow to join them.

The troop slowly walked out of the barn. Will and Nadia led the way with Shadow between them. Lacey and Jillie trailed behind and they admired their little cousin’s confidence in the saddle.

“So, Nadia must be spending lots of time here riding,” Jillie commented.

“She is here every chance she gets and she’s always with the horses, unless I give her a chore,” Lacey replied. “Will takes care of her riding lessons, so I don’t even know all that she knows. Work is never done around here, but Adam is a great help. Our cousins all come over to help whenever they’re in town. Some of the older cousins of our parents come over and help as much as possible too. So, I can’t complain.”

“I feel so bad Lacey,” Jillie said. “I cannot wait for my studies to be complete, but it takes time.”

“OMG Jillie, please don’t worry. Will and I are holding it together. When Uncle Jake and everyone return, we’ll have some additional help.”

Jillie smiled. “I miss seeing them all.”

“Lacey, Jillie,” Nadia yelled, “look at me!” Nadia was standing up on Little Girl’s saddle with her right foot planted on the saddle and the left ‘toe tipping’ the saddle horn. Tye, Tess and now Tea were all circling on the ground watching over Nadia showing off her skills.

Will looked back and shrugged his arms up. “She’s a natural.”

“Nadia, that is awesome, but please be careful,” Lacey called back.

Nadia sat back down and turned Little Girl around. “Little Girl, let’s show these two what we can do.” Nadia and Little Girl began showing off with all kinds of tricks and poses. The girls sat back and watched their young cousin ‘ham it up’.

"Okay Nadia," Will said, "let's take them for a nice run.

"You got it," Nadia said and she took off in a full speed run.

Will took off after her looking back for the girls to get with it.

"Let's show them a thing or two," Lacey said, as she gave her horse a loving pat. Lacey took off and Jillie gave Baby Boy his clue to get it going. The three cats were running all around and chasing one another.

They were all flying down the pasture near the old oak tree, when Will noticed the portal wavering as if someone was about to come through to the present time. He held his arm up for all of them to halt, but Nadia was way ahead. He whistled letting Nadia know they had stopped and she turned on a dime to see what he wanted. She saw the portal wavering too and headed back to join her troop. The three cats turned into their beastly forms and they knew something was not right. They all slowly approached the old oak tree and waited to see who was coming. No one appeared. All of them waited and waited. Nothing happened. As Lacey, Jillie and Will watched for someone from their past to return, Nadia watched for someone from the future. After about five minutes of the portal door wavering, it closed.

Lacey looked at Jillie and then at Will. "I hope that wasn't someone trying to come over, but they shouldn't be there. They are all in the mountains with our Chief Running Antelope's Wolf and his tribe."

Nadia wanted to say something, but she couldn't give her secret away. Maybe it was Lope trying to come over, but something kept him from coming. They didn't have time to explore and worry. They had too much to do with the farm.

Chapter 8: Lacey's Wedding, Nadia's Debut

The big day arrived for Lacey and Will. The farmhouse and the surrounding land were beautifully landscaped with the help of Lacey's mom. The wedding was set at the six o'clock hour that evening. This allowed any out-of-town guests to have the entire day for travel if they couldn't arrive the day before the wedding. Miguel's parents were also traveling from the mountains to see their son and Jillie in the wedding.

Lacey and Will wanted a short ceremony since they had already been married three hundred years ago. This ceremony had been put together for the sake of Lacey's parents and other family members. Lacey and Will were happy to finally be able to live as husband and wife. Lacey was excited that Will's mom and dad were able to travel back to the portal to be here. They had been escorted by several warrior scouts that would wait in their beloved village. Will brought his parents to stay with him the night before the wedding. Will had assured Lacey that he would make sure that his parents would not look too out of place or time.

When Lacey told Will that she, Jillie and Nadia would get ready at her grandparents' home, Will put a wonderful wedding surprise together for his bride that would include their parents, Lacey's brother, the cats and the horses. He brought his parents' and the warrior scouts' horses through the portal for the wedding procession.

A wonderful feast was planned for the wedding

reception. Lacey's mom and aunts had turned the farmhouse into a beautiful wedding venue. Ginger and Wayne had hired a wedding catering group that brought in staff to make sure the beverages and food would be continually refilled. The kitchen was set up with all types of beverages in beautiful gallon jugs. The dining room had so many foods displayed on every surface. The wedding cake, coffee and iced teas were in the formal living room waiting to be displayed and served on the front porch, where the ceremony would take place. Round tables, with beautiful center pieces, were scattered all around the front yard for the guests. White and yellow ribbons were dangling, and waving in the breeze, from the huge pecan trees. A long table was placed on each side of the porch steps for the wedding party.

At five o'clock, music began to fill the air. Ginger had arranged for a small group of musicians to play before and after the ceremony. Lacey's male cousins, who all knew the secret of the land, divided themselves up to either direct parking or escort guests to their seats. Right before the ceremony, these guys would all walk in together and sit right behind Ginger, Wayne, Gregory and his wife.

"It's five-thirty Lace," Jillie said, as she walked over to Lacey. "Let's get your veil on now. You know we have to get a group picture before it's time for us to make our way over to the farmhouse. Remember, we saw it on the wall in the future."

Lacey looked at Jillie. "I cannot believe you remembered that. I had forgotten all about those pictures. I've been so busy. What if it was supposed to be made over there? Maybe we should have just gotten ready there."

I think we are where we are supposed to be Lacey," Jillie replied. "Don't worry; Aunt Lucy is supposed to be coming over here with your mom. She'll take a quick picture."

Lucy and Ginger walked in just a minute after Lacey's veil was on and secured. "Picture time," Lucy said. "Let me do this and get back over there. I cannot wait to see the grand entrance."

Lacey looked at her aunt. "It's not that grand."

Lucy had seen Will getting the horses all ready and knew he had a wonderful surprise coming in just a moment. "You're a bride. It's going to be grand." Lucy took a few pictures and quickly left. Lucy smiled to herself and knew that she would have the picture of Lacey, Jillie and Nadia beautifully framed as a wedding gift. They looked so beautiful and connected to her.

Ginger hugged Lacey. "You're so beautiful."

"Thanks mom," Lacey said.

"You're all beautiful," Ginger said, as she looked at Jillie and Nadia. "The dresses looked as if they were made for this wedding."

Jillie and Nadia both smiled. Jillie walked over to the front door and saw the entourage of men and horses approaching. She waved Nadia over.

"What are you two looking at?" Lacey asked.

"I want to see too," Ginger said, as she took Lacey's hand and guided her to the big living room window.

"OMG," Lacey whispered, as she saw Gregory, her dad, Will and Miguel all upon beautifully decorated horses. Each rider was guiding another horse beside them. "Jillie, Nadia, did you two know about this?"

"We all did," Ginger said. "Will asked us if we would help him give you a grand entrance."

Lacey looked at Jillie and Nadia. "I have a grand entrance!"

"Girls, don't forget your flowers," Ginger said, as she handed each one their flowers.

As Gregory approached on Storm Cloud, Nadia walked out the front door. Gregory dismounted, took the basket of yellow and red rose petals and helped little

Nadia mount Little Girl side saddle. Gregory remounted. He and Nadia moved so that Wayne could assist Ginger upon her horse. Ginger giggled and looked at her daughter. "I had to practice this a few times." Everyone laughed.

Wayne remounted; he took a hold of Ginger's reign and led them a few steps away. "I better hold onto your mom. I don't want her to give the horse the wrong message and go galloping off into the wild, blue yonder."

Everyone laughed while Ginger smirked at her husband. "You sure it shouldn't be the other way around mama's little boy. I got your number."

Next, Miguel moved Baby Boy near the front porch. He smiled and whispered. "You look beautiful Medicine Woman." He dismounted, took her bouquet of yellow daffodils with white baby's breath and sat them down. He offered his hand to Jillie and helped her to mount Baby Boy side saddle. Miguel handed her the bouquet and got back on his horse. They moved away side by side for the bride to be next.

Will's eyes were locked on Lacey, as he rode up on his black stallion guiding Warrior Girl to his bride. He gallantly slipped off his horse, walked over to Lacey and held out his hand for her flowers. He gently placed them down and held his hand out for Lacey. Lacey put her hand in his and allowed him to guide her to Warrior Girl's side. Lacey reached up and took hold of Warrior Girl's saddle horn with her right hand. Will gently put his arms around Lacey's waist and lifted her upon her saddle. He straightened her beautiful wedding gown so that it flowed over the back end of her horse and then he placed the bouquet of yellow roses, white gardenias and baby's breath to the opposite side of Lacey hanging from the saddle horn. "I'm ready, are you?" Will asked.

"So ready," Lacey said with pride.

Will jumped upon his stallion and he called out for the cats to assume their positions. Will held his hand over to Lacey. She took his hand and they moved to their last place in the procession. Gregory raised his hand to alert Aiken that the wedding procession was ready. Seconds later, the band began playing a wedding processional march. Gregory led the procession and walked his horse down his grandparents' driveway, along the roadside and up his great-grandparents' driveway. He walked the horse to the back of the tables and moved slowly through the middle of them. When he reached the front, he guided his horse over to the right side of the porch.

Wayne and Ginger were met by Will's parents. The two mothers went side by side with their spouses riding right behind them. As Lacey's and Will's mothers stopped their horses, the two fathers dismounted and assisted their wives down. Aiken, Andrew, Chase and Adam all came and took the horses. They each mounted a horse and road to the far end of the yard behind all the tables of guests. Aiken and Andrew stood side by side on one side while Chase and Adam stood side by side on the other side.

Next, Jillie and Miguel came in a bit faster showing off their equestrian talents. When they reached the four cousins mounted upon horses, they slowed their horses as they smiled towards the guests and their parents. The guests giggled as they saw Tess sitting pretty behind Jillie and Kai sitting behind Miguel. When they got up to the front, they backed their horses up to each side of tables and stayed mounted. Miguel fell behind Gregory. Tess jumped down and stood between Baby Boy's front legs. It was an unbelievable sight.

Now it was time for the flower girl, Nadia. When the wedding party and the guests turned to see who was next, the 'aaahs' were heard over the music. Nadia was standing in her saddle with Tea seated upon Little Girl's rump. Nadia gently tossed rose petals as she made her way to the front. As she tossed the petals, she told the meaning of the flowers. "I toss many yellow rose petals that honor the special friendship born unto Will and Lacey. I toss a few red rose petals for the love that unexpectedly began and will grow stronger everyday for the rest of their lives." When she reached the front, she gracefully bent to her knees and sat herself side saddle. She voiced a quiet command and Little Girl side stepped in front of Jillie. Tea stayed seated. Jeremy and Stacey were so proud as relatives gave them 'thumbs up'.

The music stopped and the crowd all stood up. As the wedding march began, Lacey and Will slowly guided their horses up the driveway and between the four cousins. Tye sat like a statue upon Lacey's gown that draped over Warrior Girl's rump. As Will and Lacey came to the front of the yard, they joined hands and stayed mounted on their horses. Tye remained behind his Lacey. The minister moved to the top of the porch and smiled out over the crowd. He raised his hands and began the short ceremony. When it came time for the rings to be exchanged, more show for the guests came.

Gregory whispered a command to Storm Cloud as instructed by Will and Nadia. Nadia whispered the same command to Little Girl. The horses took a few steps forward in unison to bring the rings. The rings were tied to yellow ribbons that were weaved into Storm Cloud's and Little Girl's manes. Lacey looked at Will and smiled. They both untied the other's ring. Will voiced a command and the two horses moved back to their previous positions.

Lacey leaned over and whispered into Will's ear. "Thank you for the surprises and making this wedding so grand."

"Our lives will be filled with many surprises and love," Will replied. "It will always be grand." He looked at the minister and nodded for him to carry on with the ceremony. As the minister announced that Will could kiss his bride, he dismounted and offered his hand to

Lacey. He helped her down and sealed their wedding promises with a kiss. The minister announced to the crowd, Mr. and Mrs. Will Hayes. The guests all stood up and cheered.

Will held up his right hand, as a chief would do to silence the guests. "I hope you will stay and enjoy this feast, I mean the reception. But first, please be seated as our little Nadia has a special gift for Lacey and all of you." Will guided Lacey to sit on the front row with their parents. Gregory led Jillie and Miguel to follow him and join their cousins with the other horses.

Nadia jumped off her horse, pulled off her beautiful dress to reveal a satin white and yellow riding outfit. The crowd chuckled in delight. Jeremy was the most excited and he stood up. "That's my daughter."

Nadia looked at her dad and blew him a kiss. She remounted Little Girl. And the show began. Nadia showed off her equestrian talents that she and Will had been working on just for the wedding. Little Girl moved at Nadia's commands and they dazzled the crowd with elegance and grace.

Lacey looked at Will. "You have certainly been working hard with our little cousin. She's like ready for show."

"Exactly," Will replied. "I think she has found a calling for sure."

The crowd all cheered as Nadia raced Little Girl away. She and the boys all took the horses to the barn and quickly took their saddles and decorations off. Adam and his cousins quickly worked and returned to the reception.

The reception only lasted two hours. Everyone seemed to be tired and ready to go home; especially Will's parents and the guests that had traveled from far away. Will and Lacey's dear friend from New York, Vance Service, wished them his best and gave them a huge check to help with the farm. Miguel's parents left soon after they ate to head back to the mountains. Little Nadia, after being treated like a celebrity, was exhausted and left without any argument. Gregory helped his sister and made sure their parents and grandparents didn't stick around so they could get Will's parents back to the village three hundred years ago. Miguel and Jillie, along with Miss Virginia, Tye and Tess, left with Will's parents to return to their village and to their warrior scouts three hundred years in the past. Miss Virginia would continue traveling with Will's parents and the warriors as they would make their way back to their temporary home in the North Carolina Mountains. Aiken, Andrew, Chase and Adam stayed around to help get things all straightened up. They knew the importance of the secret and they were there to help. They stayed at their grandparents' home and would make sure Miguel and Jillie returned. Will and Lacey got to stay in the farmhouse as husband and wife.

Chapter 9: Elementary for Nadia

Third grade arrived for Nadia and she was extremely excited. She loved seeing her friends that she didn't get to see over the summer and she loved learning. On the very first day of third grade, Nadia got to show her reading skill once Miss Flint had everyone seated after lunch.

"Okay students, this year I would like to take thirty minutes each day to review everyone's work from the day before to see if I need to review the material again. In order to do that, I will need one of you, and I hope all of you participate, to read to the rest of the class from one of your required readers. This way, you will all get one book read to you. So, you have to pay attention, take notes if you need to and ask questions at the end. Who would like to be my first assistant teacher?"

"Assistant teacher," Nadia thought with excitement and she threw up her hand.

"Okay, so I have a reader. Thank-you Nadia; here is the book I want you to read to everyone. It's all about our very first President. Nadia you have the floor from the front of the room."

Miss Flint took her stack of papers and positioned herself at the back of the room. Nadia rushed up to the front of the room and looked at all her classmates. She felt a bit nervous with so many eyes on her and took a deep breath. She noticed Tea sitting on the ledge of the back window. She knew she was there because she felt scared. "Okay class, if I mess a word up, help me out please."

Miss Flint looked up after hearing Nadia's remark. "That's right class, help one another out. What a great teacher you would make Nadia."

Nadia beamed with pride from that one comment of praise. She relaxed and began to read. She read with such enthusiasm that soon the teacher noticed that Nadia had captured an audience. She sat back and enjoyed the story. Nadia only struggled with a few words and Miss Flint was so impressed how Nadia walked over to the board and wrote the word for everyone to see. The class all helped her sound out each word as a team. She was so impressed. When she noticed twenty-five minutes had flown by, she quietly got up and walked up to Nadia.

"Thank-you Nadia; I think we all enjoyed listening."

Nadia's classmates clapped and one student called out. "I think Nadia should read to us everyday."

Nadia smiled. "I would love to." She looked at the back window and Tea was gone.

"Well Nadia, I may just have to rearrange my thoughts now. I so enjoyed you reading, I think I want to hear everyone read."

Some of the class, especially the boys, didn't like that and called out for Nadia.

"Okay class," Miss Flint said, as she held up her hand. "I want everyone to try at least once. It's good practice to be in front of a crowd. If you struggle, we'll help you. Just like Nadia said, she wasn't sure she knew every word. Look how you all helped her. Nadia is a bit advanced in her reading skill, so I don't want anyone to feel like they have to read that well. I wouldn't be needed if you were all reading like that."

That day made a huge impression on Nadia. She wanted to become a teacher one day. The rest of the year was awesome for Nadia. Her class had their moments, but with the help of Miss Flint, they worked out their struggles of getting along and learning how to deal with differences. Miss Flint helped them realize how not everyone learns at the same pace or level and she wanted everyone to respect one another. Miss Flint introduced the students to many subjects and saw that some students were already unbelievable artists or promising musicians.

During November, she helped the students write a play for Christmas that they would perform for their parents. The name of the play was "Friends Are Special Angels". Each student played an angel, except for one boy. Roger got to play the main part. The teacher realized that Roger had a talent for drama. He was good at memorization and he quickly learned his lines with enthusiasm.

Nadia was so excited about being an angel that she asked her dad to help make her special wings. Jeremy was more excited than Nadia. He loved making things. Nadia and her dad made her the biggest and shiniest wings from coat hangers. That was also part of the excitement, each student got to make their own wings.

Jeremy bent the coat hangers in the shape of wings and helped Nadia fit them right over her shoulders. Nadia asked her mom to get her gold foil and white tissue paper. With the help of her dad, they covered the coat hangers with the white tissue paper using lots of tape around the ends. Once they had that secured, they used the gold foil to fit all around the metal that outlined the white tissue paper. They were amazing and the play was a hit. The parents gave a standing ovation. Jeremy taped the entire play and gave a copy to each student as a present to their parents.

Nadia's third grade year was half over and she was loving school. Christmas break came and went. The second half of third grade was great. She even got to bring Tea to school. The teacher allowed any student to bring in their pet if they wrote a short essay about them.

Nadia wrote how Tea had come to her home and her classmates loved hearing the story. Nadia wanted to tell so much more and bring in one of the horses from the farm. But she knew that her secrets could not be told; at least not now. She didn't even share much about her riding talents. She was too busy having fun just being a kid.

Fourth grade came and almost all of the same students were in her class. School was fun from the start. Nadia's fourth grade teacher wasn't very young, but she was nice. She liked to read to the class herself and she was very enthusiastic and animated. The only thing that Nadia and her classmates hated was when there was a sad part. Their teacher cried like a baby. Someone, usually Nadia, handed their teacher a tissue. That was another person who made a great impression on Nadia. Her fourth grade teacher showed the students how to be compassionate. No one could be mean to poor Mrs. Petree.

Mrs. Petree, like Miss Flint, loved the students' creativity. She also encouraged the students to write. Nadia and a few girls wrote a play together. Mrs. Petree was so impressed. She told them they could cast it and perform it in front of all the fourth and fifth grade classes. Nadia learned how hard it was to select classmates for parts in the play without hurting others' feelings.

Nadia was also introduced to the world of clicks. Her feelings were hurt when she was ousted on the playground by several girls. Tea showed up a few times when the boys were chasing the girls around the playground. Nadia had to learn to control Tea with her thoughts and not allow a cougar loose on the playground.

Fifth grade was a tougher year for Nadia. In order to get the students ready for middle school, the students changed classes for certain subjects. Nadia wasn't with many of her friends and Nadia was very fearful of her fifth grade teacher. Tea sensed the fear and showed up in the classroom almost every day. Nadia would open her room locker and there she would be quietly sitting.

One day, Nadia saw Tea peeking out from behind the supplies cabinet when the teacher was yelling at the entire class for not being neat. Nadia about fell out of her seat when Tea made a low growl and the teacher whipped around looking towards the strange sound. The classroom was so quiet you could have heard a pin drop. Mr. Yellman stood there for a few seconds and then returned his attention to the class. Everyone was quietly sitting and waiting for something to happen. He burst into laughter. "I think I'm going to start growling to get everyone's attention." The students joined their teacher in a good laugh. When Mr. Yellman held up his hand, they all quickly quieted down. "Students, I apologize for yelling and I would appreciate it if you would try harder to keep your desks neater."

It was also during fifth grade that Nadia began noticing some of her classmates were starting to act differently. She wasn't sure who she should call her friends. She realized that she was not being invited to many of her old friends' homes. She had no idea that her intelligence was causing her peers to not like her. She felt sad, but having Tea around kept her entertained and she began asking her parents if she could spend her weekends on the farm. Her parents worried, but she always came home so happy from working on the farm or riding the horses that they decided it was okay. "

"Not everyone needs to be part of a big group," Jeremy would tell his wife.

With her spending so much time at the farm, she didn't have time to get into trouble with other children. It was during her summer following fifth grade that she began seriously riding. Her father even agreed to have an English riding teacher come to the farm. Lacey loved having Nadia there and she loved watching her ride.

A wonderful part of Nadia's fifth grade year,

Uncle Jake returned with most of the people that had fled to the safety of the unknown and hidden Appalachian Mountain tribe. Sir Edward Miller and his wife, Anna, had returned from England as planned. They had purchased the land. Will began teaching Nadia about his people and he began taking Nadia on educational trips back and forth across time. Nadia began to read more and more history books. She became intrigued with history. She spent more and more time on the farm. Once the summer arrived, she didn't want to miss a day on the farm.

Jillie and Miguel came home to the farm for a weekend break from their studies and Nadia was there waiting on them. As so many times before, Nadia, her cousins, Will, and now Miguel took all five horses out for a nice ride. They planned on checking the fences, look over the planted fields and enjoy a picnic. Miguel also brought Kai along.

As they all loved to do, they were all racing down the pasture near the old oak tree, when Will noticed the portal wavering as if someone was about to come through to this time. He held his arm up for them all to halt. They all slowly approached the old oak tree and waited to see who was coming. Fours beasts were now circling their people. Three felines and one black wolf were watching over Nadia and her family.

Seconds went by and it was their Uncle Jake's best friend, Son of Running Deer, who was startled to see them all right there. Will, also known as Tame Tiger, jumped off of Shadow and ran over to his dear friend. Son of Running Deer grabbed Tame Tiger in tight and began talking in their native language. Lacey and Jillie tried to understand, but they couldn't understand every word. But Nadia did and she jumped off her horse. She ran over to the two men with the four beasts circling around the two men and the little girl. Lacey and Jillie looked at one another in amazement.

Nadia ran back over to her two older cousins. "It's Uncle Jake's son, Twoson and it's not good news. He's very sick and they think he has what I had, but they are not sure. We have to do something."

"How did you know what they are saying?" Lacey asked.

"Tame Tiger teaches me whenever I'm here. We only speak in our native tongue now when it's just us two."

"Okay then," Jillie commented. "So ole smart one, what should we do?"

"We must go to our family in the past and say prays over our cousin. It's the only thing we can do."

Jillie looked at Lacey. "Why can't we go forward and find Lope and do what we've done before for someone else?"

"Uncle Jake says no," Nadia replied. "Son of Running Deer and Tame Tiger are discussing that now and Uncle Jake fears that we cannot run to the future to solve all of our problems or we may face certain destruction. I would have gone myself to get Lope if they were game."

Jillie looked at Lacey and then at Nadia. "You know someone named Lope?"

Nadia cringed. She didn't know if she should spill the beans on Lope or not, but she couldn't lie to the two people she adored the most. "Yes, I met Lope in the barn. He's my best friend. Please don't be mad at him. He loves coming and playing with the horses at night. He only comes when he's on the farm."

Jillie and Lacey looked at one another, but didn't say a word. Nothing surprised them any more after all the things they had learned about their own lives.

"Okay, let's head over with Son of Running Deer," Lacey said, as she slid off Warrior Girl. "We'll take the horses with us too so we can go quickly to the village."

"Nadia, you're going to see something so wonderful," Jillie said.

"I've been there lots of times," Nadia quickly replied. "Tame Tiger and I go back there a lot. You know how we're always working on the fences? Well we do, but we also go back to the village. I play with all my friends there. They are our family you know."

Lacey and Jillie shook their heads. "And we're supposed to be all apart of this destiny," Lacey said with a bit of hurt in her voice. "I guess it's for a reason." She mumbled some other words to herself as she frequently did when she was upset.

"Well Lace," Jillie said, as she put her arm around her older cousin's shoulder, "we knew that Nadia is something special and I guess we just need to let her destiny take her where she needs to go. We cannot make the rules, as we have not been able to do so with our own lives."

Nadia looked at her cousins with a puzzling look. "You're not mad at me are you?"

Lacey shut her eyes and shook her head 'no'. "No little girl, we're just confused. It's all good. Come on; let's get ready to cross over. Hold onto Little Girl and go with Son of Running Deer.

Nadia did as Lacey directed and moved next to her uncle's best friend. He took the horse's reigns in his left hand and held out his right hand for Nadia. Tea was on Nadia's right side. Will motioned for the girls to go next and their protectors were right by their sides. Miguel, Kai and Storm Cloud stayed back. Miguel wanted to watch over the farm and head off any relatives that would happen to drop by the farm.

Just before son of Running Deer was about to walk into the portal, Jillie yelled. "Wait! I must go back and get my medicine pouches. I won't be but a few minutes." Jillie jumped back into her saddle and took off on Baby Boy before anyone could argue."

Son of Running Deer patiently waited for Jillie to return. Somewhere between five and ten minutes Jillie returned, jumped off her horse and resumed her position. Son of Running Deer, Nadia, Tea and Little girl walked into the wavering portal. Jillie guided Baby Boy and Tess behind Nadia. Lacey pulled Warrior Girl in tight and looked down at Tye. “Let’s go boy.” Will and Shadow went through the portal last and the wavering door quickly closed behind them.

Chapter 10: Jake's Nieces Unite

As they all arrived three hundreds years in the past, they all regrouped themselves making sure the animals were all unharmed. Will excused himself and vanished further into the cave. When he reappeared, he was Tame Tiger once again and in his native dress. Lacey looked at him, smiled and gave him a hug. She knew what he was sacrificing for her. He looked down into her eyes and smiled back. Son of Running Deer spoke and brought them back in tune with everyone else. "Everyone mount up and let's get on our way."

Jake's best friend led the troop and went full speed ahead. Jake's son's life was in danger and he had to be there for this child that was sick. He had to be there for Jake. Nadia stayed close to Son of Running Deer. Jillie, Lacey and Will were all side by side with their horses racing to the edge of the woods. The cats, in their beastly forms, ran all around them. Before long, Virginia came out of nowhere and joined them in her lion form. When they reached the edge of the woods, Son of Running Deer continued to lead with Nadia right behind him. Nadia was followed by Jillie, Lacey and then Will. The feline beasts were everywhere. They made sure nothing would come in their way.

Finally, they reached the end of the woods, where they sounded out their bird calls alerting the village of their presence. Calls were returned and they knew it was safe for them to advance to the village. Lots of security had been set up since they were ambushed by the British

Dragoons.

As they came into the village, many young men came to take the horses for food and water. They each hugged Tame Tiger and the girls. Son of Running Deer hurried to Jake's teepee. Tame Tiger talked with the young men for a few minutes and all three girls waited for them to finish. Nadia listened to every word and shook her head as she was listening. Lacey and Jillie looked at one another again. They understood most of it, but they could tell that Nadia knew it all.

"Okay, let's go," Tame Tiger said and the four of them rushed to Uncle Jake's teepee. Tame Tiger's mother was waiting there on her son and smothered him with hugs and kisses. Then she hugged and kissed Lacey, Jillie and little Nadia. Soon, the Chief came too and welcomed them all.

"Healing Heart has been with him all day," Chief Fierce Tiger explained. "I am glad you all are here for your uncle and his family."

Jillie moved forward. "Do you think I can join them? I brought all my medicines."

Fierce Tiger held open the teepee flap for Jillie to enter. "Healing Heart can use your medicines, as you may have something from the mountains he does not have."

Jillie rushed into the teepee and Fierce Tiger let the flap fall down. He spoke to his son and left.

Lacey looked at Tame Tiger with a questioning look. "He told me he would like to speak with me. I'll be back."

"Okay," Lacey replied and she turned her attention to her little cousin, Nadia. "You okay?"

"Worried," Nadia replied.

Lacey smiled and pulled her cousin in tight. "Let's go find a quiet place and pray for our cousin."

"That sounds like the right thing to do," Nadia replied.

Lacey and Nadia strolled arm in arm to the edge of the village. No one bothered them and they found a beautiful spot next to the stream. The two cousins sat down on a huge rock. Lacey took Nadia's hand in hers and they sat in silence for a few moments.

"Do you want me to say a prayer Lacey?"

Lacey softly smiled down at Nadia and whispered. "Yeah, that would be wonderful."

Nadia stood up, raised her hands to the sky and her left foot to her right knee. When she finally spoke, Lacey couldn't help but look up at her cousin. She sounded so grown up and so wise beyond her years. She took in every word that her young cousin spoke as she asked for the health of their cousin to be restored. Lacey's heart filled with joy, as she felt so much faith. Nadia lowered her right hand for Lacey to hold. Lacey reached up and squeezed her cousin's hand, as Nadia continued praying. Nadia returned the squeeze, closed her eyes and felt like something wonderful was going to happen. When Nadia finished her prayer, she sat back down and the two cousins sat in silence listening to the stream's soothing trickle. Some time went by and voices from the village interrupted their meditation. Lacey stood up and saw Jillie running towards them. Lacey ran towards Jillie with Nadia close behind her.

"Twoson broke his fever. He's sitting up and he's eating like nothing was ever wrong."

Lacey looked at Nadia and then back at Jillie. The three girls clung together for a few moments. "Come on," Jillie said. "Uncle Jake sent me to get you two."

The girls ran all the way back to their uncle's teepee. The flapped door was thrown back and they went right in to see their cousin awake and talking. Twoson looked at his three cousins. "I saw you in my dreams. I saw each one of you. Jillie, you were a panther, just like Tess. You understood my death was near and held on to me with your healing energy. Lacey, you were a tiger like Tye. I could feel your healing strength holding me steady. Nadia, you were a cougar like Tea. I could feel your fury and your power. You overpowered my sickness with your words of healing. You all became one and you were a lion like Virginia. She told me to let go of my worries. I did and I woke up.

The girls all looked at one another and then at their Uncle Jake. There were no words needed to be spoken. Jillie's necklace lit up beneath her shirt. Lacey reached over and pulled it out where they could all see. The three stones were brightly glowing.

From that moment forward, Nadia wanted to be on the farm even more. This was where she belonged. Tea, of course, loved being on the farm. She was around her older brother and sister. Virginia visited often and the four felines would follow Nadia's every step. Nadia's elementary days had been filled with such special love. The love of the most powerful beasts surrounded her with the most magical love.

Unlike all the years before, Nadia wasn't excited about returning to school. She didn't want to deal with fitting in and trying to make friends. Jeremy and Stacey had to enlist the help of Lacey and Will to talk with her about the importance of going to school. Will expressed his fears for Nadia to Jeremy and Stacey. She was so wise beyond her years; she was far more grown-up than her classmates. Lacey agreed more with her uncle and aunt. Lacey felt that Nadia needed to learn to socialize with people her own age. Therefore, Nadia begrudgingly began her middle school years with fear and negativity. Tea was on guard to protect her Nadia.

Chapter 11: Sixth Grade Sisterhood

First day of sixth grade came too fast for Nadia. The only reason Nadia was happy to see her sixth grade year was Jillie's and Miguel's wedding was being planned. Jillie would be finishing up her final year of her veterinarian degree. Lacey and Will were already working with Miguel to build a vet office on the farm for their practice. Nadia was helping design the spaces for cats.

"Okay Nadia," Stacey said, as she pulled up to the middle school drop-off spot, "have a wonderful day and please put a smile on that face."

Nadia looked at her mother through the rearview mirror. "The only reason I am happy that sixth grade is here is because the faster it goes, the sooner Jillie's and Miguel's wedding will be. And, Lacey and Will are letting me design the cat rooms for the new veterinarian clinic and boarding service Jillie and Miguel will offer."

"I hope you continue to keep your mind on your studies too Naddie Girl. I know you will make us proud as always."

"Mom, as far as my grades go, you don't have to worry," Nadia said, as she opened the door and quickly got out. When she slammed her door, she tapped on the passenger side, front window. Stacey rolled down the window. "It's the other students you better worry about. You know how the junior high years can be. It can just be a treacherous experience for those of us who actually like school."

Stacey held back her smile at her daughter's serious response. "You'll do great Nadia and just remember that you don't have to be popular to make something of yourself. Stay true to yourself and good things will happen."

Nadia rolled her eyes, turned around and glanced for any sign of a friend. "Just breathe," Nadia thought to herself.

Stacey beeped and pulled away. Nadia quickly walked to find her homeroom class. Some of the eighth graders were standing with signs to help the new students. Nadia smiled at one of the older girls holding up a sign, "Need help, ask me."

"Can I get help finding my homeroom?" Nadia asked.

"You bet. What is your name?"

Nadia gave her name and the nice girl walked her to her room. "My name is Veronica Flowers. If you need any help this year, just let me know."

Nadia smiled. "Thanks Veronica. I am a little scared of the whole middle school thing."

"Get involved in clubs, sports or both and you'll have friends in no time," Veronica replied, as she saw another lost soul wondering the halls. "Better go help that one, he looks really lost."

Nadia smiled and turned her attention to her homeroom class. She walked in and saw several kids she knew from elementary school, but no one waved or smiled at her. Nadia took the first seat she came to and sat down all alone. Students were filing in one after another and no one said a word to Nadia. When the teacher finally came into the room, Nadia noticed her beautiful scarf with cats all over it. It made Nadia relax and she thought of her cat, Tea. She knew Tea would be there for her, but she didn't want to do anything to make her show up.

"Okay class, let's settle down."

Students began sitting down and the buzzing of voices soon vanished.

"My name is Gloria Morning. Please say 'here' when I call your name. After roll call every morning, you have fifteen minutes to chat, finish some homework or study. When I say chat, that means from your chair to your closest neighbors and it must be done quietly. If you are absent for one or two days, you need a parent's note. If you're out for three or more, you must have a doctor's note. Any questions?"

No one raised their hands. "Okay, enjoy your next ten minutes and be ready to get to your next class when the bell rings. Eighth graders are in the hallways to help you find your class."

The buzzing resumed, but Nadia sat quietly alone. Miss Morning noticed Nadia sitting and staring straight ahead. She walked over to Nadia's desk. "Nadia, wasn't it? Is everything okay?"

Nadia sat up straighter than she already was and smiled at the teacher. "Yes m'am; I just don't really know anyone here very well. I'm not the usual sixth grader Miss Morning."

The teacher smiled. "Nadia, just give it a chance. Middle school can be a challenge for those of us who are not as outgoing or as popular. You'll find your friends. If you find yourself worried or confused, please come and see me. I think you and I are a lot alike."

"Do you like cats Miss Morning?" Nadia asked with excitement.

"Oh yes. I have two cats. Their names are Salt and Pepper. They are siblings. I bet you can guess that one is white and one is black. Their mother was black and white. So funny how genetics work."

"Oh yes. I have a cat named Tea. She is grey and white with huge golden eyes. I noticed your scarf. I love it."

"My mother gave me this Nadia, because I am so

nuts about my cats."

Nadia laughed and the bell rang. "I better get going Miss Morning. Thank you for spending time with me."

"You have a good day and remember I am here if you need me."

Nadia felt wonderful as she quickly walked out of homeroom all alone. "Two nice people so far," Nadia thought to herself. "Maybe I was too quick to judge."

Just as Nadia was feeling good about herself, someone pushed her forward. Nadia swung around and was face to face with two girls laughing.

"You're a nerd, we can tell," one girl said.

Nadia didn't know what to say. She moved out of their way and let them pass. One of them gave her a mean smirk. Nadia was shaken, but no one asked her if she was okay. Students just walked by her as if nothing happened. Nadia asked one of the eighth graders for directions to her next class and she almost ran. When she got to that class, she found an old friend from third grade sitting alone. Nadia sat to the girl's right side and smiled.

"Do you remember me, Susan?" Nadia asked.

"The best reader ever," Susan answered.

Nadia smiled. "So you don't think of me as a nerd?"

"Nadia, if I could be as smart as you I wouldn't care what others thought."

"Thanks Susan. You just made my day. I hope we have more classes together. What's your schedule?"

Susan pulled out her schedule and the two girls compared their days. "Oh look, we have Phys Ed and History together. To change the subject, what did you do all summer?"

"I spend a lot of time on my great-grandfather's farm riding horses," Nadia answered. "Do you like horses?"

"I have a horse and I love to ride, but not many

people do you know."

Nadia was so excited that she found someone that was more like her. "Maybe we can get together and ride sometime. We have enough horses on our farm or you can trailer yours over. You gotta come and see this place. We're getting ready to build a vet clinic and boarding kennels and stables. It's going to be so cool. Do you want to come see it one weekend?

"Uh yeah," Susan answered. "This weekend is good for me."

"Let's exchange numbers and we'll ask our parents. I also have to call my cousin, Lacey, who lives on the farm. She and her husband live there and they are fixing it up more and more. It's so much fun Susan."

"Oh Nadia, I cannot wait and…"

Susan was interrupted by the teacher turning on and off the lights to get everyone's attention. "Enough chattering everyone; I know you all have lots to share. I think you all know that my name is Mrs. Reader. I love English and I love creative writing. For your first English assignment, I want each of you to write a short story, with an illustrated title page, all about your summer. You will have a chance to read it aloud, so make it fun or make it a mystery. And if you have to fiction it up for some excitement, then by all means make it exciting. I'm grading your grammar most of all. The story is yours. No vulgarity of course and I hope I don't have to even say that again. So, take today to think and make an outline of a story. If you need help, raise your hand and I want you to say it to the class. That way everyone hears the same answer. Make this fun, but take it seriously. We are here to learn the English language."

Nadia looked at Susan and they exchanged smiles. Nadia's day wasn't so bad and she wasn't watching the clock to go home.

Nadia and Susan became best of friends and were inseparable. Tea seemed to like Susan and won Susan's affections too. Lacey and Will loved having both of them on the farm. The girls rode and groomed the horses as well as cleaned the stalls. When Susan's parents, Lucille and Earl Scout, learned more about the up and coming boarding plans, they put their name for one of the first stalls for Susan's horse. Susan soon became a constant around the farm when her horse, Shining Star, was moved over to one of the first stalls. The girls' help allowed Lacey and Will to concentrate more on the construction of their boarding facility, which they would run while Jillie and Miguel would run the animal clinic. As the building of the veterinarian clinic progressed, Jillie and Miguel were traveling home a lot to help with any questions or problems.

One weekend when Jillie and Miguel were home, they all decided to come up with a name. Lacey and Jillie decided to ask Nadia and Susan what they thought the name of the clinic and boarding facilities should be named. The girls were so excited that they ran off to come up with some suggestions.

"Come on Susan, let's take the horses out for rides and look for ideas inspired by the farm."

"Sounds great to me," Susan said. "I'm sure Shining Star wants a good ride. Which horse are you saddling up first?"

"I'm going to take Warrior Girl out for Lacey. We'll let all the horses out to graze. We'll have to give them all a good ride and grooming today. I'll do Shadow and Storm Cloud and you can do the twins."

The girls let Shadow, Storm Cloud, Little Girl and Baby Boy out into the pasture to roam and graze at their leisure.

Once the girls saddled Warrior Girl and Shining Star, they guided them out of the barn and allowed them to slowly walk so they could chat back and forth.

"Nadia, who does Storm Cloud belong to? I never hear anyone talking about belonging to Storm

Cloud."

Nadia thought about it for a moment. She was so young when Blake went missing and had never really thought much about it. "Wow, you just brought back a memory that is so sad. Lacey actually had a long time boyfriend, Blake. You know, I don't really know what happened to him. I was so young and I really only remember Lacey and Will being together. I think Storm Cloud was his. I'm not sure I want to ask."

"I don't blame you," Susan replied. "I don't want to bring up any sad memories for Lacey. Come on, let's give these two a good run and look around for a great name for this place."

"Let's go!" Nadia called out as she gave Warrior Girl the go ahead to run like the wind leaving Susan and Shining Star behind.

"Wait up!" Susan yelled. Shining Star took off and Susan's long blond hair blew back with the wind.

Nadia slowed down enough for Susan to catch up. When the horses were side by side, the girls looked at one another and gave their horses an easy kick to let it fly. The horses raced down the pasture until they neared the big oak tree. Warrior Girl led the way around the oak tree. Nadia studied the place that she knew took her to wonderful places.

"I got it," Nadia yelled out. "I know what we should name the farm. I think we should name the place, Oak Pastures. This old oak tree has been here for generations from what I understand. And, we have to name the animal clinic something and the boarding facility something. Both should flow with Oak Pastures."

Susan stared at the oak and looked all around the pasture. "I like that."

"Come on; let's take Warrior Girl and Shining Star for a little more riding. We need to give the others some fun too and maybe we'll come up with the boarding facility name next."

The girls walked the horses further down into pasture lands and brought the horses back on a different trail that ran along the fence that Blake and all the cousins had helped fix. Nadia thought about the stories she heard from Adam and she smiled. "I've got the boarding facility name, B & B Boarding. I'll have to run this by Lacey and Will to see if it's too painful."

"What's the other B for Nadia?"

"You know Will is Native American and someone in the past was named Beautiful Butterfly." Nadia could not tell the family secrets. "I think she was one of his ancestors or something."

"Oh," Susan commented. "You better ask them for sure. If these two people were really important, then I bet they might like it too. Now, what about the clinic name?"

Nadia smiled when she thought about Miguel's family. Jillie had told her about her studies with Calm Water. "I think the animal clinic should be a neat name from Miguel's family. They do a lot of conservation work in the mountains."

Susan looked over at Nadia with a confused look. "Isn't Miguel Native American too?"

"Yeah, what's the chance of that? It's like what they call destiny."

"Wow," Susan said. "I never even thought about that. How neat is that?"

Nadia smiled inside. "Kind of weird, but life is full of surprises."

"This place is magical to me Nadia," Susan said.

Nadia looked around acting like she had never thought about it. "I guess any place like this would be magical. It feels like freedom. It feels like safety. And, it's full of history."

Susan nodded and smiled. "Yep, I think that sums it up. So, what name are you thinking? I don't really think I am the person to help name this place. It's your family."

"Wild or Calm Animal Care," Nadia softly said. "I don't know just yet, but I'll run that by them. Let's get these two horses cooled and brushed down."

The girls spent the rest of the day taking care of the horses only stopping to eat a bite of lunch that Lacey brought down to them. Nadia and Susan spent almost every weekend together taking care of the horses. They even fixed up a place in the loft as their weekend bed and breakfast. They both loved living above the horses even when the winter chill enveloped the barn. They began giving Lacey and Will suggestions how the kennels and stalls could be better for the animals. Lacey and Will already had their first employees before they even opened their doors to the public.

Sixth grade flew by for Nadia and she soon settled into middle school. Tea didn't have to make any emergency visits and scare the pants off of anyone. Occasionally, Tea would show up in her locker and make her smile. The only thing she didn't like is when she saw others being bullied and made a mental note that she was going to do something about that. But, being on the bottom of the totem pole was not the time. A plan had to be developed. She didn't even share her plan with Susan. She wanted to talk with Will and Lacey to get a grown up's point of view to help her do the right thing.

Summer was coming and so was Jillie's graduation and wedding. Nadia, her two older cousins and Jillie's two other bridesmaids, Courtney and Alexi, spent a Saturday afternoon shopping for their dresses for Jillie's wedding. Jillie's colors were lavender, white and grey. Purple lilacs were being planted all around the front yard of the old farmhouse. Nadia could not wait for another summer.

Chapter 12: Jillie's Celebrations

"Come on Nadia, if we're going to make Jillie's graduation celebration, we need to hit the road," Stacey called up the stairs.

"I'm coming," Nadia yelled back. "Are the boys all ready?"

"Yes," Stacey yelled again. "The boys and your dad are in the car."

Nadia gave her hair one more flip and rushed downstairs. "How do you think I look mom?"

Stacey gave her daughter a big smile. "You look beautiful and way too old."

"That's the idea mom," Nadia answered. "I want to look older."

"Don't rush it my dear. You are only going into the seventh grade and I'm not ready for you to be all grown up. Although, you are so much more mature than I ever was at your age."

Nadia looked at her mom and smiled. "I cannot imagine you a silly teen mom."

"Well, I was and I'm glad I don't have to go through that age again."

"Mom, was junior high in your days as frustrating as it is now?"

"It was so frustrating Nadia; junior high was so frustrating for me too. Are you having troubles sweetie?"

"So far, it's okay. I just don't love it like I did school when I was younger. Some kids are trying to be cool by the partying thing and some kids are not very nice. But, I have made a few friends. Susan and I are very busy studying during the week so we can be on the farm all weekend. It keeps us out of trouble, but we don't know many people. I think people think I'm a nerd, but I'm really not."

"Don't worry Nadia. Stay on your own course and don't let not being popular worry your pretty head. When you become an adult, you will be happy you were a nerd and studied hard. Just be nice to everyone too. Even if someone is mean to you, you don't have to be mean back. You never know what other people are going through in life."

Nadia thought for a few minutes absorbing everything her mother said. "Mom, that is so much like what Will and Lacey tell me too. Thanks mom."

Stacey hugged her daughter in tight. "Come on; your dad is probably singing out there and your brothers are probably ready to take flight."

Nadia and her mom laughed, as they rushed out the door.

Jillie's and Miguel's graduation celebration was going strong when Nadia and her family arrived on the farm. There were lots of Jillie's and Miguel's friends there from college. Nadia didn't know a lot of them, but she ran off to find Lacey, Will, Jillie or Miguel. Jeremy, Stacey and the boys found family to join.

"Jillie, Miguel," Nadia called out when she saw them walk out of the farmhouse.

Miguel held open his arms for Jillie's younger cousin. "How's one of my favorite people?" Miguel asked, as he hugged Nadia in tight.

"Congrats you two," Nadia said, as she wiggled out of Miguel's clutches and hugged her older cousin.

"Thanks little cuz," Jillie said. "So glad you're here. We were hoping you would help give tours of the clinic and the boarding facilities later so we can visit with friends and family."

"You bet I would," Nadia said. "Notice how much older I look today?"

Miguel looked down at Nadia with a big smile. "I was thinking something looked different about you. I am going to make sure none of my friends think you're old enough to date."

"Yes, we better do that," Jillie added. "Now come on and we'll introduce you to some of our friends who may be coming here to work now and then."

The day went by so fast. Nadia had tons of fun giving tours of their veterinarian clinic and boarding facilities. Jillie's and Miguel's friends were so impressed with Nadia. Susan arrived toward the latter part of the celebration and helped Nadia. When the tours were done, the girls changed and began their work with the horses and the stalls. Several of the guests, who were new veterinarians themselves, hung out with Nadia and Susan. They enjoyed watching the girls work with so much love and care. The day's celebration went without a glitch.

There was no rest for the weary as the farm buzzed with tons of activity. Last minute touches were being done to the new clinic and boarding facilities and a wedding was being planned. It was taking all hands on deck. When no one was around, other than Will, Lacey, Miguel and Jillie, Uncle Jake, Son of Running Deer and Crazy Horse were all there to lend a hand. On the weekends, Nadia, Susan and any family or friends who were free came to help. The wedding was set for August 1st and opening day of the clinic was set for September 1st.

During the last weekend of June, Nadia talked her parents into letting her stay on the farm twenty-four seven. Lacey and Will backed her up and promised they would keep a good eye on her. Tea also made sure Nadia was always safe. Lacey gave Nadia the upstairs, huge bedroom as her own place. Miss Virginia, Tea, Tess and Tye stayed up there with her almost every night. Lacey and Jillie continued to see how much command Nadia had over all four cats. All of the horses loved her too. Whenever she talked, they responded. You couldn't help but notice her gift. It was as if she had a gift of communicating with animals. Lacey remembered what Nadia had told her she was going to study. Animal whispering had made her laugh, but maybe she already had mastered the gift.

As July came to its last week, Uncle Jake came and invited the three girls, Will and Miguel to the village for a special celebration for Jillie and Miguel. On the last Friday of the month, and the weekend of their wedding, they left after dark to travel back in time for a special family gathering. They left the cats to guard the farm. A special wedding ceremony was planned for Jillie and Miguel, as Lacey and Will had been given. Nadia took it all in and dreamed of the day she would have her wedding with their village family too. Nadia was always drawn to Lope's mother and father. She loved spending time with them and they loved sharing stories of their son. Lacey and Jillie noticed how much time she spent with Son of Running Deer and his wife. The pull of destiny was so great and Nadia had no clue what Lacey and Jillie knew. Her ancestors were drawn to her and her descendant returned to save her. The secret was safe and never spoken of between Jake, Lacey, Will and Jillie. They did not want to mess with destiny.

After four hours of celebrating, the five of them had to return to their time. The cats were waiting at the portal. When they saw Nadia, they all changed into their wild, feline beasts and circled all around her.

"Okay Nadia, Lacey said, "they shouldn't be doing that."

Nadia laughed. "They read my mind. I wanted them to change."

"Tell them to return to their cat forms please," Lacey requested.

Within seconds the four beasts were sweet cats again. Nadia took off running with all four cats at her heels. Lacey, Jillie, Will and Miguel all laughed.

"I think we are getting old, because there is no way I can take off running. I'm beat," Lacey said. "I'm feeling a bit light headed from that time travel."

Jillie grabbed Lacey's arm. "You have never said that before now."

"It's nighttime and I'm exhausted," Lacey replied. "Let's keep walking so I can hit the hay."

Will reached out for Lacey's hand. He was thinking exactly what Jillie was thinking, but tonight was not the time to discuss it. He wanted to talk with Lacey in private.

Sunday quickly came. Lacey, Will and Nadia were up early. They enjoyed breakfast and tended to the horses together. All four cats were walking around the horses and purring so sweet. Nadia stayed back to ready the horses with braids and flowers. Not only were the horses part of the processional parade, they were also part of a show that Nadia and Susan were giving as a gift to Jillie, Miguel and all the wedding guests during the reception. Susan arrived in time to help Nadia with Baby Boy and Little Girl. The girls chatted and giggled the entire time they were working with the horses. Lacey returned to let the girls know they needed to finish up so Nadia could get ready.

"The horses look amazing girls," Lacey commented, as she walked over to Warrior Girl and gave her a big hug. The other horses neighed for Lacey's attention and all three girls laughed. "Okay, okay," Lacey said, as she pulled out carrots for all. Lacey offered a carrot to each horse and gave each a hug.

"Okay, we're done," Nadia said. "Let's go Susan. I need help with my hair."

Lacey and the two teens walked back to the farmhouse together discussing more plans for opening day. "What an exciting summer?"

"It's been the best summer of my life," Nadia replied.

"I cannot wait to begin teaching riding lessons," Susan added.

"I don't know what we would do without you two," Lacey said. "You know we need to hire someone to work during the week for those people who want to come for lessons. Jillie is hoping one of her classmates may want to join us. They will help with the horses' veterinarian care and teach riding lessons."

"That would be great," Nadia said. "I would like to meet them too before they are hired. I want to see how the horses react around them."

Lacey looked at Nadia and smiled. "Of course, we know how much those horses mean to you." Lacey also thought to herself. "I know how you seem to be able to communicate with them too. Of course they will tell you who they like or don't like."

Nadia looked back at the barn. "Yeah, they will let me know."

Lacey smiled and thought to herself. "Yep, she's an animal whisperer."

The three reached the house and wedding excitement took over. "Guests will be arriving in two hours." Lacey warned the girls.

Nadia and Susan ran upstairs to get ready. Nadia had to put on her new bridesmaid dress. Susan even had a part in the wedding too. She would be reading a beautiful poem written by Nadia and herself for the special couple.

Lacey and Will made a last minute walk through the front yard as they remembered their special day that came together so quickly. The yard was beautiful with purple, pink and white flowers adorning the aisle that Jillie would walk. Rows of chairs were on each side of the aisle with lavender bows tied to the end chairs. As they had done for Lacey, ribbons of lavender and white were gently blowing as they dangled from the tree limbs. The large pecan trees' limbs and leaves held the August sun's heat at bay. Large white awnings had been set up all around the perimeter of the yard with huge fans gently blowing so that guests could sit and enjoy their time without melting from the heat.

As Lacey and Will walked under the awnings, Lacey fluffed up the delicate, purple lilacs they had placed in the center of each table covered in white. Lacey brought a centerpiece of lilacs to her nose to smell the sweet flower's scent. Instead of enjoying the sweet aroma, she felt so nauseated and sick that she almost dropped the group of flowers. She quickly sat the vase of flowers down and ran over behind a bush. Will quickly followed her and watched his wife toss her cookies.

"Lace, are you okay?" Will asked, as he gently rubbed his wife's back. "You know I didn't ask you about your lightheaded comment the other night, but I am wondering if…"

Lacey stood up and smiled as she took Will's hand and placed it on her tummy. "Oh yes, we're going to have a baby."

Will stood there for a moment without moving his hand.

"Will, are you okay?" Lacey softly asked.

Will looked deep into his wife's eyes and then he gently picked her up as he was going to carry her over a threshold. "I'm more than okay my little, warrior wife. I am the happiest man on earth. My first son will be joining us soon."

Lacey remembered the picture too. "Yeah, our first son and we know he's going to be so cute. We have seen him!"

Will stood there holding Lacey for a few more moments and Lacey placed her head on his shoulder. Their dreamy moment soon ended when they heard Nadia calling out for Lacey. Will gently placed his wife and child back down; he took her hand and led her back to the day's celebration. He wanted to shout his joy to the world, but today he and Lacey would enjoy their wonderful, tiny secret.

"Jillie wants to see us Lace," Nadia called out when she saw Will and Lacey smiling. "You two look like you have been up to something."

Will laughed and gently pushed his wife. "Oh yeah, we've been up to something."

Lacey looked at her husband with wide eyes. "We've been reminiscing about our special day. Come on Nadia, let's go see Jillie. I want to make sure my hair looks good too."

Nadia smiled at her older cousin. "You look radiant Lacey."

Lacey smiled and glanced back at her husband. She smiled at him and walked on with Nadia to celebrate more than just a wedding. When the two walked into Jillie's house, they both were stopped by her beauty. She was wearing the same dress that Lacey had worn. The dress that had been custom made by Beautiful Butterfly centuries ago. Jillie's long, blond hair had been swept up with tiny, long ringlets falling down her back.

"OMG," Lacey whispered, "Jillie, you look so beautiful. I forgot how truly gorgeous that dress is and it fits you better than it did me. It's so special.

"Will you two help me with my veil? My mom and the other two left to go get the bouquets."

Lacey and Nadia walked together and helped their cousin with her veil. Unlike Lacey's grand entrance, Jillie was going to arrive in a horse drawn carriage that would be pulled by Little Girl and Baby Boy. The other horses, now four including Miguel's stallion would be leading the carriage, the bridesmaids and Aiken. Nadia, Will and Susan, of course, had been working with them to get the procession set. When Karla and Jillie's two other bridesmaids walked in, they all stopped and admired the bride.

Karla walked over and hugged her daughter, but not tight enough to ruin her hair and make-up. "The guests are arriving and the carriage is making its way over, horses and all."

Nadia rushed out of the house to see Susan and Will driving the carriage over and all the horses walking in sync just as they had taught them. "Lacey, come and look at this."

Lacey and Jillie walked to the front door and walked out onto the porch. Jillie had tears in her eyes and she grabbed Lacey's arm. "Lace, we are so blessed you know."

"I know little cuz. It's been a wild ride, but the blessings have far out weighed the challenges."

Will smiled at his wife. "Okay ladies, it's time to get this procession ready to go."

When the carriage came to a stop, the door opened, Kent and Aiken jumped out. They held out their hands to help Jillie and her mother into the carriage. As Jillie descended down the steps, she grabbed her father's hand. Kent looked at his daughter and smiled. "Cannot believe you're all grown up"

Jillie smiled at her dad and then looked at her older brother. "Glad you could make it home from your mission. Aiken had joined his older cousin in the Air Force and flying in a special squadron known as the Air Angels.

"I wouldn't miss it for the world," Aiken replied, as he winked and then looked at his mom. "Mom, you look beautiful."

Karla smiled and joined her husband and son at the bottom of the porch steps. Both men helped Karla into the carriage with her daughter.

Next, Will jumped down and helped Susan descend down from the carriage front seat. "I'll go make sure the musicians are ready and everyone is seated," Susan said and she walked back to the farmhouse front yard.

Kent climbed up onto the front seat waiting for Will. Will and Aiken helped the bridesmaids sit upon the horses that would now lead the carriage. Will helped Lacey upon Warrior Girl and Aiken helped Courtney upon Storm Cloud. Aiken then helped Lexi upon Susan's gentle horse. Will and Aiken helped Nadia upon Will's huge black stallion. Last, Aiken pulled himself up onto Miguel's stallion and he moved his horse in front of the girls. All four cats leaped up to the top of the carriage and assumed their positions of facing North, South, East or West. Kai was with Miguel.

Will looked at everyone's saddle and pulled on them to make sure all was connected for safe rides. He walked to the opened door of the carriage and looked at Jillie and her mother. "Ready to become a married woman?"

Jillie smiled and nodded her head. "I'm ready papa."

Will looked at her, smiled and shook his head. "She couldn't wait?"

"Oh yes she did, but I know a pregnant person when I see one," Jillie replied.

Karla looked at Jillie and then at Will. "Congrats," she whispered.

Will closed the carriage door shut. He glanced at his wife and climbed to the carriage seat like he didn't have a tuxedo on at all. He looked at Kent sitting there looking at him shaking his head. "What old man? Don't you wish you could climb like me?"

"You and Miguel are like peas in a pod. No wonder my daughter fell for someone like you."

Will laughed. "And that's a bad thing? Don't you worry your 'good old boy' head; your daughter will have the most wonderful life working side by side with her husband doing just what they love doing."

Kent stared into Will's eyes and smiled. "Yeah, I think you're right and I'm going to be here to make sure of that."

Will nodded his head forward with a quick jerk, made a wild bird call and the horses from the back moved forward to guide the carriage. Kent closed his eyes and sat back to embrace his daughter's crazy, exciting day and life.

The music started and all the chatter ceased as the guests all stood up to watch the beautiful procession of horses, bridesmaids and a beautiful horse drawn carriage. The procession slowly made its way down the driveway of the house that would now be Jillie's and Miguel's home. Police officers were there to hold any oncoming traffic to a stop as the procession walked the paved road that ran in front of the two houses. Once the carriage was off the road and making its way up the farmhouse driveway, cars slowly passed with quiet beeps of blessings.

When the horses arrived at the beginning of the aisle, Lacey's brother and cousins were standing there to help the girls down. Aiken descended down and waited for the carriage to pull up. He would be helping his mother out of the carriage and escort her down the aisle.

Courtney slowly began her walk down the middle of the rows. Once she turned the corner to find her spot at the front, Lexi began her walk. Nadia was next with all four cats in tow and everyone giggled at this amazing sight. Then, it was Lacey's turn to walk down this aisle again. When all four girls were in place, Aiken walked his mother down the aisle and assumed a place up front. Will escorted Miguel's mom down and stood behind Aiken. Next, Miguel, his father and Brad walked out to join Aiken. Miguel and his father took their place in front of Aiken while Brad took his place behind Will. They all stood ready for Jillie and her father to make their way down the aisle.

The music changed and Kent held his arm for Jillie to descend from the carriage. As she made her appearance, Miguel smiled towards his bride. As Jillie linked her arm into her father's, Kent leaned over and whispered in her ears. "I'll still be checking on that wild man."

Jillie giggled and that actually helped her relax. "I am counting on it dad. Let's go, so you can start your plotting. Just don't let mom know."

Kent laughed. "Let's go. I'm ready."

Jillie and her father walked with big smiles. Jillie was ready to be Miguel's wife and Kent was ready to give his new son-in-law a run for his money. It was a match made from destiny.

The minister spoke about love and how God blesses couples. Before it was time to exchange the rings, music softly played and Susan walked up from the front row. She didn't have anything in her hands but one beautiful red rose. She walked next to the minister and smiled at Jillie and Miguel. "A special gift of words..."

THE LOVE BETWEEN

The love between-
No one will ever know.
The love between-
Started so long ago.

Sometimes our love takes us-
To dreams far away.
But our love will always take us-
To the home where we will live and stay.

The love between-
Will grow stronger in our hearts.
The love between-
Will never fail when hardship starts.

The future leads us-
In directions yet to go-
And where the paths should lead us-
Only destiny and time will surely know.

The love between us-
A friendship of many years.
The love between us-
Will conquer any hidden fears.

As age creeps upon us-
We will know we both have grown.
As age will bring wisdom to us-
Together, we will continue to search into the unknown.

The love between-
No one can ever break.
The love between-
Will be held in a lifetime that we shall dream and make.

When Susan finished the poem, she handed Jillie the rose. "This is a gift that symbolizes true love."

Jillie and Miguel both hugged Susan and she returned to her chair. The couple looked at Nadia and blew her a kiss. When Jillie and Miguel turned their attention back to the minister, he began the ring ceremony. The rings were both designed and made by Miguel himself. It was from gold found in the mountains of North Carolina, the place where Jillie and he would travel throughout their lifetime together.

"I now pronounce you husband and wife. You may kiss the bride."

Everyone stood up and clapped. Miguel held out his arm for his wife, the minister announced the new couple, Mr. & Mrs. Miguel Swiftbare and they walked back down the aisle together. Karla and Kent followed behind them. Miguel ran around the rows of chairs to walk his mother down the aisle. Miguel's father held his hand out for Lacey and they walked down the aisle together chatting away and nodding their heads to their guests. Will and Nadia were next with the cats jumping all around them that made the guests laugh. Aiken and Lexi fell in behind the circus act and then Jillie's dear, childhood friends, Brad and Courtney, ended the recessional march.

The band began quiet songs so people could mingle and find a place to sit under the awnings that lined the sides of the yard. Before Jillie and Miguel joined their families for another feast, they walked around and chatted with everyone. Once everyone was seated with the wonderful food on the plates, toasts were made by many people. Some were attached to stories of fond memories and they had Jillie and Miguel laughing with tears.

Nadia waited until no one else had a toast for the newlyweds. She stood up and clanked her water glass for everyone's attention. This soon to be seventh grader warmed the crowd with her brief but wonderful speech. "I can never say all the things I truly want to say. So, the only wish I have for my cousin and her wonderful husband is that I wish them a lifetime of exciting and loving adventures and that they will leave a legacy to all those generations to come."

The guests all clapped, but Nadia held up her hands for one more comment. "Please stay seated and enjoy your food. When all the chairs have been removed from the ceremony arena, Susan and I have a wonderful gift we prepared for our two new family veterinarians and you. We hope you see how animals can bless our lives with love and adventure too."

Jillie and Miguel looked at one another. They had no idea, but Will and Lacey had helped the girls plan and practice for this wonderful show. It was another part of keeping their great-grandparents' farm alive. Jillie's and Miguel's friend and reporter, Dan, took pictures for an article to help advertise the farm and the veterinarian clinic. This was Dan's wedding present to his special friends.

After the wedding, Nadia had to return home to get ready for school. School was to begin in two weeks and Nadia's parents wanted to take a family vacation. Susan's parents also wanted to get in a vacation before school started, so Nadia and Susan got their parents to take different weeks. At least one of them would be able to go over these next two weeks. Jillie, Lacey and Nadia had hired one of Jillie's classmates, Tom Goodheart, to work with the horses and keep the barn in order with Will's help. Tom had also grown up around horses and even helped train new riders when he was in high school and during his undergrad summers. He would be starting the riding school, but he and Nadia had to help Will design the corral layouts.

As the farm began to take shape of its future life, Lacey was in charge of the gardens, where organic vegetables, herbs and grapevines were being grown. She had a co-op going with the local college horticulture departments. Students were there everyday to work the gardens. The college leased the gardens and they shared the profits with the family's farm.

Will was in charge of the buildings' upkeep as well as helping with the horses. He also helped Jillie and Miguel with the overnight animals, as he had a gift like Nadia. He helped Lacey with any tough decisions, but left the legal matters to the lawyer in the family.

Jillie and Miguel ran the clinic. Both of their schedules became booked with emergency services and new patient care. They hired one full-time office assistant, Mrs. Darling, who was an empty nester. She had fostered dogs and cats for years and now had one loyal German Shepherd, Tracker, and two cats, Whiska and Talley. They came to the farm everyday. A vet tech was also hired full-time, Jim Ellie. He was a big, strong young man. Jillie needed him more than Miguel to help with the larger animals. They also started a co-op with a local college with students who were interested in getting into veterinary school. They assisted the two doctors and ran the kennels for dogs and cats.

Nadia and Susan came whenever they could during the weeks and almost every weekend. The girls even designed a small room that Will and Miguel built at the back of the barn with bunk beds, a small wood burning stove and a few essentials for them to have for overnight sleepovers. Tom was excited to see the room being built too. He wanted a place to stay if the horses ever needed round the clock care. He supplied the barn with a nice generator as his gift to the girls for all their hard work. Susan helped Tom design the two training arenas. Nadia and Will were in charge of designing a covered arena with bench seating for shows or working with animals during intrepid weather.

Chapter 13: Bad Meets Beasts

Seventh grade began for Nadia and Susan. They didn't have one class together and they felt like their schedules had been set up to keep them separated. Nadia realized how many classmates she did not know. Her first week could not end fast enough. Tea was waiting in her locker every time she opened it up. It made her smile, but it also made her a bit nervous that someone would find out her secrets.

Finally, Friday came and Nadia was at her locker getting her books she needed for the weekend. As she thumbed through her organizer for her assignments, someone pushed her from behind. Nadia swung around and it was that girl from her first day of sixth grade. "You're such a nerd."

Nadia stood there for a moment. "Why do you feel like you have the right to push me? If you think I'm a nerd, then just please leave me alone. I don't have anything against you."

The girl got up close to Nadia's face and held up her right fist next to Nadia's head. "Maybe I feel like punching a nerd, nerd. Move out of my way. I want to see if your locker has cooties in there." The girl pushed Nadia away from her locker.

"Please don't, Nadia said, worried she would see Tea.

When the girl opened up the locker, Tea was gone. The girl started to grab a book to toss on the floor, but something scratched her hand. "OW!" The girl pulled her hand back.

Nadia took a deep breath of relief. Tea was there, but she was invisible. Nadia didn't say anything and waited for this horrible person to do her next mean thing. The girl looked at Nadia with a smirk. "Look out next week nerd."

The girl slammed Nadia's locker shut and quickly ran away. The hallway had thinned out and a teacher was making his way down the hall. Nadia tried to compose herself and get her books. She just wanted to get out of there. Tea softly meowed when Nadia opened her locker door again. Nadia read her thoughts to her. "Don't worry about her, she's nothing more than a rat and you know how I feel about rats."

Nadia smiled and thought back. "See you at home."

Tea vanished. Nadia grabbed her books, shut her locker and ran to make her carpool. On her way home, she called Lacey and Will to see if they were okay with her coming over that night. They gave her the go ahead and Will picked up the fear in her voice. Will offered to pick her up and shared his perception with his wife once they hung up. Nadia accepted before she even asked her parents. She called her mother next and didn't exactly tell her the truth. She explained that Will offered to pick her up because he and Lacey needed some help.

"You have to have your studies done before you come home on Sunday. I know you'll be so tired from riding and helping around the farm that you will come home exhausted."

"I promise mom!" Nadia excitedly replied. "Do I need to ask dad too?"

"No, he's here with me and he heard the conversation."

Jeremy pulled the phone from Stacey. "You can bring us home some nice vegetables."

Nadia giggled. “Dad, I’ll pick them myself.”

Lacey always told Nadia and Susan to take home fresh vegetables as payment for their hard work.

“You’re saving us lots of money little girl and we’re eating very healthy,” Jeremy commented. “See you when you get here and I’ll give you something to take to your cousin too.”

“Okay daddy; I’m almost there.”

Nadia thanked their next door neighbor for the ride and jumped out. Stacey walked out and waved hello to their neighbor.

“Hey mom,” Nadia said as she gave her mom a quick kiss and ran inside to pack.

“Dad, what is it that you’re sending Lacey?” Nadia asked, as she rushed into the kitchen where her dad was fixing something in his fancy blender.

“I’m making it right now. I am making you all some fresh vegetable soup from some of the vegetables you brought last week. “Here, taste this.”

Nadia opened her mouth for her dad to spoon feed her his special concoction. She wanted to spit it out, but she didn’t want to hurt her dad’s feelings. “Ummm good,” Nadia said, as she giggled and ran off. “Put it in a container. Will should be here soon.”

Jeremy smiled and shook his head, as he tasted his soup. “Best soup ever.”

Will drove up fifteen minutes after Nadia got home. He got out of his car and knocked on the back door.

“Come on in,” Jeremy yelled.

Will walked in to find Jeremy stirring something in a blender. “What’s cooking?”

“Come here Will. I want you to taste my famous soup I just blended together. It’s made with all the vegetables at the farm.”

Will took the spoon from Jeremy and helped himself, but he didn’t actually like it. “Very good, very good."

Jeremy stood up tall and smiled. "I knew you would love it. Here, this is for your dinner tonight."

Nadia walked into the room with her backpack and an overnight bag. "I see you got to taste the soup we're having tonight."

Will looked at Nadia and quickly winked. "Oh yes and Lacey is going to love it. Thanks Jeremy. Nadia and I have to rush back to the farm." Will took the container of soup and smiled trying not to laugh. Nadia, I'll get this to the car. Say bye to your parents."

Nadia smiled back at Will and winked back. "Be right there. Don't spill our dinner." Nadia turned her attention back to her dad. "Okay daddy, see you Sunday."

Jeremy hugged his daughter and handed her fifty dollars. "You don't have to spend it you know."

Nadia blew her dad a kiss and ran out the door. Her mother was outside talking with Will. "Bye mom." Nadia ran up to her mom and hugged her.

"Behave and call tomorrow to say hello."

"Will do," Nadia said and she jumped into Will's car, held the door open for Tea to jump in and pulled the car door shut.

Before Will pulled out of the driveway, he made sure Nadia clicked her seatbelt. When he did pull out of the driveway, he looked at Nadia. They broke out into laughter at the same time. "How bad is that soup?" Will asked.

"We can poor it back into the ground in the garden," Nadia replied. "There are lots of good nutrients for the new plants."

"Great idea," Will replied. "Now, why were you sounding so nervous earlier when you called us?"

Nadia took in a deep breath and told him about the mean girl. Will quietly listened until Nadia completely finished.

"I know Tea will be there to protect you, but we don't want her to have to show herself if you know what I mean. I'm going to show you and Susan, if she comes over, how to defend yourselves. Better yet, I am going to show you both how to warn someone they don't want to intimidate you."

Nadia looked at Will and smiled. "I would like that. It's not something I really want to do. But if I have to fight, I want to win."

"Oh, you won't have to fight," Will quickly replied, as he looked over at Nadia with a big smile.

Nadia smiled, sat back in her seat and crossed her arms. "Thanks Will."

Friday night was an enjoyable evening. Nadia had pizza with Lacey, Will, Jillie and Miguel. It was the weekly ritual for the farm crew. They called it quits by three o'clock and always ordered pizza to be delivered. Tom, who usually joined them, had to leave for the weekend to handle some family matters.

Lacey and Will had bought a huge sixty inch flat screen television and mounted it in their family room as they referred to it. It had been the room where the girls' great-grandparents had slept, hung out and family visited. When they removed the bed that had been in the room for many decades, it made the most awesome family room or den. Wood burning stove still remained at one end. Comfortable recliners were placed near the stove with a small table between the two recliners. Lacey and Will hung out here to relax and enjoy the warmth of the stove. Towards the back of the large, oblong room, the sixty inch hung on the wall opposite the stove. Two comfortable L shaped couches were placed along the long walls. Both couches had three reclining sections. This room became the perfect home theatre. Of course, Will was always like a child in a toy store. He was still getting used to all the amenities developed since his true time. Everyone turned in once the Friday night flick had been watched. Daytime always came early for a working farm.

Nadia beat everyone up. She put on the coffee for Lacey and Will. Then, she went onto the back porch, picked up the cat dishes and washed them all. As she was fixing food for Tye and Tea, Tess, Kai and Miss Virginia showed up out of nowhere. Nadia giggled and leaned over to pet the mother cat. "You always know when I'm here Miss Virginia, don't you?"

Tess and Kai purred and rubbed all around Nadia's legs. "I see you two. Don't worry; there is plenty of food for all." The cats all ate side by side and Nadia headed out the door to the barn.

When Nadia walked into the barn, all of the horses began neighing. She laughed and opened up all the stall gates. Nadia had troughs of hay, grains and water spread out along the barn walls. She had talked Will and Lacey into letting the horses socialize whenever the stalls were being mucked and stocked with fresh hay, grains and water. The horses would walk around and eat at their leisure. They could also walk outside the back of the barn into an attached corral where they could run, walk or hang out beneath a large Poplar tree. She and Will had placed a large salt lick beside the long trough of water.

Susan soon arrived for her Saturday work. She worked off part of her horse's room and board by coming over every Saturday, unless she was sick or her parents needed her to be at home. "Hey Nadia, I'm here."

Nadia poked her head out of Warrior Girl's stall. "Hey, start with your horse's stall and meet me in the middle."

"Okey dokey," Susan replied and she headed for her horse's stall.

The girls steadily worked until they were finished with all of the stalls. When they finished, they left the stalls open for the horses to return and went back up to the farmhouse for breakfast. Lacey and Will were at the kitchen table eating breakfast when they arrived.

"Here you go girls; we just made the scrambled eggs, Lacey said. There is plenty of bacon and grits for you both. Eat up. You have a lot to do since Tom is gone. Will would like to work with you both on a few things."

Nadia and Susan grabbed plates, silverware and helped themselves. "What's the plan man?" Nadia asked, as she looked at Will.

Will halfway smiled at Nadia before he spoke. "I want to finish designing the teaching corrals and then I want to work with you both about self defense. When I say self defense, I want to talk with you about how to walk away from a fight. But if you must fight, then as you said Nadia, you fight to win."

Susan choked on her food trying to say something. "Something going to happen and we need to protect ourselves?"

"No," Will answered, "it's my intention that nothing does happen. Nadia, you can tell Susan what happened yesterday. Lacey and I have some things with the gardens to look over this morning. You girls eat up and clean up the dishes for Lace."

The girls both nodded and kept on eating. Lacey and Will got up and left the house to drive down into the pasture, but didn't say where or why they were going.

"So what happened yesterday Nadia?" Susan asked.

Nadia swallowed her food and took a sip of milk. She told Susan about the mean girl, who Susan remembered from their sixth grade.

"Oh yeah, I've had a few encounters with her too," Susan added.

Nadia couldn't tell Susan all about Tea or the other cats, so she left it at that.

"I'm finished," Susan said, "let's get the kitchen

cleaned up and go finish up on our sketches for the training corrals."

The girls cleaned up, ran by the clinic to say hello to Jillie and Miguel and headed back to the barn. The horses had all gone back into their own stalls. The girls shut the gates and headed to their little room. They worked on the sketches and finished them up for Will's and Tom's review. When they finished, they saddled up Baby Boy and Little Girl and headed down into the pasture to catch up with Will and Lacey.

As they passed the old oak tree, Nadia saw the portal door wavering. She quickly looked around the pasture and she saw the truck parked close to the trees on the other side of the oak tree. "Susan, I forgot something. We need to go back to the farmhouse." Nadia quickly turned Baby Boy around and Susan followed.

"What's wrong?" Susan asked, as she caught up beside of Nadia.

Nadia thought as quickly as she could. "Jillie asked me to file the horses' hooves today and I totally forgot. I want to get them done before she sees that I haven't done them. She'll do them and I'll feel really rotten."

"Okay Nadia; I don't think she'll even notice, but let's go do it."

Nadia took a deep breath and ran Baby Boy all the way back to the barn. She jumped off, quickly took off his saddle and bridle and rubbed him down. Susan did the same with Little Girl.

"I'll go get the files and we'll start with these two," Susan said.

"Thanks," Nadia said and rubbed the sweat from her head. She had almost given their family secret away. She loved Susan like a sister, but she wasn't sure someone else should know a secret so important. As she paced around a bit, the cats all walked into the barn and walked around their Nadia. Miss Virginia looked into

Nadia's eyes and let her know she did the right thing.

Susan came out of the tack room and saw the cats all walking around Nadia. "Now, that is a sight."

Nadia smiled. "They are my buddies for sure." The cats ran from Nadia to Susan to help Nadia out. Nadia followed the cats to Susan and took one of the files. "Let's get filing. I know Jillie or Miguel will be down to check on the horses since Tom is gone for the weekend."

The girls worked for almost two hours filing the horses' hooves. Will came in as they were finishing up. "How is it going girls?"

Nadia looked around Storm Cloud's back end. "We're just finishing up here. We almost forgot to file the hooves, as Jillie asked. We started down the pasture to find you and Lacey, but I remembered I promised Jillie. We got down to the oak tree and I remembered."

Will looked at Nadia and didn't blink. He smiled and looked away. "Good you remembered. Lacey and I were really busy working with some of the college students. We had set today's date to meet with them over a month ago. You know we want to get ready for fall harvest and all."

Nadia knew now why Lacey and Will had left this morning. They went back to see Uncle Jake and everyone about the big fall feast. "We finished up the sketches too."

Will helped guide the horses back into the stalls, while Susan took the files back to the tack room. "Sorry, we should have told you. I'll make sure you know if we go back."

Susan returned from the tack room. "So what's next?"

"I want to talk with you two about self defense. I'm what you say an expert at self defense, but the first line of self defense is to try and avoid the fight if possible. What Nadia had to deal with is basic bullying.

Someone is trying to intimidate you to make them feel better about themselves. Just remember, it takes a lot of courage to be who you are, or who you want to be, when you're growing up. Everyone is different. And you will always encounter bullies, even when you are all grown up. The first thing you need to do is not back down and don't be a coward. One on one is fair and you need to hold your own. Ask them why they are doing what they're doing. When they think about it, they may realize there is no reason. Try and just talk it out by telling them something about yourself. You both have some great talents that are very interesting. Remember, for every action there is a reaction. See if you can get a positive reaction from your action. But, if they don't back off, then you're going to have to prove you're a strong person. If you are all alone and someone throws the first punch, then you need to either get away for help or protect yourself."

Will showed the girls a few simple and easy techniques of self defense. They wouldn't severely hurt the other person, but it would let the other person know they were not going to stand back and take it. He explained that the element of surprise would sometimes put them at an advantage.

"Now, if you are out numbered, then it is not fair. You need to enlist the help of others being mainly adults like your parents or teachers. If a group of people are given the power to be mean and hurt others, then they will continue. Your teachers or parents can help relay the consequences of their actions. If you don't say something, then no one will know you need help. Just remember, more than one is not fair. It's okay to ask for help, but get the right help.

Also, I want you two to become very aware of your surroundings. Don't be looking down at your cell phones especially when you're alone. Look around you and notice what's going on around you. If you walk into a restroom and it's filled with lots of people, you should be safe to go further. If you walk in and you see only one person hanging out, especially someone who has a bully reputation, turn around and leave. If you are alone or with only one other girl, hold something that you could use as a self defense weapon. Two small girls like yourselves could be easily grabbed."

Will looked at the girls for a moment letting them think. "What did you get out of this? Susan, you go first."

Susan stood up straight. "Keep something in my hand for defense."

Will nodded and smiled. "Good. And now Nadia, what did you hear me say?"

"I heard a lot, but I think being aware of my surroundings is a really good one. I do look down a lot and try to hide away from others."

"Very good, very good," Will replied. "What you and Susan said are both good things to remember. Look people in the eye too. They know you saw them and you're not going to be surprised. I think this is enough of self defense for today. Just let me know if I need to help either of you out. Now, let's look at those sketches."

Will and the girls worked on the training corral sketches until Lacey came down to the barn and asked them if they were starving. "It's almost dinner time."

Nadia pulled out her cell. "Wow, it's four o'clock. The day has flown by and we didn't take the horses out for rides."

"Let's get Jillie and Miguel, their day ended at three, and we'll take them all for a ride.

"Sounds like a great idea," Nadia said. "Susan and I will start saddling up the horses, if you will go get Jillie and Miguel."

"I'll help with the horses," Will said.

Lacey left to go find Jillie and Miguel. Life was sure much easier with everyone on the farm together.

When the three returned to the barn, the horses were all outside with Will, Nadia and Susan mounted and ready to go on Shadow, Baby Boy and Shining Star. Miguel took Storm Cloud, Jillie took Little Girl and Lacey climbed upon Warrior Girl.

"Once the new stables are built and ready for more horses, I want to bring my horse down from the mountains," Miguel said.

Jillie looked at her husband. "I know you must miss him. We'll get him down here as soon as possible. Will, when will the new stables be ready?"

"By next summer for sure," Will answered. "Let's get these horses going and we'll talk more about stables around dinner." Will gave Shadow a gentle kick and they headed into the pasture.

Everyone joined him and they all rode side-by-side until they had to go through the narrow opening. Once they were all through the opening, they joined together until Will gave Shadow a sign to take off and run like the wind. The others took off and let the horses have a great run. Even Lacey let Warrior Girl run, but her horse knew that she had to be gentle. When they reached the small creek, they turned around and let the horses trot and walk back to the barn. They all worked together to get the horses settled for the night, put together a nice dinner and they all hit the hay to start all over the next day.

Susan's parents came early to get their daughter the next morning. Nadia stayed around, helped with the horses and did her studies in the barn. All of the animals stayed with her until it was time for her to go home. Lacey and Jillie took their younger cousin home and reinforced how important it was for her to keep Tea from going to school. They could tell that Nadia was way beyond her years and she just didn't fit in with all the other children. Even Susan was not as grown up or mature as Nadia. They were worried about their cousin.

Nadia went to school that Monday feeling better and more prepared to deal with her new friend as she called her. She walked with her head up and looked all around her taking note of what people were doing. She smiled as she realized how much she was blocking out just because she was unhappy to be there. She was closing others out from even seeing her. Some of the other girls even smiled and said hello.

But as soon as she began to feel a little better, she saw her new friend coming toward her down the hall. Nadia looked right at her, smiled and even waved. The girl looked at her with the most confused look and walked right past her. Nadia stopped and looked back to see if she was going to get a surprise attack. But, her new friend turned the corner. Nadia went to her locker and Tea wasn't there. She smiled to herself and went to homeroom.

Days, weeks and even two months went by for Nadia and seventh grade. Once the riding school was open, schoolmates began to hear that Nadia was one of the instructors. Lacey or Will began picking Nadia up from school every Friday. Students began coming up to her and Susan to ask about their riding school. They invited everyone that asked about the school. Nadia's 'new friend' even came up to her and asked her all about it. Nadia was so excited and invited her to come out for a special tour. Little did she know, but she was being set up. Little did her new friend know, but she was going to be quite surprised herself.

It was an early November Friday and Nadia was getting her books for the weekend out of her locker. As she was closing her locker up, Betsy, her new friend walked up to her. "Hey Nadia, can I bring a couple friends and visit your family's farm tomorrow?"

Nadia was so excited. "Of course; we love to show people the facilities. I'll give you and your friends a personal tour and take you for a ride. What time and how many people?"

"We'll be there around eleven and there will be me and two other girls," Betsy replied.

"Sounds great Betsy; I'm looking forward to meeting your friends." Nadia smiled, turned around and thought to herself. "For every action, there is reaction. I hope the reaction will be a nice one."

When Nadia walked out of the school, she looked around to find Will standing by his truck. Nadia waved and hurried to get to the truck. Will gave her a quick hug and they jumped into the truck. As they were pulling out, Nadia saw Betsy with two other girls. "Hey Will; see that girl there? That's Betsy, the girl who I have had some troubles with in the past."

Will took notice of the young person and her friends, but he didn't say anything. He did not like what he felt.

"I think she's changing her attitude towards me. She wants to come over to the farm tomorrow with her friends. They want to see the riding school. Can I take them for a ride?"

Will thought for a moment. "You better shoot her a text that all three girls' parents must sign a waiver if they get on a horse."

Nadia lightly slapped her forehead. "I totally forgot about that part. I'll do that right now." Nadia sent Betsy a text and told her where to go to download and print out the waiver.

Will thought some more. "A parent would have to come with them, correct Nadia?"

"I would think," Nadia answered. "She does have an older sister who drives."

"Make sure I'm around when they arrive," Will directed.

"Sure; you're so cool. She will probably really like me once she meets you and Lacey."

"Oh I'm sure she is a nice young lady," Will said

trying not to sound sarcastic while he made a mental note to himself. "If she's not, she will be thinking twice about being mean to my little cousin after she leaves." Will changed the subject. "So, tell me what went on at school this week."

Nadia went through her classes and excitedly told him everything she was learning. Nadia loved learning and it showed. When they reached the farm, it was already four-thirty and close to the time to take care of the horses. Nadia ran inside the farmhouse, dropped her backpack and changed into her work clothes. Lacey was coming in from the pastures and they exchanged hellos and hugs. Nadia headed back to the barn to find Tom and Will mucking the stalls. Nadia saw the horses were not inside the barn. "I'm going to go round up the troop."

When Nadia began calling out, the five cats came from behind the barn and the horses came running up from the pasture. She greeted each animal and led them all back to the barn.

When Tom saw Nadia surrounded by horses and cats, he shook his head. "I think we have our very own animal whisperer."

"She definitely has a gift." Will didn't want to say much more than that. He knew Nadia had a gift, but he didn't want to play it up. She was far too young to bring so much stardom to herself at this young age. She had a lot of maturing to do, like handling people that are critical and wanting to harm her spirit. He couldn't stop thinking about the Betsy person and he was worried about her even being on the farm. But, he couldn't turn anyone away, especially a young person who may need some help or much needed direction.

Friday night was enjoyable as always with pizzas and a movie. The night passed by fast and Nadia was first one up as usual. She put on the coffee, fed the cats and headed down to the barn. Tom was already up with coffee in hand.

"Morning Tom," Nadia said, as she joined him rubbing Warrior Girl.

"Good morning Miss Nadia. I think I heard some of your friends are coming to see the riding school and check out the place."

"Yep, but I'll make sure Susan takes care of the lesson scheduled at eleven. I don't think there is another one. We usually don't double book until afternoon. She may not always be able to get here early."

"I can help you girls on Saturdays and I don't always have to leave as much as I do. I just like to go see friends and family too."

Nadia smiled. "Thanks Tom; we'll let you know for sure."

Lacey came down to tell them breakfast was ready. Before she left, she gave each horse a carrot and a peppermint. When the horses saw Lacey, they knew they would get a treat and they all got excited whenever she came down. They also sensed her delicate condition and were so gentle to her. Tom and Nadia walked back with her and they talked shop. During breakfast, they all reviewed the schedule for the riding lessons. When breakfast was over, Nadia helped Lacey with the dishes and the men folk put things back into the refrigerator.

Susan arrived by eight am and the girls had their first lesson at nine. They worked together with their young student. She was a six-year-old girl and her parents were hoping to buy her a horse that would be boarded at the new facility. Their ten o'clock student came just a few minutes before time to start getting a horse ready. Nadia helped the first student take off Little Girl's saddle and rub her down. She was put back into her stall. Nadia joined Susan with their ten o'clock student who was also six. Today was her first lesson for her to see if she really wanted to commit her time to horses and riding. Her mother had been an avid rider and wanted her daughter to give it a try. They mainly went over how to care for a horse, saddle and bridle them. They let her get on Baby Boy for about twenty minutes. The twins were extremely gentle horses and were great for new riders.

A few minutes before eleven, Will walked to the side of the corral with three girls in tow. He had been waiting and greeted Nadia's 'new friend' and her friends. He talked with Betsy and her two friends about their plans for the new stable. He talked about how hard Nadia and Susan worked to help get things all set up. He explained how early they got up to help take care of the horses and be ready for their students. Betsy and her friends sweetly smiled as they listened and watched. When Nadia noticed them standing there, she waved and let Susan take their student to the barn. Tom was there to help with Baby Boy so Susan could be ready for the eleven o'clock student. Nadia ran over to Will and her schoolmates.

"Hey girls; I see you met Will," Nadia excitedly said.

"Okay girls, I'll leave you with your friend," Will said. "Nadia, I'll be around if you all need me. And, this is Cindy and Debbie. Debbie is old enough to drive."

Nadia looked at Will and smiled. "Thanks Will. I think we will be fine."

Nadia turned her attention to the three girls. "Did you bring waivers to be able to ride or do you just want to get a tour?"

Betsy looked at her friends. "We'll just let you walk us around the farm."

"Okay, I'll show you the barn and all our horses we have. They are the most magnificent creatures."

Betsy looked at her friends and smirked behind Nadia's back. Nadia talked all about the farm's history, leaving out the truly important historical facts, and walked them into the barn. Betsy and her friends looked all around and didn't see anyone else around. They had no idea Tom was at the back of the barn working in the connected corral with all of the horses, except for Baby Boy, he was out walking and grazing in the open pasture. Tom noticed the horses' nervousness like something spooked them. He looked around and didn't see anything to cause alarm.

"Nadia, can we climb up into the hay loft? Betsy asked. "I've never really been in a real barn before today."

"Nothing much to see, but come on," Nadia answered. "Susan and I have fixed a really cool way we like to climb up there." Nadia led the girls back to the front of the barn. Just before the stalls began, there was a huge rounded log that was one of the securing braces of the building. Nadia and Susan had hammered large studs up the log to the loft. Will had secured an extremely thick rope to the main beam of the roof. The girls used the rope and the studs to scale the log to the loft. Nadia went up first and watched as the three girls joined her one at a time.

Betsy was the last one up. When she reached the top, she casually walked around the loft. Nadia followed her with the other two girls behind Nadia. When they reached the back of the loft, Betsy turned around with a weird look in her eyes. She pushed Nadia back and she landed in the arms of the two girls behind her.

Nadia was in shock. "Hey Betsy, what do you think you're doing? This is not the time or place for you to be mean to me."

"You think I'm scared of Will or anyone here?" Betsy asked, as she walked up to Nadia's face. "If you scream, I'll get you at school."

"Betsy, I'm warning you. You don't want to go any further," Nadia said, as she looked around the loft.

"What are you looking for little miss smarty pants?" Betsy demanded.

Nadia didn't answer, but she saw what she knew

would be close. She saw four tiny kittens peering out from behind a bale of hay. Betsy looked in the same direction and saw the tiny creatures too.

"Well, well, it looks like we have some little pests in the barn. I bet you wouldn't mind if I just toss them out that window."

"Betsy!" Nadia yelled, but a hand went over her mouth.

Betsy slowly walked towards the four kittens. "Here kitty, kitty, kitty..."

The kittens all hid behind the bale of hay and Betsy laughed. "They're scared and they better be scared of me."

Nadia was trying to break free of the two girls' grips, but she couldn't. So, she just stood calm and let her protectors do the work. She had never seen them in action and she prayed that they wouldn't really tear these bullies to pieces.

Before Betsy moved around the other side of the hay bale, a very loud roar was heard. Betsy jumped and looked all around. The two girls dropped their hold on Nadia. Nadia ran to the hay bale and looked behind it. There were no kittens in sight. Betsy was now behind her looking over her shoulder.

"Where did they go and what was that noise?" Betsy demanded.

Nadia quickly thought. "I tried to tell you. Those little kittens were probably some type of cub. We have been having some problem with bobcats. We have been seeing one or two coming and going around the barn. One must have had a litter. The mother must be hiding in here somewhere."

Betsy looked at Nadia with fear in her eyes. "I'm out of here. Come on Cindy and Debbie. Let's let this nerd get back to her horses."

When Betsy, Debbie and Cindy turned around to leave, Will and Lacey were standing there with their arms crossed. The look on Will's face was not the nice, gentle face Nadia had always known. The look in his eyes was fierce, like a tiger. Lacey held her hand out to Nadia. When Nadia reached Lacey, Lacey whispered something in her ear and they left Will with the three mean girls.

He stood silent for over a minute, daring one to move. Low pitched growling was heard from all around the loft. The girls were frozen in fear. Finally, Will spoke. "You're not welcome here ever again." He walked over to stare into Betsy's face. "If I hear one more word of your threats or bullying to anyone, you will answer to me." Will's gaze was so threatening and the girls were scared to move. "DO I MAKE MYSELF CLEAR?"

Betsy didn't answer. She was so frightened and ashamed. Will wasn't happy. "Do I need to repeat myself?"

"Yes," Betsy squeaked out.

Will was enraged. "WHAT DID YOU SAY?"

"Yes sir," Betsy whispered.

Will took two steps back, so that he could look at all three girls. "I don't want you to look at Nadia, talk to Nadia or speak of Nadia to anyone. Not even a word is to be spoken among you three. If you say one thing, the dark spirits will follow you the rest of your lives. If you have something to say, you better say it now." He looked at each one of them and held out his palm waiting for a word, but nothing was said. "I take that as you have nothing to say. Now leave our land and never return to my sight."

The three girls took off through the loft to the log and quickly scampered down like scared rats. Will stood there for a moment and then he turned to see all four beasts waiting to attack. He bent down on his knees and held out his arms. "Good kitties for not showing yourselves. They are not worth our magic." Then he began laughing to himself. "Dark spirits sounded good, huh? I can be a beast myself at times."

The feline beasts returned to their cat forms and vanished to go find Nadia. Will walked over to the window to watch the car tear out of their driveway. He waited until the car vanished from his sight and he hurried down from the loft. Tom was walking around from the back of the barn.

"Is everything okay in here?" Tom asked.

"Oh yeah," Will replied. "Just getting some mean rats off of this farm."

Tom laughed and knew exactly what rats Will meant. He gave his employer a 'thumbs up' and went on about his business. Tom was diligent about his work. He didn't chat much while he worked with the horses as he had done since he was a boy. Will threw Tom the peace sign and hurried to the farmhouse to chat with Nadia.

As Will had told Nadia, she never had to worry about Betsy and her friends again. Nadia's seventh grade and eighth grade years were not the best for her, but she put her mind to her studies, the farm and the baby. Lacey's and Will's baby boy was born in April of Nadia's seventh grade year. She wanted to be on the farm more than ever to help with little Wayne Jake Hayes, named after three important men. She loved Wild Wayne, as she called him. She and the cats loved babysitting him. Lacey and Will saw another wonderful characteristic in Nadia. She had a strong maternal instinct. How they knew she would need it.

Nadia, and Susan, made some new friends and soon they had quite a few schoolmates taking riding lessons and helping on the farm during the summer. The new boarding stables were completed before seventh grade summer ended. During her eighth grade year, Nadia was more consumed with the farm than trying to fit in with everyone at school. She learned to be more outgoing at school and just be nice to everyone. She didn't avoid Betsy and her friends, but they avoided her.

Tea continued to surprise Nadia to remind her she would always be there in a magical moment whether she needed a purring kitten or a ferocious beast.

Chapter 14: Unexpected Beginnings

Nadia's summer before high school was full of excitement for the family and the farm. Not only did Lacey and Will announce another baby on board, but Jillie and Miguel also announced baby number one. And, the babies were due within days of one another. Those were not the only babies coming to the farm. Miguel's stallion, Wolfriend, had finally joined the farm. The stallion and Warrior Girl were expecting a colt to arrive right around the same time as Lacey's and Jillie's babies. Nadia's ninth grade spring would be welcoming new life.

Nadia had so much to look forward to that she wanted her ninth grade year over and done. She made a personal commitment to herself that she would dedicate her time to studying hard throughout the week so her weekends were open for her farm duties and fun. Her Saturdays were always full. She not only taught riding lessons, she joined a riding troop that performed exhibitions at horse shows, rodeos and parades. Susan didn't join her, because she enjoyed teaching riding lessons and not having to commit to the events. Because her parents had so much going on with their family business and her brother Luke going to college, Nadia began getting rides from some of the other riders. One particular older woman, Mrs. Ellie, became one of Nadia's dear friends. Her circle of friends began to grow with some of them being much older ladies. They all shared a love of horses and animals.

Tea didn't seem to make many visits to school her

ninth grade year. Nadia wasn't as insecure as she had been during her middle school years and now so many people knew her and her talents. She had earned more respect from her peers. Tea became busy hanging out on the farm during the days. Jeremy and Stacey didn't even notice. And if they did, they thought she was wandering around the neighborhood. All four cats seemed to help Lacey and Will with Wild Wayne. One, if not two, seemed to watch him round the clock. Kai made his appearances now and then, but stayed around the clinic or in the mountains with his wolf family.

During the ninth grade fall season, Nadia was so busy working with her riding troop. They were preparing for a huge Thanksgiving Parade at the state's capital. Nadia was so excited. She was working on her outfit and she had exceptional tailors to help her. Uncle Jake would come and get Nadia to take her back in time. Her aunt and Lope's mother were helping her design, and sew by hand, a beautiful outfit. Nadia's group would be meeting riders from all around the state. Will, Lacey, Miguel and Jillie had already planned to close down the farm, the clinic and the riding school. They were renting a huge bus to take plenty of family and friends to the big event. Will had arranged for Uncle Jake and a few of his 'old' friends to come across time and watch over the farm with the help of some sweet, lovable cats.

Two weeks before the parade arrived, Nadia was floating on air. Nothing bothered her until she began feeling ill. Jeremy and Stacey noticed their daughter's dark circles under her eyes and they both remembered their daughter's past illness. Nadia tried to convince them she was fine, but they kept her out of school and made an appointment with her oncology physician. Lacey and Jillie joined their aunt and uncle at her appointment. They couldn't believe they would have to worry about this again. They thought they had put it all behind them. They waited outside of the examination room and they both paced the hall. When they finally saw Nadia come out of the examination room with a big smile across her face, they both almost burst into tears of joy. "It's nothing," Nadia called out. "It's just sinus and ear infections and I have let them go too long. I have strict orders to stay at home for a couple of days and let the antibiotics take effect. I am really tired and I'm feeling chilled. This is not going to get me down. I have too much to do."

Lacey and Jillie laughed and they both hugged their younger cousin.

"Go home, get in bed and don't worry about anything but you," Lacey demanded.

"I second that," Jillie added. "We'll see you later when you're better and not a minute before young lady."

Nadia smiled and looked back for her parents, who were just coming out of the room with her doctor. "I'm heading to the car."

Jeremy held up his hand and nodded. Her parents continued to walk and talk with her doctor.

Lacey waved at her uncle and aunt. Jillie did the same. The two older cousins took a place on opposite sides of Nadia. The three walked out of the hospital talking all about Nadia's new outfit. Nadia had finally brought it to the farmhouse and it was amazing. "I'm going to be the belle of the ball I think," Nadia said.

"I think you mean the princess of the parade," Jillie said and laughed.

Lacey and Nadia joined her laughing until they got Nadia to her parents' car. Nadia keyed in the code to unlock her dad's SUV and climbed onto the back seat. "I'm going to lie down and start my recuperation right now."

"Great idea," Lacey said. "We'll check in."

Lacey shut the door. She and Jillie slowly walked away quietly talking about their concerns. But as they had seen in the future, they knew Nadia would be okay.

The future had promised them.

Nadia did make a quick recovery. After a couple days of fever and chills, Nadia's health returned with the help of the antibiotics, a few teas from Jillie's cabinet and lots of rest. She did not return to the farm for a week. She went to school, worked hard during her breaks to make up some of her missed work and took all of her books home with her. When she returned home, she ate a quick snack and retired to her room to get started.

When Jeremy came home that Friday, Stacey asked him to get Nadia for dinner. Jeremy knocked on his daughter's door and walked into her room to find his daughter talking out loud to herself and balancing on one leg with her arms up in the air. He stood there and listened to his daughter talking in some foreign language. He walked over, tapped his daughter on her shoulder and she jumped. "I didn't mean to startle you, but I didn't know how to say anything to the foreigner in here." Jeremy chuckled and Nadia shook her head at her dad. "We want you to come down and have dinner with the family. Luke is here from college and you need a break and some fuel."

"*Oui*," Nadia answered in French. "*Je suis affame papa*," Nadia added.

"I know you said yes, but what was the other part?" Jeremy asked. "And, does it help to balance on one leg?"

"I'm famished dad," Nadia interpreted. "And, yes it's a meditating thing I do dad."

"Okay and how do you say 'me too'," Jeremy asked.

"*Moi aussi*," Nadia replied

"My ousi," Jeremy said in a very southern twang.

Nadia laughed. "Stick to southern dad."

"The only language I know," Jeremy said, as he put his arm around his daughter's shoulder and they walked down to the dinner table. Nadia loved hearing all about Luke's college experience. It gave her something to work toward and look forward to higher learning.

Nadia didn't go to the farm over the weekend either, because she had scheduled practices that Saturday and Sunday with her riding troop. Ellie Sondeerun picked her up and dropped her off both days. Mrs. Ellie, as Nadia affectionately called her, loved Nadia. Mrs. Ellie was hoping to introduce her grandson to Nadia. She talked about him and how great a rider he was. Nadia heard all about her grandson. He was part of an all men's riding troop in the mountains of North Carolina and would be in the big state, holiday parade with his grandfather's troop. Nadia was so busy keeping up her studies during the week and working on the farm on the weekends; she had not even given boys a second thought except as friends. She didn't tell anyone, not even Susan, because she didn't want the hassle.

The school week was a short one due to the Thanksgiving holiday. Lacey, Will, Jillie and Miguel were hosting the holiday meal. They also invited all of their farmhands, clinic employees and any family that could come. Nadia also invited Mrs. Ellie and her husband. Mrs. Ellie and her husband accepted and asked if they could add their grandson. His parents had to go visit their older son and wife in another state and he wanted to participate in the parade. Nadia knew that Lacey and Jillie wouldn't mind and told her 'the more the merrier'.

Nadia talked her parents into letting her go over Wednesday night and explained how she needed to help take care of the horses for Lacey and Jillie, who were both expecting. And, she loved helping with Wild Wayne. Lacey and Jillie could concentrate on the food, the clinic and the farm. People would be arriving early on Thursday to bring different dishes and to visit. Will gladly picked his best helper up. They even stopped on the way home and picked up take-out barbecue, coleslaw and hush puppies. They bought a lot with two expectant mothers and famished men.

During dinner, Lacey asked Nadia more about Mrs. Ellie and her family. Nadia told them how they were from the mountains and had moved to be closer to their daughter in Burlington. She told them they had another daughter, who lived near Boone, and it was her son who was coming with Mrs. Ellie.

"So, what's his name," Jillie asked.

Nadia looked away for a moment. "You know, I cannot remember his name. It's kind of different, but I cannot remember it. We'll find out tomorrow."

"Do you know how old he is?" Lacey asked.

"I think he's in eleventh grade and he's planning to go to Appalachian State for college. He loves the mountains Mrs. Ellie says all the time."

Will swallowed a big bite of barbecue. "What's Ellie's name again?"

Nadia put her glass of sweetened, iced tea down. "Sundeerun."

"I kind of know that name," Miguel said. "Maybe they belong to our people. That would be very interesting, huh?"

"We'll find out tomorrow," Nadia said. "I'm sure Mrs. Ellie would love to tell you all about her family. She loves to talk."

"I'm looking forward to meeting her," Miguel said.

After dinner, Nadia, Will and little Wayne walked down with Tom to the barn and stables to check in on all the horses. Everyone turned in early to get up before sunrise on Thanksgiving Day to start the turkeys, take care of the kennel animals, the horses and last minute set up for all the guests.

Thanksgiving Day came early for everyone. As always, Nadia had coffee brewing when Lacey and Will walked into the kitchen. Lacey had to give up the real stuff again and was fixing decaf teas now. Will always fixed a thermos of coffee and drank it during the course of the day. He was still enjoying the simplest luxuries like the thermos. Tom, Will and Nadia worked fast to take care of the horses. Miguel took care of the cats and dogs that were being boarded or needed veterinary care and were staying in the clinic. Lacey and Jillie were trying to get as much done before Wayne woke up.

Friends and family began arriving by eleven and the house was buzzing with chatter. A huge coffee maker, holding thirty cups, was ready with hot coffee on the back porch. Carafes of hot chocolate and hot water for tea were also placed on the back porch. The chilled guests were stopping to get their warm brew as they entered the house. Cold drinks and dishes were set up in the kitchen while the hot dishes were set up all around the dining room. The house was filled with delicious and inviting smells.

The blessing was to be delivered at twelve sharp, so everyone that had dinner plans with other friends and family could enjoy this meal and be ready for another one that evening. Will and Miguel would have to return to their farm and clinic duties and they wanted to be able to enjoy their guests.

Lacey and her mom held Wayne Jake up to ring the dinner bell that they had found hidden in the granary while clearing it out for the renovations to make it Jillie's and Miguel's clinic. Will had hung it outside the back porch and it was brought back to life. Some people had wandered off to see the veterinary clinic, boarding kennels and stables. It was five minutes to noon and the food was ready to be devoured. Everyone heard the bell.

When Nadia came bounding into the house, she announced that everyone should be inside. She looked around for Mrs. Ellie and didn't see her friend and her family. They couldn't hold everyone up and Lacey began her welcome from the dining room. Miguel's dad, Skip, was introduced and he blessed everyone and the food with a special prayer. Nadia let everyone else get their food as she watched out the dining room window for her guests.

"Nadia, they may have been held up in traffic," Lacey said, as she joined her cousin at the window. "Does she have a cell phone?"

"I'll check mine for any messages. She does have my number." Nadia ran through the dining room and upstairs to check her phone. No messages. She walked over to one of the upstairs windows and looked out from there.

"Nadia," Jeremy called up, "come on and eat with your family."

Nadia slowly walked back downstairs. She was really bummed that her wonderful friend had not shown up. Jeremy was standing at the bottom of the stairs smiling up at his daughter. "Mrs. Ellie will call or she will show up. You need to eat and fuel that ever running engine of yours."

Nadia gave her dad a half smile. "Okay dad." Nadia filled a plate, joined her family and picked at her food.

"Nadia, you have to eat to stay healthy," Stacey quietly told her daughter. "Please don't pick at your food."

Just as Nadia was going to take a big bite of potatoes to make her mother and father happy, she heard car doors shutting. She jumped up and ran back through the house and out the back porch. Her friends were walking up to the front porch and Nadia yelled. "Come this way!"

Mrs. Ellie saw Nadia and smiled. "So sorry, we're late, but we got off to a late start. Someone here didn't want to get up."

Nadia looked at the person she was pointing towards and finally got to see this wonderful grandson, who looked absolutely miserable. "Hey, I'm Nadia."

"Nadia," Mrs. Ellie quickly interjected. "This here is my husband, Jake and my grandson, Miguel Lope Letour, but we call him Lope."

Nadia stared back and forth at Jake and Lope. Three names she was so familiar with hearing. Her Uncle Jake she knew so well. And Lope, the name that was used for two different people in two different times. She didn't know what to say and just stared.

"Nadia," Jake Sondeerun said, as he held out his hand. "So nice to finally meet you and I'm very excited to see your farm and meet your cousins."

Nadia tried not to totally lose it. "So sorry, I spaced out for a minute. I'm famished. Come on; let's get you three inside where it's warm and enjoy some of the wonderful food."

"Oh Lope, get our dishes we brought," Mrs. Ellie politely told her grandson.

Miguel Lope went back to the car and pulled out a box of foods.

Nadia led them inside to find Lacey and Jillie waiting in the kitchen to greet Nadia's special guests.

"Oh, so nice that you made it Mrs. Ellie," Lacey said, as she held out her hand and also locked her eyes on the young man who stood there holding a box.

Jillie stood speechless, as she stared at this young man too.

Nadia broke the silence. "Lacey, Jillie, let me introduce my wonderful friend and co-rider, Mrs. Ellie Sondeerun, her husband, Jake, and their grandson, Miguel Lope Letour."

Lacey still had a hold of Mrs. Ellie's hand. "Your names are so familiar to us."

Jake took Lacey's hand from his wife. "Hearing all about Nadia and her cousins, I believe we may have some mutual ancestors from centuries ago."

Lacey stared into Jake's eyes and then looked at

his grandson again. "Are you by any chance a descendant of someone named Son of Running Deer?"

Jillie's heart was racing and Nadia was a bit amazed and excited. She knew Son of Running Deer.

Jake smiled and nodded his head. "Let's say we get together another day. You have so many guests and we do not want to take up all of your time."

Lacey smiled and took her hand back. "I think that is a great idea. Please help yourselves to all the food, find a spot and we'll make plans to meet later. Thank you so much for the dishes you prepared." Lacey turned to Nadia. "Nadia, please help your guests and introduce them to your parents." Lacey took the dishes from the young man.

Nadia smiled. "Sure thing; Mrs. Ellie and Mr. Jake, come on and follow me. Miguel Lope, I'll show you the stables and our horses later if you want."

"That would be the best part of the day," Lope answered.

"Lope, mind your manners," Mrs. Ellie reprimanded her grandson.

Nadia laughed. "Oh don't worry Mrs. Ellie. It really is the best part of any day for me. I'm not much of a people person like my cousins. I kind of like the animal world."

Miguel Lope smiled and winked at Nadia. "That's exactly how I feel too."

Nadia led the three family members away leaving Lacey and Jillie standing in a state of shock. Lacey looked at Jillie. "Can you believe this?"

Jillie shook her head. "Let's go find our husbands and fill them in on this surprise. Maybe they can go sit with JAKE and LOPE. I hope our husbands don't faint."

"I almost did," Lacey replied, as the girls went to find their husbands and place the wonderful dishes for all to enjoy.

The Thanksgiving meal couldn't end fast enough

for Lacey, Jillie and their husbands. Meeting the Sondeeruns had been exciting and so unexpected. Nadia devoted most of her time to her parents and her special guests. She and Mrs. Ellie talked shop and were both excited about the holiday parade.

"Nadia, if it's okay with your parents, why don't you come and stay with us Friday night," Mrs. Ellie said, as everyone at their table enjoyed their dessert.

Nadia looked at her dad's expression and just knew he was going to say no.

Jeremy looked at this wife. "Well, what time do you have to be there?"

Mrs. Ellie cleared her throat and took a sip of coffee. "They want all of the parade participants there by ten am. The parade officially starts at twelve noon. They are having a quick meeting and snacks for all of us. They want to review any changes of line up and we have to make sure our horses are all ready and we have time to get in our beautiful parade costumes. It's a very busy day for us horse riders. Since we live closer to Raleigh, you won't have to get up so early or try and find something to do while you're waiting for the parade to begin."

Jeremy looked at Nadia and then at the young man sitting next to her. "I'm not sure about this."

Nadia stirred in her seat, but kept her cool. "Dad, it's okay. You'll just have to be at the farm by seven am. I'll have the trailer hooked up Friday night and I'll stay here overnight. I'll get Little Girl all ready to go and to be sure everything is ready to head out when you get here. Mom and Luke can come later."

"Well, I could sleep a bit later and drive to Raleigh with your mom," Jeremy reluctantly said.

"Oh," Stacey added, "let her go. I think she will be in great hands and I can tell Mr. Jake and Mrs. Ellie will take good care of Nadia and her horse."

Nadia was holding her breath.

"Okay," Jeremy replied. "You better behave

yourself young lady and we want to hear from you."

"No problem dad!" Nadia said, as she pushed back her chair and rushed to hug her dad.

"Mr. Jeremy," Jake said, "My grandson and I will come to the farm tomorrow afternoon. We will take care of Nadia and her horse."

"Can I take Miguel Lope to see the horses before you leave today?" Nadia excitedly asked.

Jake Sondeerun stood up. "I would love to see the horses and the facilities too."

"Great," Nadia replied, "let's go."

Nadia led Jake and Miguel Lope back through the house where they ran into Will and Miguel. Nadia did quick introductions. She wanted to show off the farm. "I'm going to give Mr. Jake and Miguel Lope a tour before they leave. Oh, they're coming back tomorrow and picking Little Girl and me up. Mom and dad are letting me stay with them tomorrow night so they don't have to get up so early and ride together to Raleigh."

Will looked at Miguel. "Wow, seems like you have it all worked out."

"Oh and you two don't mind helping Tom with the horses Friday night and Saturday morning do you?" Nadia begged.

Will and Miguel both laughed. "I think we can handle it, since we have had to take up your slack whenever you're in your riding exhibitions," Will replied.

"You're the one that got me into the whole riding and showing off thing," Nadia replied. "Come on; help me show them our wonderful place."

Nadia led the group and did all the talking. Will and Miguel enjoyed hearing Nadia's history of the land and being so careful not to share their wonderful family secret. Although, they both knew that this young man they just met would one day be joining them and their family quest. The future had shown them his face.

***

Parade day arrived. Nadia was having the time of her life with Mrs. Ellie, Mr. Jake and Miguel Lope. She loved calling him Miguel Lope. She could tell he was not enthused with her formality, but they didn't really know one another. Nadia was trying to be grown up, but Miguel Lope thought she was rather immature. Friday had been full of horse care, a fun dinner sitting around a fire pit and roasting marshmallows. They were all up very early to enjoy a continental breakfast and more horse care. Mr. Jake's small barn had wonderful gas heaters that made getting the horses ready more enjoyable on a cold November morning. Little Girl seemed happy to see Nadia and excitedly neighed to tell Nadia she missed her family. Nadia laughed. "I know Little Girl, but you have new friends here."

Mr. Jake quietly watched Nadia with her horse. He knew she had the gift and sensed it the night before when they were all caring for the horses. Their horses would not settle down until Nadia visited each of them. He heard her whisper to each horse and he heard each horse respond with soft replies. Once she attended to Little Girl, she again made her round to each horse. The promising tale handed down to every generation of his tribes' people was coming to life. His ancestor, Running Antelope, told his children and his grandchildren to continue to tell each generation the tale of the wonderful family, and the three beautiful cousins, who would bring their lands back to their family.

Miguel Lope and Nadia got all four horses into the combined elaborate truck and horse trailer. Little Girl was placed in the first mobile stall so Nadia could be near her and open a window to check on her. Nadia opened the sliding window and found Tea nestled into Little Girl's mane. Nadia smiled and knew Tea would be gone when they all reached their destination. Nadia shut the window, turned around and relaxed. She looked over at Miguel Lope and he had gone fast asleep. She decided to get a cat nap herself. She knew they were all in good hands.

When they arrived at the parade's unloading site, Mr. Jake awoke his three sleeping passengers. The four went into the huge indoor conference center to meet up with their riding members. It was here that Nadia realized that Mr. Jake and Mrs. Ellie were the two people who had started these two riding troops. She saw that they were connected to many people and they were well respected among many of the parade participants. The Sondeeruns introduced Nadia to many people. Miguel Lope already was well known. Once they were up to date on their parade line up positions and light snacks were enjoyed, everyone headed to get their costumes on and the horses ready.

Nadia's parents met up with Lacey with a bundled little Wayne, Jillie, Will, Miguel and almost everyone that had been at the Thanksgiving feast. Mr. Jake had made sure they were all escorted to a wonderful platform. They were going to be able to take in all the sites of the parade. Most importantly, they were going to see Nadia.

The parade drums started. Jeremy noticed they were seated right at the beginning of the parade. "Wow, how did we get this spot?"

Lacey and Jillie looked at one another with big smiles. "I think your daughter has made friends in high places."

Jillie laughed and winked at Lacey, as she thought about her mountain family she now called her family. "Literally, high places."

"I'm glad I said yes to her staying with the Sonnn," Jeremy stopped trying to remember how to pronounce Mr. Jake's last name. "What was that name of theirs again?"

"Sondeerun," Will quickly answered and looked

at his wife. He leaned over to his wife and whispered in her ear. “I should tell him it’s really Son of Running Deer.”

Lacey shook her head and smiled. “Don’t you dare do that. Remember how my dad and Jillie’s dad reacted to you two? Don’t get him thinking or worried for Nadia. She has a lot of growing up to do and we are not even going to mention Miguel Lope to Nadia or her parents. You know we know more than we’re supposed to know.”

Will looked directly into his wife’s eyes. “Maybe we were supposed to know.”

“Enjoy the parade and stop thinking,” Lacey quietly said.

The Grand Marshall’s car was coming with a huge band behind him. The drums were loud and the crowd was cheering. Nadia’s family and friends were excitedly waiting for their family star. The parade was huge and groups from all over the state were participating. The theme of the parade was always North Carolina’s history. A group from the North Carolina Highlands always made a huge presence. A bigger presence was the North Carolina American Indians.

Soon, Nadia’s troop was making its way to where her family patiently waited. Jeremy spotted his daughter first and she led her troop. When he saw her, he was totally taken back when he saw his daughter dressed in a beautiful costume. Lacey and Jillie grabbed one another’s hands.

“OMG,” Jeremy said. “Look at my daughter. She looks so grown up and…”

“I know hun,” Stacey added. “Her outfit, it’s the most beautiful thing I have ever seen.”

Wayne Jake got so excited when he saw Nadia. “Naddie, Naddie!”

Will smiled with so much pride. “She is dressed in the royal dress of a chief’s daughter. An American

Indian princess you might say."

"I am the chief of the house," Jeremy said, as he laughed at himself. "And, you are my woman," he said to his wife.

"Watch it chief or you will be doing the dishes all week," Stacey said and laughed. Others joined in and got a good laugh on Chief Jeremy.

Nadia looked over at her family as she slowly guided Little Girl near them. She waved at them and blew her dad a kiss. She gave little Wayne 'a thumbs up'. Jeremy snapped a ton of pictures. Lacey and Jillie looked at one another again, as they remembered seeing this day hanging on the wall centuries in the future. Nadia looked grown up beyond her years. Mrs. Ellie looked so beautiful and proud in her winter Indian leather dress and leggings. Everyone watched her troop until they disappeared from sight.

"Okay, what now?" Jeremy asked.

"We have to wait and see the entire parade," Lacey demanded. "We haven't seen Mr. Jake and Miguel Lope yet."

"Well, it's not like they are going to be around much except at some of the shows and parades. I know Nadia likes Mrs. Ellie, but she has high school, college and the farm to take up her time."

Lacey and Jillie winked at each other and smiled. "We want to stay Uncle Jeremy, but you can leave whenever you want. We'll make sure Nadia gets back to the farm. We'll bring her home tomorrow."

"Thanks Lacey. I think we'll take you up on that. I'm beat and it's cold out here."

"Thin skin," Will commented."

Lacey pushed her husband. "Shush."

Will quietly chuckled and looked at Miguel. They loved picking on Nadia's dad. He was not like his brother Jake.

Jeremy, Stacey and Luke took off after a few more minutes. They didn't wait to see Miguel Lope leading the men's riding troop. He was decked out in a deer skin tunic and pants with the grandest chieftain headdress made out of leather and duck feathers. He waved at his new friends as he slowly guided his group by Nadia's family. He did not smile, but he kept his look upon them until he would have had to turn his head. Mr. Jake nodded and winked at Lacey and Jillie as he passed. They both waved at him and smiled with endearing looks. They knew the farm's magical and mysterious destiny was weaving more thread into its everlasting web.

Chapter 15: Stepping Stones to Success

The holiday parade had brought fame into Nadia's life. So many students had attended the parade and saw Nadia in her glory. She walked back into school after Thanksgiving with teachers and students praising her and really taking notice of this very quiet and smart teenager. She brought state wide attention to the farm and the riding school. Will and Tom had to hire more stable help when their boarding stables were filled up and a lengthy waiting list. So many of the young riding students were in awe of Nadia and they wanted a chance to join the riding troop. Nadia was so happy that she had nothing to do with such decisions. She wanted to concentrate on her studies, spend time working with the horses and continue her work with her riding troop. Mrs. Ellie and Mr. Jake became more and more involved with Nadia, her family and the farm. Mr. Jake had a green thumb and he came over several times a week and helped Lacey and Will with farming ideas. Mrs. Ellie and Mr. Jake assisted Tom, Nadia and Susan teaching riding lessons. They both helped the beginning riders and their parents to realize the dedication of owning horses. Every once in a while, Miguel Lope would come visit his grandparents on the weekends and help on the farm. Everyone noticed the friendship evolving between Miguel Lope and Nadia. They shared a love of horses. Miguel Lope even began helping in the clinic and he soon began talking about becoming a veterinarian.

When Lacey's second baby boy, Blake Fierce,

and Jillie's baby girl, Anna Grace, were born, all hands were on deck during the summer before Nadia's tenth grade. She and Miguel Lope got to be with Miguel for the birth of Warrior Girl's second filly that was promised to Nadia. Nadia named her little filly, Whispering Willow. She would call her horse Willow for the gentle tree that is truly strong and bending. Everyone loved the name.

Tenth grade arrived for Nadia and her days were full. Nadia would be turning sixteen and finally getting her license. Lacey and Jillie, along with Nadia's parents, planned a huge surprise birthday party for their young cousin. Jeremy had already scouted out an almost new truck and horse trailer with the help of Mr. Jake. Jeremy and Stacey were excited and wanted to surprise Nadia. Their plan was a bit devious, but they knew their daughter would totally forgive them once she realized how so many people were apart of making her sixteenth birthday a day she would never forget.

"Nadia, your dad and I want you to spend your birthday with us," Stacey said, as Nadia came downstairs Wednesday before her Saturday birthday. "We have picked out a few cars, but we want you to look at them too."

"Cars?!" Nadia replied. "I need a truck mom. How do you think I'm going to get my horse around?"

Stacey looked away so that Nadia couldn't see her smile that she just couldn't contain. "Well, we'll look at trucks too. Anyway, we want to pick you up this Friday and spend your birthday with you first. We will take you to the farm Saturday afternoon. I've already told your cousins that you will not be there on Friday and Will doesn't need to worry about you."

Nadia didn't say anything right away. She poured herself a glass of milk and fixed herself a bagel with cream cheese. "Whatever mom."

Stacey hated making her daughter sad, but everything was all planned out to have cake and ice cream at the farm with her cousins and the Sondeeruns.

"Come on, I'll take you to school. Don't let spending a bit of time with your mom and dad get you down."

Nadia looked at her mom and gave her half smile. "Mom, I don't mind spending time with you and dad. I just miss being on the farm. You know how I am by now."

Stacey smiled. "Oh yes my dear. You're a determined young lady and we are so proud of you. We'll have some fun. Don't worry and don't have a bad few days. We want to celebrate our daughter."

"Okay mom; I cannot wait to see the cars dad is thinking about buying me. I hope he's not looking at tiny, little cars. I really want a truck."

"That is why we didn't buy one yet. We figured you would like to have a say. I bet your dad will be okay with a truck and it seems safer to me."

"I do have a horse that I need to get around when she's old enough to join me," Nadia replied, as they walked out the door. "And mom, you won't have to take me to school."

Stacey swished her daughter's dark, long pony tail. "I don't mind taking you to school."

Nadia didn't have a great three days. She was bummed out that she couldn't go over to the farm like she did every Friday after school. Friday came and she waited outside for her mother. As she waited, she dialed Will.

"Hello," Will answered.

"Will, its Nadia. Just checking to see how everything is going over there."

Will laughed. "You think we cannot handle things without you over here?"

Nadia giggled too. "Well, you know Will. The

horses will miss me and they probably know this is Friday. Will you just go tell them that I'll be there tomorrow?"

"Of course little woman," Will said and laughed.

"Oh Will," Nadia started waiting for Will to stop laughing and listen to her. "I'm probably getting a vehicle tomorrow. I think he's got a car picked out for me. I'm going to try and persuade him into buying me a truck. Either way, I'll be able to drive over a lot more during the weekday evenings after school."

"That you will; that you will," Will answered. "Don't let your studies go down hill, because you start hanging out over here and your parents will put a stop to that."

"You don't have to worry about that," Nadia quickly replied. "I'll just sit in the barn with the horses and do my studies. They just like having me around."

"Okay Nadia. Have fun with your mom and dad. I cannot wait to see your new vehicle."

"Mom's here," Nadia said. "See you tomorrow."

"Sure thing," Will answered and hung up laughing and thinking about her face when she saw her new truck and horse trailer.

Nadia jumped into her mom's SUV. "Hey mom; let's get home and get ourselves all dolled up for my birthday dinner."

Stacey looked at her daughter. "Now that is a surprise for the girl who loves her jeans, boots and a pony tail."

"Time to grow up mom," Nadia replied with a huge smile across her face.

"Let's go get all dolled up," Stacy said, as she slowly pulled away from the curb.

When Stacey and Nadia arrived home, Jeremy's car was already there. Nadia ran into the house. She looked around for her dad and couldn't find him and yelled. "Dad!"

Stacey came into the house. "Did you find your dad?"

"No," Nadia said, as she ran to the back door to look into the back yard. "I don't see him anywhere."

"I'm going to go see what I can doll up in tonight," Stacy said and left the room. She wanted to go call Jeremy on his cell and let him know Nadia was looking for him. She, of course, knew he was helping take their daughter's birthday present to the farm. Mr. Jake had met him here earlier and picked him up.

Nadia gave up trying to find her dad and headed upstairs to get herself all dolled up for her birthday dinner. When Jeremy slipped into the house before his daughter came back downstairs, he got himself all decked out for a big evening out with his wife and daughter. Nadia was totally surprised when she came back downstairs and found her parents waiting on her.

"Where were you hiding when I got home from school dad?"

Jeremy tried his hardest not to smile. "I was at the neighbor's house. They had a problem getting their garage door to open and asked me if I could look at it."

"Oh," Nadia replied. "*Je suis affame papa.*"

"*My ousi,*" Jeremy replied.

Nadia and Stacey laughed, as Nadia walked over to her dad and took his head in her hands. "Dad, stick to southern please."

Jeremy laughed at himself. "*Oui,* and you both look mighty nice."

Nadia twirled for her dad. "I'm growing up dad and out of my pony tails."

"Oh," Jeremy replied, "I love your pony tails."

Stacey cleared her throat to let Jeremy know she had to do something before they left.

Jeremy hugged his daughter and walked her out the door, so Stacey could pull out the cake she had made and decorated that day. She placed it out on the dining room table, along with a couple of small presents.

Tea came into the dining room watching Stacey. Stacey looked over at her daughter's loving cat. "Guard the cake Tea. We don't want anyone to eat it before we get back."

Tea meowed to answer "yes". Stacey laughed. "I swear you know what I am saying, but I'm not saying a word. Someone might think I'm losing it."

Tea meowed again and walked in between Stacey's legs purring to let Nadia's mother know she appreciated her too. Stacey smiled and bent down. "Be good and watch the house," Stacy said, as she gave Tea a few long strokes down her back. "Better go; they're waiting on me."

Tea walked behind Stacey and watched them pull out of the driveway. She sat down to wait for Nadia's return.

Jeremy had another surprise that even Stacey didn't know. He had invited the Sondeerun's to join them. He knew this would make Nadia the happiest little girl and it gave him a chance to thank Mr. Jake and Mrs. Ellie for all the rides they had given Nadia and helping him find Nadia's truck. They had graciously accepted and even asked to bring Miguel Lope which made Jeremy a bit uncomfortable, but what could he say.

***

When Nadia and her parents pulled into the parking lot of the Proximity Hotel, Nadia saw her friends. "Dad, did you invite Mr. Jake, Mrs. Ellie and Miguel Lope?!"

"I invited Mr. Jake and Mrs. Ellie and they invited their grandson. I hope you two are just friends."

Nadia's eyes were on Miguel Lope, who was all dressed in black slacks, a black button down and a beautiful contrasting tie. "Dad, we're only friends with similar likes and that would be horses."

Jeremy was looking back at his daughter from his rearview mirror and saw the dreamy look in her eyes. "Just keep it simple. You have lots of life before you should even think of getting serious."

Stacey looked at her husband. "That's enough. Enjoy your daughter's sixteenth and stop worrying about her wedding."

Nadia heard her mom. "Now, that's just gross. I'm only sixteen and I am going to go to college, so could you both just drop worrying about me and Miguel Lope. We are just friends. He's stuck on himself anyway and I tell him that all the time."

Stacey gently punched her husband in the arm and smiled at him. He looked at Stacey, rolled his eyes and moved his lips so that Nadia could not hear him. "I'm not stupid."

As Jeremy pulled into a parking space, Nadia jumped out and rushed across the parking lot to her friends. Miguel Lope stood mesmerized. Mr. Jake and Mrs. Ellie saw the twinkle in his eyes. Mr. Jake leaned over to his wife. "That is exactly how I felt when I saw you decked out at that summer wedding."

Mrs. Ellie pushed him away. "Do not start anything and scare our grandson, Nadia or her parents."

Jeremy and Stacey met up with everyone. As soon as they greeted one another, Jeremy led the way into the bistro. Dinner was wonderful for all of them. Nadia was the center of attention and she kept everyone entertained. She had no problem talking around the people who meant so much to her. When dinner came to an end, Jeremy rushed the check so he could get his daughter home. Goodnights were exchanged and Miguel Lope walked Nadia to the car.

"See you real soon Nadia," Miguel Lope said. Nadia had no idea he would be at the farm tomorrow for the big surprise.

"I hope so and let me know how college stuff is going."

"Let's hit it Nadia," Jeremy said out the window.

Miguel Lope held the door open for Nadia and slowly shut it once she was all settled. He smiled big at her and then saluted Jeremy. Jeremy cracked his window. "You got that right son."

Stacey and Nadia broke out in laughter and so did Miguel Lope. Jeremy motioned for him to watch out and he took off to take his little girl home.

***

Tea was waiting for them when they walked in the door. Nadia bent down and picked her beautiful cat up and hugged her tight. "Let's go change."

Jeremy came up behind her. "Wait Nadia; there is another little something for your birthday. We'll go car hunting another day. I just said that so you would not weasel out of going with us tonight. And, I had invited your friends."

Stacey walked by with matches to light the cake. When Jeremy and Nadia entered the dining room, Stacey had the candles all lit. She began singing "Happy Birthday" and Jeremy piped in too adding his silliness. Nadia smiled and waited for her parents to end the grueling tunes.

"Open your presents sweetheart," Stacey said, as she picked up and handed her daughter a present.

Nadia grabbed her present and quickly ripped off the gift wrap. "Oh mom and dad, this is so great." Nadia held up the license plate frame with horses all around it. "I love this and it would look really good on a truck, hint and hint."

"Open that one too," Jeremy said, as he pointed to the smaller present.

Nadia tore into it and pulled the personalized

keychain out. "Is there a car sitting in the driveway or something?" Nadia ran to the front door, swung it open and ran outside. She quickly returned. "I guess not. Thanks mom and dad. Sorry I got so excited, but I thought you had the real surprise outside."

"Don't worry Nadia," Stacey started, "we'll help you get a car."

"I would really like a truck."

"We'll see when we go looking Nadia," Jeremy said and walked out before his face gave it all away.

"I'm going to change," Nadia said, as she scooped up Tea again and started out.

"What about cake?" Stacey asked.

"Later mom," Nadia called back and kept on going.

Jeremy came back into the room with a big grin. "She's going to be so surprised and I cannot wait."

"Tonight is going to be a long night around here," Stacey added and left to go change.

Saturday came and Nadia had her parents up early bugging them to take her to the farm. Jeremy called Lacey when he couldn't take it any longer to ask if they were ready for her. Lacey laughed and told him to bring her on over. They were just waiting for the Sundeeruns to arrive.

Jeremy, of course, had something to say about that. "Oh, of course, let's not leave out the boy who is after my daughter."

"Why do you think that Miguel Lope is after Nadia Uncle Jeremy?" Lacey asked.

"You can see it in his eyes. If you all would open your eyes, you would see it too."

Lacey tried not to give the future away and remembered the picture of Nadia and her family on the walls of the farmhouse three hundred years from now. "Don't worry Uncle Jeremy. Nadia is a very smart girl. She will make the right choices and she will have a wonderful future."

"Whatever," Jeremy answered. "We're on our way, Tea and all."

***

Jeremy slowly pulled into the farm's driveway. He didn't see any cars and realized they were going to really surprise Nadia.

"Dad, I'm going to run down to the stables and check on the horses. Are you and mom going to go see Lacey and Will?"

"Yeah, I thought we would visit for a few minutes," Jeremy answered, as he wondered where they had hidden the truck and trailer.

Nadia quickly got out of the car and ran all the way down to the barn and stables. Jeremy and Stacey rushed into the farmhouse to find everyone in the dining room waiting for Nadia.

"Nadia had to go down and check on the horses," Stacey said.

"Oh," Lacey said, "we wanted her to come in here."

"I'll go get her," Miguel Lope said and he quickly ran out of the room and out of the house.

Jeremy looked at his wife and she just smiled without saying one thing. "If they're not back in five minutes, I'm going down to get them."

Everyone laughed at Jeremy and Mr. Jake came over to him. "Don't worry Jeremy; I would never let anything happen to your daughter. She is much too special."

Jeremy looked at this older man. "Thank you Mr. Jake. I know you know what I mean. You have two daughters."

Lacey and Jillie looked at one another with big eyes. Before anything else could be said, they heard the back porch screen door close. Seconds later, Miguel

Lope walked in with Nadia behind him. They all yelled "Happy Birthday!"

Nadia brought her hands up and covered her mouth. "Another party; this is turning out to be a great sixteenth. Let's eat cake. I never ate my cake last night."

Jeremy looked at his wife and she smiled with anticipation of what was to come.

Everyone sang the birthday song and Nadia said her wish so everyone could hear. "I wish for a truck!" She blew out her candles and looked at her dad with such a sweet and begging look.

Jeremy just smiled back without saying a word. Lacey started cutting the cake and handing it out. The two little ones were both in a playpen and Wayne Jake was devouring his cake. Tye, Tess and Tea were all sitting around the babies.

Miss Virginia was not present today and Nadia noticed. "I guess Miss Virginia is out scouting the farm."

Lacey smiled. "You know Miss Virginia. She loves to wander far away."

Nadia smiled at her older cousin. "She's probably having a wonderful day."

Everyone enjoyed the cake and ice cream social hour. When Jeremy noticed everyone was finishing up with their cake, he looked at Will. Will excused himself and made an excuse to leave the house. Minutes later, a horn was beeping outside and everyone stopped talking.

"Is that Will or does someone need you guys outside?" Jeremy asked.

"I have no idea," Lacey said, as she picked up Wayne Jake and handed him over to Stacey. "Let's go see." Lacey and Jillie picked up their babies from the playpen.

Nadia went over to Stacey and held out her hands for little Wayne. "Let's go see if your daddy is being silly."

Jeremy and Stacey led the way outside. Nadia was one of the last ones and everyone was waiting to see her reaction. When she saw the white Ford truck, with a Willow branch flowing down the side, hooked up to a horse trailer, she was speechless. She looked at her dad and her mom, who both stood there with big smiles across their faces.

Everyone yelled, "Happy Birthday Nadia!"

Nadia handed Wayne Jake back to her mom and ran out to the truck. Will was getting out and handed her the set of keys. "Your dad and mom went to great lengths to keep this surprise for today. I hope you appreciate this wonderful gift."

"OMG," Nadia yelled. "Dad, you got me a truck." She ran back and hugged her dad and then her mom. "I love the Willow branch. It's the best gift since I got Whispering Willow. She is going to love her new ride. Can I drive it down into the pasture?"

"I'll go with her," Miguel Lope called out.

"Come on Miguel Lope," Nadia replied. "Don't tell me how to drive it either. I've already taken driver's education and I just need to get used to MY truck."

"Go for it girl," Miguel Lope replied.

The two teenagers jumped in the truck. Nadia looked out the window and held up her left thumb giving her dad a 'thumbs up'. She started the truck and slowly pulled it through the gate to the pasture, horse trailer and all. Will and Miguel whistled and made some native sounds.

And when Mr. Jake joined in, Jeremy looked at all three of them. "Ya'll are definitely not right." Jeremy looked at his nieces and shook his head. "You married some wild men."

Lacey walked up beside of Will and put her arm around him with the little one in the other. "Best man ever."

"I second that," Jillie commented.

"Third that," Mrs. Ellie chirped in.

Jeremy looked at Stacey. "Okay dear, you need to fourth that."

Everyone laughed. Nadia soon returned with smiles so big that it melted her daddy's heart. "Dad, you're the best."

"Don't forget it either," Jeremy replied, as he glared at Miguel Lope.

Miguel Lope knew he had to say something at this moment. "I second that."

Everyone broke into laughter again.

Nadia's sixteenth birthday was just one of many wonderful days Nadia had in high school. With her truck, her trailer, her hose and her Tea, Nadia never worried about anything. She had one thing on her mind and that was Whispering Willow and the horses on the farm. She devoted all her time to her studies, especially general science, biology and chemistry. She had very little time for teenage anything. Her time was too valuable to waste on partying. She had a goal and that was to become the best equine veterinarian, keep the riding school thriving and becoming a national renowned equine specialists. Jeremy and Stacey gave up trying to get Nadia to be the silly teenager long ago and supported her with her endeavors. They had no idea how important their roles were in raising the most important link to the survival of their family's farm.

Chapter 16: At Last, Graduation!

Nadia did extremely well throughout her high school years. The only thing is that she never truly loved high school. She never fit into the 'in crowd' and didn't want to participate in any school sports. She just wanted to be with Willow, the other horses or her riding troop. She spent countless weekends with Mrs. Ellie and Mr. Jake or on the farm. She did hang out with Miguel Lope, but she never thought of him more than as her friend. Miguel Lope had girlfriends that came and went and they never lasted past half a year. Nadia was always there to listen to his heartaches. Miguel Lope sometimes dropped hints of them dating, but Nadia never got the hint. Her mind was totally on her future. Everyone that cared for Nadia accepted her the way she was and that was one serious minded individual.

February of Nadia's senior year, Nadia was walking to her last class of the day one Thursday. Darrin, a boy in Nadia's last class, caught up with her.

"Nadia, how about actually having a little fun and joining me for the basketball game this Friday?"

Nadia knew Darrin and thought he was nice. "I don't know and why me?"

Darrin looked down at Nadia. "I think you're a cool girl and I just finally got the nerve to ask you out."

Nadia looked up at her classmate and smiled. "You were nervous about asking me out? I'm flattered. Write your number down and give it to me after class."

"You got a deal," Darrin said, as they walked into

class together.

Nadia didn't see Darrin give one of his buddies 'a thumbs up'. She couldn't stop thinking about it either and couldn't wait to tell Susan

When the bell rang, Darrin escorted Nadia to her locker and gave her his number. "I hope you'll say yes Nadia."

"I'm definitely thinking about it Darrin."

Darrin left Nadia standing at her locker. Nadia grabbed her cell and sent Susan a text to wait for her outside near their trucks. Nadia practically ran to go tell Susan that Darrin had asked to take her out.

Susan was just as excited for her friend. "Just go Nadia. Prove to everyone that you're not so nerdy and have some fun."

Nadia looked at her friend. "You think I'm nerdy?"

"Of course not silly, but I hear what people say about you. Prove them wrong."

"Okay, I'll say yes," Nadia replied with a huge smile on her face. "I know my mom and dad will be happy. I can only hear them now if they don't faint."

Nadia and Susan laughed, said their good-byes and headed out from the school parking lot. Nadia went home thinking how she would say it, what she would wear and what kind of fun they would have at a basketball game. She was pretty ignorant when it came to sports. As she had predicted, her parents were ecstatic that she had a date. Nadia knew they just wanted her to have some fun.

Nadia waited until after dinner to call Darrin.

"Hello," Darrin answered.

"Darrin, it's me Nadia."

"I hope it's a yes," Darrin said.

"It's a yes Darrin," Nadia replied. "Are you picking me up or should we meet at the school?"

"I'm picking you up for sure," Darrin excitedly said. "I'll see you tomorrow at school and I'll pick you up at six sharp."

"Sounds cool," Nadia replied, "see you tomorrow."

Nadia hung up and truly realized that this was the first date of her life. She looked at herself in the mirror and shook her head. "Where have you been for the last four years?" Nadia studied as best she could and went to bed early. She was too nervous and too excited to concentrate.

Friday morning came too early for Nadia. She finally fell asleep around two in the morning. She was excited and worried about her date. Tea was exhausted too, because she couldn't stop worrying about her Nadia. "Sorry Tea, you just sleep in this morning. I'll put your food out."

Tea held her head up and looked at Nadia with sleepy eyes. Nadia gently rubbed her cat's head and let her sleep. Nadia slowly made her way to the bathroom. She was not as excited as she had been last night. She was too tired. Nadia briefly talked to her parents before she fixed herself a cup of hot tea and a PB&J. Before she left for school, she checked in on Tea one more time. Tea was still fast asleep.

When Nadia pulled into the school parking lot, she saw Darrin talking with some other guys. He saw Nadia's truck and rushed over to greet her. "Hey girl."

Nadia told herself to be nice, but she wasn't in the mood for small talk. She hoped she had not made a mistake. "Hey Darrin; how are you?"

"I'm great," Darrin said with a huge smile. "You okay? You look like you stayed up studying all night."

Nadia didn't want to tell him that she was so excited and worried that she couldn't sleep. "Just reading a good book and couldn't put it down."

"I wish I had your study and reading habits,"

Darrin replied. "Maybe you'll rub off on me. Come on, I'll walk you to your locker."

Nadia smiled. "Reading can take you to places all over the world or to events that happened centuries ago."

"I guess that is a good way to look at it," Darrin replied and then he talked the entire time it took them to walk to Nadia's locker. Nadia tried to be nice and not so nerdy. "Nadia, are you listening to a word I say?"

Nadia quickly shook her head. "Of course; I'm just thinking about a test I have today." She did have a test, but that was not what she was thinking about at all."

"Okay, I'll let you think," Darrin said, as he helped Nadia close her locker. "I'll see you after school and then I'll pick you up at six."

Nadia looked up at Darrin, but she didn't feel like she did yesterday. "Sounds like a plan Darrin. See you later." Nadia rushed off to her homeroom.

The day moved slowly and Nadia yawned the entire morning. Lunch finally came and she decided to take a power nap. She grabbed a pack of peanut butter crackers and a green tea beverage from the front vending machine. She practically inhaled the crackers and the drink. She went to the library and found a quiet corner. She fell into a deep sleep and she didn't wake up to make it to her next class. She missed her test and the teacher didn't even worry about her. Nadia was such a dedicated student the teacher just took it for granted that she was out sick or had gone home sick. Nadia woke up to the librarian shaking her; she jumped up and looked at the clock.

"OH MY GOSH," Nadia called out. "I've missed my test."

"Nadia, are you not feeling well? Maybe you should go to the office and go home."

Nadia thought for a moment and then noticed Tea across the room. Her fear had caused Tea to be there to check on her. "I'm not feeling very well. I think I will go to the office and go home." Nadia quickly walked toward her cat sending her a thought to go home. Tea disappeared. Nadia cleared herself to leave and drove home. When she walked into the house, her mom was there waiting on her.

"So sorry you're feeling bad Nadia," Stacey commented.

"I'm just tired mom. I didn't really sleep last night."

Stacey walked over and gave her daughter a hug. "Go lie down for a while and I'll wake you around five. Are you still going out with that boy?"

"Sounds good," Nadia said, as she dropped her backpack on the floor just before heading up the stairs. "Oh, I'll text Darrin to call after five."

Nadia went straight to her room and fell into bed. Tea climbed in beside her and joined her in sleepy time. She was in a deep, deep sleep when Stacey came in to wake her up.

"Nadia," Stacey said, as she shook her daughter, "it's five o'clock."

Nadia stirred a bit and turned over without opening her eyes.

"Nadia, Nadia," Stacey said again while she rubbed Nadia's hair away from her face.

Nadia turned over, looked at her mom and quickly sat up. "OMG mom; what time is it?" Nadia nudged Tea to move so she could get up.

"It's five," Stacey replied, "and time for you to get up if you want to go out tonight."

"I don't even know mom, but I cannot let Darrin down. I guess I'll go. I'll check my phone to see if he's called or not."

Nadia saw that Darrin had called her and sent her text messages seeing if they were on or off for the game. Nadia called him and told him they were on for the game. She jumped out of bed and took a quick shower to wake up. She carefully selected some cool jeans, a kind of new shirt and her cowgirl boots. She wasn't going to wear anything else.

Darrin arrived right on time and Nadia invited him come in to say hello to her parents. Jeremy and Stacey were just so happy to see their daughter go out on a date. They made small talk until Nadia directed Darrin it was time for them to get to the game. Darrin opened the car door for Nadia and that was something Nadia wasn't expecting. She liked that. When they arrived at the game, Darrin opened the door again for Nadia to get out. The evening went great. They both had a great time and even joined some friends out for pizza following the game. Nadia had a great time with Darrin. And, Darrin had a great time with Nadia. This date became the beginning of Nadia's senior high romance; a romance that took Nadia and everyone by surprise.

Nadia's dreams changed over night. Because she wanted to spend every free moment with Darrin, Nadia began leaving her responsibilities of Willow and the farm behind. Lacey and Jillie both understood, but hated to see their little cousin quickly go in a total opposite direction. Darrin seemed like a nice enough guy, but he totally turned Nadia away from the things she had always loved. Even Tea had a hard time with Nadia and Nadia a hard time with Tea. Everyone tried to get Nadia to bring Darrin into the world she had always loved, but she stayed away whenever she was with Darrin. He had a hold over her. She said it was true love, but Lacey and Jillie knew it was jealousy and envy on his part. Even Stacey and Jeremy began seeing a different daughter they didn't know, especially when she turned down invitations to spend time with Mrs. Ellie and Mr. Jake. Even Susan had been forgotten by Nadia.

Nadia needed saving again, but this time from something more than a life threatening illness. She needed saving from herself. No one would ever believe that Lope would be the one to save her again. No one even knew they had been secretly meeting for years. Nadia's own great-grandson, many times removed, had grown up seeing his great-grandmother that he saved when she was a young girl.

After three months passed, Lope knew something was not right. Nadia and he had a special place they left notes stating times they could meet. Lope arrived one Saturday around five in the morning and hid in the hayloft. Nadia should have been there, but all he saw were Tom and Will. He couldn't take it any longer. As Will was cleaning out Willow's stall, Lope climbed down to confront Will about Nadia.

"Will, Tame Tiger" Lope started, "don't freak out. It's me, Lope."

Will jumped and couldn't believe his eyes. "You're; you're all grown up Lope.

Lope took a deep breath. "Where is my, I mean Nadia?" Lope demanded. "I haven't seen her in months and I need to know if she is sick again."

Will shook his head, smiled and stuck the pitch fork into the ground. "I think we have some talking to do. I think Lacey and Jillie might need to hear what you have to say."

Will made Lope stay put while he went to find Tom. He didn't want to 'give the farm away', so he made up an excuse that Lacey had called him up to the house. Susan would be arriving soon to help. Will rushed Lope up to the house to find Lacey and Jillie playing with the little ones. Miguel was at the clinic tending to the animals needing overnight care. When Lacey and Jillie saw the young man with Will, they both thought it was someone here to check out the facilities. Lope had a huge smile across his face and Will looked totally bewildered. Lacey noticed the look on her husband's face and looked at Lope again.

"How are you?" Lacey asked, as she stared into

the eyes of this young man.

"I'm doing great Lacey," Lope answered smiling even more.

Jillie froze and Lacey stood up. "Lope?"

"In the flesh," Lope answered standing proud. "Please don't faint on me Jillie."

Will cleared his throat and walked over to take his youngest son from Lacey's hands. "I think you two may want to sit down for this."

Jillie and Lacey looked at one another and then at Lope. "How old are you now Lope?" Jillie asked.

"I'm twenty-five now," Lope replied. He didn't give them a chance to ask any more questions. "I'm worried about Nadia."

Lope went on to explain how he and Nadia had been secret friends since he was thirteen-years-old and she was just seven. As he told them all that he and Nadia had done together, the girls looked at one another. It all made sense now. All those times Nadia disappeared and her excuses were always about school projects. Lacey and Jillie both shook their heads as Lope 'spilled the beans'.

"So bottom line," Lope finished, "I just want to know if my great-grandmother's health is okay or not."

Lacey took in a deep breath. "Lope, Nadia's health is perfect. It's her mind that is a bit messed up. It's all about a boy and she is just so 'in love' as she tells us all. He's got this hold over her and we hardly ever see her. She's left all of the things she always loved behind. She is eighteen now and we don't like to talk with her parents about it. They are both so distressed over all of this. They feel guilty, because they were always worried about her not being the normal, giggly teen and now they are worried. Let's just say none of us know what to do about it. We're just hoping that she is not in the partying scene, but her grades are perfect. Jeremy and Stacey feel like he wants her to do everything he wants and he doesn't respect what she likes to do."

Lope stood in silence for almost a minute. His mind was racing. "You all know he is not the person for Nadia. So, we can let it play out. Or maybe, we throw Nadia a bone."

"And the bone would be?" Jillie asked.

"I know everything there is to know about my great-grandmother. The loves of her life are Tea and Willow. That is of course until she realizes 'you know who' is her soul mate. Tell her someone is interested in buying Willow. If she's not really into her, she'll realize that it's only fair to Willow that she has someone who loves her. I think she may just come back to reality."

"You think 'true love' will fall to the horse?" Lacey asked.

"He's not her true love", Lope sternly answered. We all know who will be her true love. The future has already been written. I am living proof and I'm not vanishing into thin air for no one."

"Okay then," Jillie replied, "who are we going to say wants to buy Willow? Lope, you know your great-grandmother so well. Who should we say is buying her horse?"

"That's so easy Jillie," Lope said smiling. "The Sundeeruns would definitely want Willow, but they don't even have to pay us anything. Just ask them to go along with our little charade."

Jillie walked over to Lope and gave him a big hug. "They are worried about her too. You are so smart Lope and they will be here today to help out with the riding lessons."

"Can I meet them?" Lope begged. "You know they are my ancestors too."

"Not as Lope," Will chimed into the conversation. "I don't know if it's a great idea, but it's our way of saying thank-you for being there for Nadia, your great-grandmother." Will looked at Lacey for her approval.

Lacey smiled. "Don't look at me. He's been coming over here without our approval for all these years. I wouldn't have it any other way."

Lacey joined Jillie and they hugged Lope in tight. "Thank you Lope for being here when we needed you again. One day, I think Nadia will figure you out and she'll be so happy to have known you."

Miguel walked in from the clinic and was a bit in shock when they all filled him in on Lope. They were all apart of a huge destiny and it kept getting better.

When Mrs. Ellie and Mr. Jake arrived, Lacey and Jillie filled them in on their idea. And, they introduced Lope as a prospective boarder, John James. Mr. Jake kept looking into Lope's eyes, but he never said a word. He felt something, but he knew it couldn't be more than that; a funny feeling that he shook off.

The plan was put into action. Lacey made the call to Nadia. Of course, her voicemail picked up. So, she left a quick message and left it at that. Nadia called her cousins back and told them she would think about it and she would be there Sunday.

On Sunday afternoon, Darrin drove Nadia over to the farm. She didn't bother to call Lacey that she was on her way, which was her norm since Darrin entered the picture. Darrin was with her and not Tea. Lacey and Will were so excited to see her. They gave her hug after hug and finally gave Darrin a hello. It was obvious to Nadia that they did not approve of Darrin.

"So, you think I should sell Willow?"

"She needs someone to love her Nadia," Will calmly answered. "She went from being the most loved horse on the farm to the horse that everyone feels sorry for now."

Nadia turned her head away. Tears were welling up in her eyes. Lacey and Will noticed, but didn't say a word. "I need to go see her."

Tea showed up, but she hid from Darrin's view.

Darrin cleared his throat. “Do you think you should really do that Naddie? Won’t that make it that much harder to say good-bye?”

Will tensed up. He sensed Darrin’s control over Nadia. “She should see her to make sure it’s what she wants to do.”

“Come on Darrin,” Nadia quietly said, “I want you to meet her.”

“I’ll wait in the truck. Make it fast. We’re meeting our friends you know.”

Lacey was about to come unglued. “Darrin?” Lacey questioned. “Do you have something against horses?”

“NO,” Darrin quickly answered. “Nadia and I have better things to do than hang out with horses and waste our time on this farm. Nadia and I are planning on moving to a big city and ditching this place.”

“Nadia, is that how you feel?” Jillie questioned. “You owe it to her to say good-bye.”

“It’s a horse for goodness sake,” Darrin shouted.

Tea became a cougar and Will saw her. Will put his palm to his side and motioned for Tea to stay put and calm.

Nadia looked at Darrin. For a split second, Lacey thought she saw fear in her younger cousin’s eyes. “I’ll go quickly, I promise.”

Darrin stormed out. Nadia stood frozen not knowing what to say. “He says he cannot live without me. He says that if I truly love him, I will spend my time with him. I don’t know what I am supposed to do.”

Will moved in front of Nadia and looked down into her eyes. “Has he hurt you?”

Nadia shook her head. “No, but he just says weird things and then he apologizes and he says it’s all my fault.”

Tea moved to Nadia’s side, which startled Nadia. “Tea, I told you to stay home. I didn’t want Darrin to hurt you."

"Nadia, he cannot hurt Tea," Lacey sternly said. "Tea is there to protect you."

"He makes comments about not liking cats or any animals," Nadia replied.

"Nadia!" Jillie yelled. "He's manipulating you. If he truly cared for you, he would allow you to be you. Remember, it takes courage to become who you want to be."

"He says he loves me," Nadia cried out.

"No he doesn't Nadia," Will calmly responded, as he took her and hugged her tight. "Do you miss us? Do you miss Willow? Do you miss coming here and exploring?"

Nadia pulled away and looked up at Will. She thought about Lope and how she just stopped communicating. "Oh I miss everything, but he's my boyfriend and I have to be loyal."

"No Nadia," Will said, "he's not being loyal to you. He's convinced you somehow that you are nothing without him. You're everything and more. He's a coward Nadia. Please, let Tea handle him. You know she will not harm him, but she will make sure he's out of your life. That is if that's what you want."

Nadia broke into tears. "I have been so scared. He demands too much of me, but he always ends our time together telling me how much he loves me. I just want to go back to the way I used to be. I cannot take the texting all hours of the night. I'm exhausted."

Nadia bent down and hugged her cougar. "Tea, I need your help, but please don't hurt him."

Tea roared and when she did, a lion, a white tiger and a black panther all joined her. Tea looked into Nadia's eyes. "It's a family matter." The four beasts disappeared before their very eyes. Seconds later, they heard tires screech as Darrin pulled out of the driveway.

Nadia broke down and cried, as she told her

family how wonderful Darrin was in the beginning and how awful it became. The beasts were all around her pacing and growling in low tones. Lacey, Jillie, Will and Miguel all sat with her in total silence.

"Nadia," Lacey began, "we're here for you always. We totally understand what happened, but remember no one should fear another person, especially someone who supposedly loves us. There are so many people that can help you to make the right decision. Not everyone has a Tea and just how did you get her to not do anything?"

"She wanted to, but I commanded her to stay away. I wasn't sure she wouldn't get hurt. I was stupid Lacey, but it was my first boyfriend. I really had no idea that Darrin was the way he is. I don't know what to expect tomorrow from him."

"Don't worry, Miss Virginia and her kittens will be there for you the rest of the year," Will said. "Now, how about you running down to the barn. I think there might be a horse that has been very sad."

Nadia wiped away her tears, quickly hugged everyone and ran down to the barn as quick as she could. There waiting for her was Willow and Lope. Lope held out his open arms to his great-grandmother. "We've missed you little woman."

Lope spent an hour filling Nadia in all the things he and Willow had been doing. Lacey, Jillie, Will and Miguel stayed happily in the farmhouse knowing Nadia was with the one special person who would always be there for her.

Graduation day finally came and Nadia couldn't wait to say good-bye to that part of her life. Darrin never talked to her again. Nadia let him tell whatever he wanted to tell his friends, because she knew he would never be able to tell the truth. She heard through the gossiping grapevine that he told his friends that she was too smart for him. Susan was thrilled to have her friend back. Graduation for Nadia consisted of family celebrations in the present, in the past and in the future.

Chapter 17: Destiny's Fear Conquered

Nadia slept in after a week full of graduation parties. Parties that were, how do you say it, out of this world. She was exhausted and so was Tea that followed her everywhere she went. Today started a new chapter in her life with a little introduction called 'summer before college'. Nadia had so much planned that she made a list of all the things she had to do before she left to North Carolina State, where she planned on becoming an equine expert. Even the best made plans get interrupted by destiny. It was Sunday and Nadia wanted to head to the farm for the week.

"Where are you heading today Nadia?" Jeremy asked.

"The farm that I neglected; I have a lot to do before I head off to college. And, I want to train one of my riding students to be in charge of Willow for me. She's great with the horses and I can tell the horses really like her. By the way, I'm staying on the farm all week."

Jeremy chuckled. "I guess the horses tell you those kinds of things?"

"They do dad; they have a language and I understand it and they understand me." Nadia was a bit agitated with her dad for always questioning whether animals can really communicate. "You just have to be open to it and you would be able to do it too."

Jeremy walked over to his daughter and gave her a hug. "I'll leave that all up to you. I think I do well with Tea."

"You mean she does well with you dad," Nadia replied. "She's got you all figured out."

"I'll have to trip her up with some of my magic," Jeremy added and laughed, as Tea entered the kitchen.

"Speak of the little de-, I mean angel," Jeremy said.

Tea looked at Jeremy and locked her eyes with his.

"Okay, forget it." Jeremy said, "She is too intimidating for me. She wins."

Nadia burst out into laughter. Stacey heard her daughter laughing from upstairs and came down to see what was so funny. It was the sweetest sound she had heard in months. Nadia was laughing again.

"What's so funny down here?" Stacey asked, as she came into the room.

Nadia pointed at her dad. "Dad is totally scared of my sweet Tea mom."

Stacey looked at Tea staring her husband down. "I believe she is sending your father a message. Watch it buster."

Once Stacey and Nadia began laughing together, Tea shook her head and strutted away.

"Did you see that?" Jeremy excitedly questioned. "That cat just snubbed me."

"Dad, don't get so defensive," Nadia answered. "She's always snubbed you. You just never paid her any attention."

"I'm going to work where I am the king," Jeremy said with a cute, sad face. "I'm not being hunted down by a small, not-so-nice, cat."

"Dad," Nadia responded, "Tea is just playing with you. She really loves you."

Jeremy held his hand up. "Talk to the hand my child. I know a vicious beast when I see one."

Tea turned around and looked at Nadia. "I can be vicious," Tea thought out.

Nadia gave her a big-eyed look letting her know that she better not. Tea tossed her head up in the air and left.

Jeremy headed out the door and turned around before he pulled it shut. "Hey cat, you can't catch me!"

Nadia looked at Tea daring her to vanish. Tea meowed. She wanted to have a little fun with daddy. Nadia shook her head 'no'.

"Okay mom, Tea and I are off to the farm. Not sure if I told you, but I'm staying on the farm all week. I have lots to get back in order. I let a lot of my responsibilities go for all those months. I cannot believe I was so incredibly stupid to give up on my OWN dream."

Stacey walked Nadia to the back door. "A huge lesson learned my sweet daughter. Drive careful little woman and at least text us a few times and maybe call once."

"Got it mom," Nadia said and gave her mom a hug. "Thanks mom for all the freedom you and dad give me. It makes me feel like you really trust me."

"We do sweetie," Stacey replied. "It's the other people we have a hard time trusting. You're growing up and I think you understand one important fact of life now. If anyone expects you to give up everything for them, they are not for you. Correct?"

"Absolutely, most definitely and I'll never do that again." Nadia hugged her mom, picked up her duffle bag and called out for Tea.

***

When Nadia and Tea arrived at the farm, Nadia got a strange feeling. She went to the farmhouse to find Lacey. Tea took off towards the barn. Nadia found Lacey busy with her Blake Fierce and Anna Grace. "Hey Lace; it looks like you could use a hand. Where is Wild

Wayne?"

"OMG Nadia," Lacey began, "I haven't gotten one thing done all day. Our nanny is sick today and Jillie had to help in the clinic. Want to hang out and help me a bit? Wayne is upstairs playing some video game. He got tired of babysitting."

"Of course I would," Nadia said, as she sat down on the floor and began to play with the little ones. "Where are all the cats?"

Lacey looked around. "You know, they are usually here, but I've been so busy I haven't even noticed they are not here."

Nadia thought out for Tea to come, but she didn't. "Lacey, have you thought out for Tye?"

"No, but let me try." Lacey thought out for Tye, but he didn't show up.

"I just thought out for Tea, who was just with me. Lacey, you stay here. I got the strangest feeling when I drove into the driveway. I'll go by the clinic first."

Lacey looked bewildered. "I've been so busy today with these two. And, Will hasn't come by to check on me now that I think about it. I don't want you to take a chance. I'm worried now. Let's take Wayne, Blake Fierce and Anna Grace and go through the tunnel. I feel like we should peak into the barn."

"Great idea Lace," Nadia said, as she picked up Anna Grace.

Lacey picked up her youngest son and called for Wayne Jake to go with them. "Let's go fast, but let's go out the front of the house and around to the side where we can go under the house. There is no way we'll get these two into that closet and down those steps."

"I agree," Nadia replied.

The girls rushed out the front door of the house. No one could see them from the barn. They rushed around to the side of the house where an opening led under the house. Nadia opened up the hidden door leading to the tunnel that would take them to the barn. When they made their way to the earthen trap door under the barn, Nadia climbed up the steps to the earthen, trap door. She pushed on it ever so slowly where she couldn't see out, but she could hear. She heard strange voices, but they were not close. She pushed the trap door up a bit more. She didn't see anyone, but heard them laughing. She heard the horses whining and someone trying to soothe them. Where were the cats? Something was truly wrong. She had to do something. She gently let the trap door back down and climbed back down to Lacey.

"Lacey, something is dreadfully wrong. I hear strange voices. Whoever they are, they have done something to our cats. The horses are very nervous, but one of them is trying to soothe them. We have to go get help."

"We'll go get Uncle Jake, Son of Running Deer and Crazy Horse," Lacey quickly replied.

"Let me go up one more time. For our cats not to come to us, we are dealing with extreme danger. I'll be right back. They are not in the back of the barn. I know how to climb into the hayloft and go see who is there."

"Oh Nadia," Lacey said, "I wish I could help you, but I have to protect our children."

"I know Lace; stay put and give me just ten minutes tops. Do you have the arrowhead?"

"No, not on me," Lacey answered.

Nadia pulled her shark tooth necklace from around her neck. "I never go anywhere without it. Here, put it on and use it to go to the past for help if I'm not back."

The girls hugged and Nadia quickly vanished into the barn that she knew so well. She and Lope had secret hiding places where they would meet. Lacey softly sang to the two younger children to keep them quiet. Wayne Jake was looking all around the earthen room. Lacey kept looking up for the trap door to open. Finally, it did and Nadia quickly climbed down and pulled the trap door shut tight.

"They are from the future Lace. They must be some bad people that found out about our portal. Lope mentioned that there are people that still want to own our land, because it's known to be magical. You have to go for safety with Uncle Jake. Take the children and stay there. I am going to find Lope and get help for our family. We cannot risk Uncle Jake and our people in the past or none of us exist."

"Nadia, you are the best and now we know why you and Lope stayed connected. We need him again. He's our gatekeeper."

The girls took the children down to the big oak. Nadia scampered up the tree to the limb that would take her forward. Lacey waited to open the portal giving Nadia enough time to be ready.

"Okay Lace, I'm ready to go. Sorry you have three little ones to handle on your own. Be careful."

"You too," Lacey said, as she put the shark's tooth into the magical spot. When the portal opened, she grabbed the two little ones and told Wayne Jake to hold onto her shirt. In seconds they were all whisked away.

***

Lacey and the children made it safely three hundred years in the past. She had a long walk ahead of her with three little ones, but she knew she would make it. The future wrote the story. She just had to persevere and endure walking in the darkness. Her saviors were village scouts that were scouring the land for any danger to their tribe. Lacey heard movement coming from the woods that she was about to enter to reach the village. Lacey had learned long ago the sounds that would let her family know she was someone that belonged. Upon hearing Lacey's familiar bird call, village scouts found her and the children. The scouts rushed her and the three children back to the village.

***

Nadia made her way to the future. She slowly climbed down the huge oak tree. She decided to use the hidden tunnels that still remained intact and use an old, oil lamp left by Uncle Jake. She moved fast and ran all the way to the barn. She just didn't know if Lope would even be on the farm. She had seen him the previous week when he helped her celebrate her high school graduation. She pushed the earthen, trap door open and peered into the barn. She decided to crawl out of the tunnel and check around the barn. When she peered around the corner, she saw other young adults who she imagined were Lope's cousins. They were busy working on things around the barn. Some were talking and petting the horses. She stood frozen for a moment thinking what she would do next. Just as she was about to descend back into the tunnel, she heard Lope's voice. She jumped up, ran to the corner and quietly peered around the corner. Lope was with his mother and they were pulling a wagon filled with bags of feed. The other relatives all acknowledged them and they all chatted back and forth. Nadia patiently waited for her chance to get Lope's attention, as he and his family unloaded the wagon. Everyone finally left the barn, except for Lope and his mother. When Lope's mother turned her back, Nadia jumped out waving at Lope. He saw her and she quickly moved back for cover. Lope knew something must be wrong for Nadia to show up here. He saw fear across her face.

"Okay Lope," Euzelia said, "I think we're done for the night."

"I think I feel like hanging out for a while mom. You know how I love to explore. I'm thinking about camping out down the pasture tonight."

"Okay, but let me hear from you when you get your camp set up. Why don't you invite one of your cousins?"

"No; they always wimp out and I end up having to bring them back. No thanks."

Lope's mom smiled and blew him a kiss. "See you tomorrow."

"I'll see if I can bring back something grand from my explorations in the morning mom."

Lope's mom held up her thumb and walked out of the barn. Lope rushed to the back of the barn where Nadia was patiently waiting. "What are you doing here?!"

Nadia fell into Lope's arms. "Something is drastically wrong in my time. Lacey took Wayne Jake and the two little ones back to Uncle Jake. There are men, dressed in clothes like you wear, in our barn. We think they have Will, Miguel, Jillie and maybe Tom held captive somewhere. The cats are not even responding to Lacey or to me. Could there be people from here in my time?"

Lope held Nadia tightly in his arms and thought for almost a minute before he spoke. "Oh no Nadia; there are some modern day explorers wanting to do something with our land because of the oak tree and the legends. It's the only untouched land left for miles. I overheard my mom and some of her relatives talking. They have been finding people sneaking onto the land. I cannot believe these people have made it back to you."

"If they did, and they are explorers, why would they be holding my family and our animals hostage?" Nadia cried.

"I don't know Nadia, but I'm going to find out. Let's go."

"What if they are really bad? I saw at least three strangers in the barn."

"Let me see for myself and then we'll come up with a plan Nadia. We'll go back and get Uncle Jake or I'm going to have to blow my secret and recruit more of your descendants."

"Oh no Lope; we cannot make this more involved than it already is. You and I have been so careful."

"I know gra-, I mean Nadia," Lope said, as he shook his head.

Nadia looked at Lope. "Did you just start to call me grandma?"

"I'm older than you are silly," Lope answered.

"Lope, I'm not a little girl. Don't you think I wonder who you are to me?"

"You have never asked me or even brought the subject up in all these years," Lope answered, as he looked at this young woman, his great-grandmother, many generations removed.

"Well, when I was little I just thought it was so cool. Now that I'm older and somewhat wiser, I don't think I want to know. I have only hoped that it made you a better person for knowing us three cousins, our love for this land and the hope for our families' future. I have so much more to learn myself, Lope."

"Don't you worry about it at all. Let's just get back and see who has traveled and why."

"Sounds good for now Lope," Nadia replied, as she took Lope's hand in hers.

Lope smiled and held up the trap door. They both jumped down into the tunnel. Lope grabbed the oil lamp and they ran back to the oak tree. When they climbed out from the hidden tunnel, they saw the portal was wavering as if it was at work.

"Let's hide Nadia," Lope said, as he took off pulling Nadia behind him. He took her into the edge of the woods. They fell to the ground near a huge tree that would shelter them. It was dark, but the moon lit up the sky enough for them to see outlines. They waited to see who might emerge onto the huge oak limb.

After a few minutes, they heard Jillie's voice asking that she be allowed to return to her time. It was obvious that Jillie was not here on her own wishes and she sounded very strange. Lope noticed the man had a stun laser in his hand. He touched Nadia and leaned in close. "He's got a stun laser. It's a way of making someone move extremely slow. He's obviously stunned her."

Nadia watched Jillie as she slowly moved down the tree and saw what Lope had explained. She moved almost hypnotic-like. "What can we do?"

"Well, he has no idea we're watching. I want you to stay close, but behind me and ready to run. I am going to try and run up on him. I'll jump him, hold him down and you can grab the stun gun. We'll use it on him and I'll reverse Jillie's hit."

Nadia nodded in agreement. "Ready when you are Lope."

Lope took off and Nadia stayed behind him, but not too close. Lope worked his way closer and closer behind the stranger. Just as he was about to make his final move, the man swung around and stunned Lope. Lope collapsed and Nadia froze in place. The man slowly moved his aim toward Nadia. Nadia couldn't move, but she said a quick prayer for a miracle.

Within seconds, four beasts came out of nowhere and pounced upon this man. When he fell to the ground, he dropped the stun gun. Nadia rushed to grab the gun and then she ran over to Lope. She fell to the ground and held up his head to place it on her lap. She called his name over and over as she rubbed his hair back across his head.

"Lope, Lope, please wake up. I need you, your mom and dad need you and our families need you." Nadia sobbed, as she looked down at Lope.

The beasts were all licking Jillie's face until she

finally came to her senses. “What in the world?” Jillie began, as she looked all around. “Nadia?”

Nadia looked up to see Jillie slowly walking towards her. Jillie held out her hand to her cousin. “Jillie; it’s Lope and we’re in his time.”

Jillie was still a bit dazed, but she understood everything and was beginning to remember things. “Nadia, we must get back. Some other people have Will, Miguel and I think they stunned our cats.”

Nadia and Jillie looked at the four cats. Nadia realized they were not their cats, but the newest generation. “They are not ours Jillie.”

Jillie remembered seeing double years ago when she came with Lope when he was just ten-years-old. “Uh yeah; I remember.”

Nadia looked at Jillie with a puzzled look. “How did you know? Have you ever been here Jillie?”

Jillie’s mind was still fuzzy, but she knew she didn’t want to say anything else about her visit here years ago to save Nadia. “How’s Lope? We need to get back Nadia. Will and Miguel are in trouble.” Jillie stopped and became horrified. “OH NO Nadia; Lacey and the children are in danger if they are not already.”

“Lacey and the children are just fine Jillie. When I arrived, I felt something strange. Once Lacey realized she had not seen Will or the cats, we knew there was possible trouble. We took the tunnels to the oak tree. She took the children to Uncle Jake and I came forward to find Lope. I just hope she made it to the village.”

Jillie’s body went limp and she fell to the ground. Lope was still down, but sitting up. Nadia got up and held her hand down to help Jillie stand. “Can you try and get up Jillie?”

Jillie nodded and took Nadia’s hand. “Boy, that stun gun of theirs is really weird. You know what’s going on around you, but you cannot do anything. Let’s try and help Lope up.”

Jillie and Nadia slowly walked back over to Lope. "Lope? Jillie asked. "Do you think you can get up?"

"The gun," Lope started, "give me the gun."

Nadia handed the gun over to Lope. He moved a dial and handed it back to Nadia. "Now point it at me and shoot again."

"WHAT?" Nadia asked.

"It's okay; it will quickly reverse the effects. Just shoot me."

Jillie didn't have time to wait for Nadia to do what needed to be done. She took the gun and shot Lope. Then she handed the gun back to Lope. "Can you hit me too? I'm feeling really weak."

Lope took the gun, turned the dial, aimed and shot Jillie.

Jillie shook her head. "That is advancement in technology."

"There are no more guns like you have in your time. But, we don't have time to get into all the technological advances. Let me see what I can learn from this man."

Lope pushed a couple of buttons and turned the dial again on the gun. He shot the man and in seconds the man was sitting up, but he wasn't trying to get away.

"What are you and your friends up to snooping on our lands?" Lope demanded.

"The man looked at Lope. "Just following my orders."

Jillie rushed in front of the man. "WHAT ORDERS?"

The man looked at Jillie and smiled. "I am an employee of All About This Land. We try and find anything unique about our country. We develop documentaries. My boss is a friend of someone who runs this sanctuary. He felt that a family that has held onto land for as long as this family must have something wonderful to keep."

"Who else is holding my family hostage?" Jillie demanded.

"We were not there to do any harm. You and your family just happened to find us sneaking around, so we stunned you. I brought you forward to make sure no one hurts my colleagues."

"What is your name?" Lope asked.

"I'm so sorry buddy; my name is Walter Tripp."

"Walter or Lope," Jillie began, "can you communicate with your cubes to your friends? What about our cats?"

Walter stirred and looked directly at Jillie. "May I stand up?"

Jillie looked at Lope, who nodded it would be okay.

Walter stood up. "Your cats; you mean your beasts? They will be fine too, but we put them down for a while."

Jillie looked at Lope. "You agree? Our cats will be fine?"

Lope nodded. "Yes Jillie, we have to put animals down for different reasons and these guns are used for many different things. Technology is a wonderful thing."

"Lope?" Nadia asked wanting everyone's attention. "What do we do with this man?"

Walter cleared his throat. "You don't have to worry about me or my colleagues. We're only explorers! We don't want anything to happen to your land either. We're all about preserving whatever we can. We're just a curious bunch and we like to write about incredible history. This land is all about history."

Jillie crossed her arms. "It's not public land, so you had no business coming onto it and exploring."

Walter looked at her with a serious look. "Your family has a traitor, because we were given free reign to roam around for a price."

Lope's face reddened. "Who was it?"

"Your cousin, Frederick Barron, gave us permission."

"He's not my cousin. He's married to one of my cousins. I'll take care of him," Lope said, as he looked at the beasts and thought out to them all.

The beasts all darted towards the barn. Anna and Frederick were on the farm. Lope was sending the cats on two missions: the lion to go follow Frederick and the other three to go help three hundred years in the past.

"You're going back with us and you're going to make sure our farm is never bothered again." Lope commanded.

"I am at your command," Walter said, as he saluted.

"Leave out the dramatics," Nadia added.

"Let's go," Jillie said.

The four of them went back to the huge oak tree and climbed out across the limb that would take them three hundred years in the past.

***

When they arrived, Uncle Jake, Son of Running Deer and Crazy Horse were also arriving from the past. At least they were all in daylight now.

"Uncle Jake," Jillie called out.

Jake looked up and saw his other two nieces and two unknown young men. The three men waited for the four young adults to climb down. Jillie and Nadia ran to their Uncle Jake's arms. "Who are these two and what's going on here?"

"Uncle Jake, it's me Lope."

Jake looked into the eyes of this young man. "Well now, it has been quite a few years, hasn't it? And, is this another cousin?"

Nadia didn't give Lope a chance. "No, he's a snoop Uncle Jake. His name is Walter Tripp and he's part of some company that is hoping to tell everyone about our wonderful farm. He and his buddies think it's something magical."

Son of Running Deer and Crazy Horse immediately surrounded Walter with spears in hand. Walter's eyes about bulged out of his head.

Jake stepped in front of this stranger. "Where are my other family members that my niece has told me she feels are in danger?"

"Wait a minute man," Walter said. "I'm here to help you and your family. Are you from another time even further back in time?"

Jake looked at his two nieces and then at Lope. "Where are they?"

Two spears were pushed into Walter's back. "Okay, okay; please let me assure you all that I was only doing my job."

"Your job has landed you in a very serious situation young man," Jake replied. "Now, let's head up to the farmhouse. How many people were with you?"

"Just two others and trust me they are not going to hurt anyone. We're just scientific, history geeks and we're just seeking the truth."

"Let's go," Jake directed.

Son of Running Deer pushed his spear into Walter's back. Walter moved forward and didn't stop until they reached the barn where he had left his colleagues sitting watching over Will, Miguel and the four beasts. There was no one to be found. Jillie ran over to the spot she remembered Miguel's lifeless body was laying.

"WHERE ARE THEY?" Jillie demanded, as she got in Walter's face. "If something happened to my husband or Lacey's husband I will make sure your life will never be the same."

Lope pulled Jillie to his side. "Maybe it's his colleagues who are in trouble now. Let's head up to the house."

Jillie and Nadia took off running ahead. When they reached the house, they practically ran into Will running out of the house. He was looking for Lacey and the little ones. They all started talking at once, but Will hushed them when he saw his family and the other strange man. Will ran up to the man and grabbed him. "WHERE ARE MY WIFE AND OUR CHILDREN?"

"WILL," Nadia yelled. "She and the children are safe in the village."

Will swung around looking at Nadia.

Crazy Horse rushed up to his best friend. "Where the two men?" His friend's English was coming along.

Will hugged his childhood friend. "Inside; everyone come inside. These three men need to be dealt with right now."

"Dealt with?" Walter excitedly cried out.

Jillie looked at this strange man. "You should just be quiet or I'll deal with you myself right now." Jillie rushed in to find her husband.

When Jillie, Nadia and the rest came into the house, they found seven beasts holding the two men at bay. Miguel was sitting back with a huge smile on his face. Lope rushed forward to the three beasts he knew well.

Will stepped out from the crowd and turned to his family. "These two guys were holding Miguel, our cats and me in the barn. These three beasts showed up and took the two men down." Will looked at Lope and knew exactly who this young man was that was standing with a big smile. "Lope, you sent them here?"

Lope smiled. "I wasn't exactly sure it could happen, but it did as we see. The magic and the mystery of our land continue to keep her safe."

"What do we do with these three?" Jillie asked.

Walter stepped forward. "I'm sure we can come to some kind of agreement."

"What is your meaning of agreement?' Nadia asked.

"Money talks," Walter replied.

Jake became infuriated and grabbed this man by his neck. "You're trying to take money from my family for our secret?" Jake didn't release his grasp until Son of Running Deer pulled him back. "Not worth."

Jake looked at his nieces and then at Will and Miguel. "We need to talk in private." Jake looked at his best friend and talked in their native tongue.

Son of Running Deer and Crazy Horse pushed the three men together and held them at their spear points. Jake led his family out of the house.

"Lope, I need you to go back home and find out about these three men. I need to know everything you can find out about them. If you don't find us here, you know how to get back to the village?"

"Yes, of course I know how to get to your village. I'm on my way," Lope said, as he looked at the three beasts he had sent from the future. "Let's go home." The beasts turned into cats and followed Lope as he took off back to the oak tree.

"Now, what do we do with these three men?" Jake questioned. "I don't think it's safe for them to stay here. There is too much activity. I think we should take them back to our village. They would be safe with us and they couldn't really run anywhere and give away the farm."

Will looked at Miguel and then at Jillie. "I agree with Uncle Jake. I don't think we have a choice."

"I agree," Miguel replied.

"Me three," Jillie answered.

"I'm in too," Nadia added.

"Okay, Jillie and Nadia can return with me to the village," Jake directed. Lacey needs some help with the children. We'll make sure the three men will remain with us until we hear more from Lope. I imagine it will take him a few days. Will and Miguel, you both stay here and take care of the farm and the clinic."

Jake went into the house, leaving Nadia, Jillie, Will and Miguel outside. Miguel hugged his wife and comforted her that everything would be okay. Will walked over to Nadia and put his left arm around her shoulders. "Thank-you for helping Lacey get the children to the portal."

Nadia shook her head. "We have to talk with Lope about securing the portal. Maybe he knows more about this sort of thing than we all do. So many scientific advances compared to this time and definitely compared to our ancestor's time."

The conversation was interrupted when Jake returned outside with the three men being pushed by Crazy Horse and Son of Running Deer. Walter and his colleagues were not happy about their situation and where they were being taken. Jake reminded them that they chose to prowl around private land and they didn't have a say-so in anything at this point.

"Will, give us a ride down to the oak tree please," Jake directed. "We need to get these three men out of sight."

Will didn't hesitate and ran for the truck with the open bed. Will backed the truck so that the men could all crawl into the truck's bed. Nadia crawled in the passenger side and moved next to Will. Jillie hugged her husband. "I'll be back soon." Miguel gently kissed Jillie's forehead and pushed the passenger door closed once she was in the truck's cab.

Will didn't waste anymore time. He put the truck into drive and took off down into the pasture. When they arrived at the oak tree, Tye, Tess and Tea appeared to travel back to the village. Virginia remained on the farm with Miguel. Jake instructed the three men to jump out. Jillie and Nadia quickly climbed out of the cab. Will hopped out on the driver's side and ran back to say farewell to his dear friends. Crazy Horse spoke to Will in his native tongue assuring him he would return if they chose to bring the three men back. The girls looked at one another, as they understood what was being said. Nadia quickly handed her cell phone to Will to hold for safe keeping.

"Let's get going," Jake commanded. "I'll take this one," Jake said, as he grabbed Walter's arm with a strong grip. Crazy Horse grabbed the one closest to him and Son of Running Deer pulled the other man along. Jake motioned for the girls to go first and ran to the back of the tree to place his magical arrowhead into the hidden spot on the oak tree. The portal wavered and the three beasts moved in close to the girls. The girls walked hand in hand into the portal surrounded by three large feline beasts. Jake and Walter followed next; Crazy Horse and his captive and then Son of Running Deer with his captive closed the portal. Will and Miguel waited for the portal to close. They went back to work to keep their minds from racing with things that could go wrong.

***

Once everyone arrived three hundred years in the past, the three men from six hundred years in the future were all weak in the knees as they were in total darkness. Not only were they amazed at the change of time, but they were also amazed the days were opposite. They whispered between themselves and Jake could sense the fear in their voices. Nadia commanded the felines to light up the night and their eyes glowed so bright that the three men nearly fell over one another.

"If you're thinking we are going to take your lives, you can rest assured we don't take pride in such action," Jake said, as he looked at Walter, then the other two men. "If you are the decent men that you claim, you will become our ally. If you don't agree to do what we ask, then each one of you will answer to my friends and me whether here or in your time."

Walter cleared his throat. "Why did you bring us here?"

"Just wait until you see the people who walk this land now and their link to my nieces' time and to yours. I think you will realize that anything you may want to write about our land could bring grave danger to many people. So, follow us and cherish this chance to truly understand the amazing changes and advancements our land has survived."

Jake shrieked out a bird like noise. Seconds later, warriors appeared out of the darkness. They were mounted upon horses and three horses trailed along behind them. Words were exchanged, as the warriors greeted Jillie and Nadia and stared at the three strange men. Once Jake, Son of Running Deer and Crazy Horse mounted their horses, Jake held out his hand to Nadia while Crazy Horse pulled Jillie upon his horse. More words were spoken and three warriors were assigned the three strangers to haul to the village. With hands held out, the three men knew what they were supposed to do. The party headed for the village. The strangers tried their best to see where they were going, but they were at a total loss.

Once they reached the end of the woods, bird calls were sounded and replies were heard. The village knew they were returning from their mission and the people were gathering to welcome their loved ones and find out the news. Jillie and Nadia saw Lacey and the children in the brightness of the village fire. Jillie begged Crazy Horse to get her to her daughter. Jillie fell off the horse and took Anna Grace in her arms. Lacey wrapped her arms around Jillie and Anna Grace. Nadia came running and wrapped her arms around her older cousins. Tears of joy rain down on their faces.

"Let's go home," Lacey demanded.

Jillie looked around to express her gratitude to everyone for watching over her child. The girls' aunt and cousins came running to great Jillie and Nadia. Oneson and Twoson, as they were now called by everyone, were young men. They encircled Nadia and gave her big bear hugs. Two young women, known to Nadia and her cousins as Blossom and Fawn, joined Jake's sons. The young men announced their plans of marriage to Nadia and Jillie, as Lacey had already been told the wonderful news upon her earlier arrival. Lacey, Jillie and Nadia all knew the girls, but only Nadia knew of any serious courtships. Blossom was just a year older than Nadia and Fawn was three years older. Over her years of returning with Will, Nadia had befriended all the young girls of the tribe. Nadia pulled Blossom and Fawn close and whispered into the two girls' ears. They all three had a private chuckle. Nadia looked at Lacey and Jillie. "We're coming back for a fun bachelorette party."

Lacey and Jillie both laughed away their tears, but Lacey didn't feel like celebrating at this moment. "I want to get home to Will," Lacey said.

"And, I want to get back to Miguel," Jillie added, as she thought about her untold news she was carrying. She had not even told Miguel that she was expecting yet. She was already over six weeks along and the doctor had heard two heartbeats. She wanted to get back to Miguel and share her news. But most of all, she also needed some rest.

"Crazy Horse will escort you all back," Jake said, as he walked over and gave his nieces a quick hug.

"I want to stay here," Nadia replied. "I want to wait for Lope and hang out with Blossom and Fawn. We have a big wedding to plan."

"Very well," Jake answered. "I am sure your cousins and their girls would love some wedding help." Jake turned his attention to her two older nieces. "Crazy Horse will head up a party to take you all back to the portal. I must take our new friends to see our chief."

Lacey looked at Nadia with a concerned look. "You'll have to come back soon. Your parents will be looking for you at some point."

"Well, I am kind of covered. I told mom and dad that I was staying on the farm all week. You know to catch up on all the things I didn't do for months. And, I left my cell phone with Will. Will you text mom and dad hello for me? I know it's wrong, but you know I'm safe. They will at least have peace of mind. I'll call as soon as I get back. My mom does always remind me that she wants to hear my voice at least once or twice to know it's really me."

Lacey, Jillie and their three youngsters all said their good-byes and were escorted back to the portal door by Crazy Horse and five warriors. Tye and Tess, in their beastly forms, ran ahead of the travel party to make sure their family was safe from any unforeseen dangers lurking in the darkness. The land was now secured by Sir Edward, but that didn't mean there weren't others trespassing through his land.

Jake led the three men to the tent where Chief Fierce Tiger, Chief Charging Bull and many others waited to discuss and deal with their unexpected visitors that had now traveled six hundred years to the past.

Nadia waited and watched until the lights of the traveling party were almost out of sight. Nadia took off with her grey and white cat at her heels. On her way, she almost collided with Sir Edward.

"Wow, little lady," Sir Edward said, as he grabbed Nadia's shoulders keeping her from plowing into him.

Nadia looked up and smiled. "Well hey there Sir Edward. What's happening?"

"Pardon me my dear," Sir Edward said, as he bent down and gave Tea a few friendly strokes.

"Sorry Sir Edward, let me rephrase that for you.

"How is your evening sir?" Nadia tried to keep from laughing but she couldn't. "I have got to teach you some slang Sir Edward."

Sir Edward shook his head and held Nadia out at a distance. "Or maybe I should have Anna teach you some proper, English etiquette."

"This is America Sir Edward, developed by your own and many others from all over the world. It's a 'hodge podge' of all kinds of things now. You better stay in this time, where you can slowly and gracefully grow old." Nadia laughed at her comment.

Sir Edward joined in and laughed too. "I think that is a smart idea. And you my dear enjoy your 'hodge podge', quirky lifestyle. I am glad to have been a part of your guidance. Maybe I will have rubbed off and you will never know."

"If you do, I will surely embrace it," Nadia said, as she curtsied.

Sir Edward removed his hat and bowed. "My lady, have a pleasant night."

They both laughed together and ended with a loving hug. Sir Edward was now part of the tribal counsel and he hurried to join their important meeting that had urgently been called. Nadia picked up Tea into her arms and rushed on to find Blossom and Fawn. Nadia spent almost two hours with the two brides to be. She helped them sew their light-weight, deerskin pieces together to form a dress. Nadia had learned the entire process and was becoming an expert. As the girls worked side-by-side, Oneson came looking for Nadia to take her to the tent of elders. Most of the responsibility had always been placed on Lacey and Jillie. It was Nadia's time to assume more responsibility of their destiny. On this night, she had to be a part of some major decisions.

As Oneson and Nadia slowly walked together, Oneson caught Nadia up on what had been already discussed. Excitement amongst some of the people caught Oneson's attention. He held up his hand for Nadia to stop. "Let's go see what's all the -, how do you always put it Nadia?"

Nadia chuckled. "You mean 'ruckus'?"

Oneson nodded his head. "Yes. Let's go see what all the ruckus is about with the people over there. The village is sure filled with excitement this evening."

The two of them hurried to see why so many people had gathered together. They could both tell excitement was in the air. Oneson and Nadia politely moved into the crowd that had formed. When they reached the center, neither one of them knew the man, who seemed to be thirty-something that everyone was hugging. Being that it was dark, they couldn't really tell who he was. When they saw Son of Running Deer's wife run into the crowd and grab hold of this man, they knew it must be Running Antelope, who many had said their good-byes to years before when they returned to the village they had known from childbirth. He had returned again.

"We have to go get his father," Oneson said to Nadia, as he turned around and ran to the elder's tent. Nadia stayed put to witness this glorious reunion.

Oneson tore into the teepee and fell upon Son of Running Deer nearly pushing him into the small fire. Oneson reached out his hand. "You must come with me. Your son, he's here!" Son of Running Deer didn't hesitate one second. He jumped up and tore out of the teepee leaving everyone in his dust.

Chief Fierce Tiger held up his hand in total calmness. "I will have these men watched until we can see for ourselves if the winds have brought back our Running Antelope." The chief slowly rose, but no one else made a move. The chief walked out of the teepee and within in minutes he held open the teepee's flap. He looked at Jake to interpret his words to the three strangers.

Jake nodded and repeated the chief's words in English. "You three men must go with my warriors for now. No harm will come to you, unless you bring it upon yourselves. I'm sure you must be thirsty and hungry. Food and water will be sent to your teepee."

Everyone patiently waited for the three strangers to be led away. The chief looked directly at Jake. "Well, let's go see what this is all about." Jake jumped up and so did all the other elders. Even Sir Edward understood enough of his Indian brothers' language to know Running Antelope had returned.

As Chief Fierce Tiger, Chief Charging Bull, Jake and the village elders walked into the crowd, the people parted allowing their leaders to see for themselves and welcome home Running Antelope. Jake could not believe his eyes. He walked up and grabbed this man, who had been like a son, and hugged him in tight. Jake held out his hand to Nadia. "Running Antelope, this is little Nadia. She's all grown up."

Running Antelope, who Nadia had grown up knowing as Lope, smiled and held out his hand. When Nadia reached out her hand, the strong warrior grabbed her in and gave her a bear hug.

"Have we met?" Nadia replied in the native language as she pulled herself away.

Lope smiled that she had learned his language. He had not remembered any English Jillie had tried to teach him. "I would join your uncle and my father to travel and watch over you three girls," Lope spoke in the native tongue. "Especially at Thanksgiving; I saw you run around with three cats all around you."

Nadia looked all around and didn't see Tea. She called out for her and in seconds Tea came bounding into the crowd. "Lope, this is my Tea."

"Your own protector I see," Lope said, as he picked up the small, grey and white cat. "And, what is your beast?"

"Put him down and you will see," Nadia replied, as she took Tea from Lope's arms and gently flung her back to the ground. "Tea, I need my cougar."

Within seconds, a large, tan cougar was circling Nadia making gentle roars. Lope held out his hand for the cougar to smell. "She's beautiful and powerful"

"A celebration must take place tomorrow," Chief Fierce Tiger said, as he interrupted Nadia and Running Antelope. "Let's allow Running Antelope's family to have him all to themselves tonight. Tomorrow the day will be used to prepare a feast."

Running Antelope stepped towards the chief. "Chief Fierce Tiger, I have not come alone. I have my warriors waiting to join. I didn't want to cause panic with strange warriors approaching during the night hours in fear of uncontrollable reactions."

Chief Fierce Tiger looked at this man, who left as a boy, returned and saved his family's tribe and now returns again. "Have you returned to your home Running Antelope?"

Running Antelope moved to face a man that had shown him great leadership. "I have not returned to stay. I am now Chief Running Antelope's Wolf of the Appalachian Wolf Tribe that you all called home for a brief time. I married Shining Star, our chief's only child as you may remember. Chief Running Wolf has fallen very ill and he has passed his rule onto me. That is why I have returned. I wanted to return to my home one more time. I wanted to see for myself that our people made it safely back and Sir Edward kept his promise to our people. I did not come alone. I have a war party waiting in the woods for my direction."

The chief looked into this young chief's eyes and saw a gentleness that would make him a great chief. He also saw a man that had come to revenge any wrongs done to his family. "I welcome you my son and you will make a strong and gentle leader. For now, spend time with your mother and father. They will tell you all you have come to know. Our destiny took you away for a very important purpose. You have many descendants that join in securing our families and our lands together. Your sacrifice made you a legend." The chief bent his arms across in front of his chest and clasped his hands together. "We are one. Take a few men and go bring your warriors to their village."

Running Antelope looked at his dad and then Jake. "Will you two ride with me?"

The two older men didn't say a word. His father joined his son's right side and Jake joined his left. Together, these two dear friends walked arm in arm with a mighty leader that they had raised side by side. Lope yelled to his mother that he would be all hers when he returned. Then he yelled to Jake's sons that he wanted to see their skills tomorrow. The village was full of chatter. Once Running Antelope, his father, Jake and his warriors returned, people were waiting to welcome new family. Families took in Lope's warriors, fed them and gave them a soft place to sleep. Lope stayed up most of the night with his parents. He wanted to know about Jillie.

Nadia didn't want to be alone and she invited Blossom and Fawn to spend the night in the special teepee that her cousins had been given years ago. They chatted and giggled late into the night. Exhaustion finally took them over. Tea snuggled close to Nadia once she was finally went to sleep. The entire village fell quiet to only sounds of the night. Tomorrow would be a day to write in history.

Chapter 18: A Magical Moment In Time

Morning came too early for many in the village. But the older women, who were always up before the moon set and sunrise, were up and bustling around the camp. Fires were lit, water was boiling for their herbal teas, blue corn hotcakes were being made and meat was frying over the open flames. Quiet chatter could be heard, but the women whispered to keep their secrets safe amongst their click. Nadia, still anxious about everything that was happening, came out of her teepee rubbing her eyes. She ran to relieve herself and quietly joined the women around the campfire. She loved getting up early and having an entire day to accomplish as much as possible. A woman handed her a wooden cup of hot brew. It was a mixture of teas that woke you up and helped you digest your foods. Nadia quietly thanked this woman. She sat back and enjoyed her tea listening to the village gossip. The women never even thought not to share with Nadia there. They spoke of everything from child care to passing onto their next life. Whatever was happening in the village, they discussed and gave their opinions. Nadia was offered a hotcake and she gladly accepted it. When the woman noticed how quickly Nadia ate the first one, she handed her another, smiled and whispered to her in the native tongue. "Your body needs this food for fuel. Never skip your morning meal."

Soon, more people began moving about the village. The chiefs and their wives always took breakfast together around the huge fire. Here they quietly mingled with their people and shared peaceful conversations. Nadia's Uncle Jake and his family didn't mingle as much in the morning. He liked having his time with his family. Nadia waited until her cousins came looking for her and their girls. Blossom and Fawn were both exhausted. Nadia had talked their ears off and they stayed awake as long as they could. She went and woke them up. Her cousins were waiting for them at the morning breakfast fire.

Jake came out and found his niece. "I believe we should get word to Will, Lacey, Miguel and Jillie about our celebration tonight. They will be calling it a day soon. They could get up early and join us."

"I'll go," Nadia offered. "Do you think Running Antelope would want to go with me?"

Jake looked towards his dear friend's home. "I don't think that would be a great idea. With Jillie in her condition and all, it might not be the right time to surprise her like that."

Nadia looked at her Uncle Jake. "What's her condition? Is she sick?!"

Jake shook his head. "Oh, me bad; my wife told me that Jillie is expecting. She knows these things."

"You're kidding?" Nadia asked. "I wonder if she even knows. She has not said a word of it. You are right Uncle Jake. Having Running Antelope show up after all these years may prove to be too much for her. No wonder she looked so bad yesterday."

"I think you and I should go back in just a bit. We'll take your cousins. They have been dying to travel with me. In the future, you will all need to take care of one another."

Nadia nodded her head in agreement. "Okay, just let me go wake up my silly cat. I wore her, Blossom and Fawn out last night. She was still curled up when I went to wake up the girls." Nadia took off to get Tea and also brush her teeth with some of the special limbs they stored in their teepee.

Nadia and Tea raced to her Uncle Jake's home, where she found her uncle, aunt and cousins excitedly talking about Jillie's babies. "Babies?" Nadia asked.

"Now don't say a word Nadia," Jake directed. "We don't want to spoil her news, before she has decided to tell everyone. Maybe, if she returns with us, she will share her great news. Son of Running Deer tells me that Lope's wife, Shining Star, is expecting and they think she may be carrying three!"

"OMG," Nadia replied. "There is so much to celebrate. Let's get going. I want to see if Jillie will share her news, how she will react to Lope's return and if Miguel will want her to return."

"What are we waiting for?" Jake excitedly asked. He seemed like a child himself.

"What about those men?" Nadia quickly asked.

"They can wait," Jake said with a smile. "We're going to invite them to our big celebration tonight. I see good in them Nadia. Let's give them a chance. One never knows; they may be like Vance or Dan. Your Lope can use some allies in his time you know my dear."

"Lope!" Nadia excitedly said. "I hope he's okay."

"Do you know that boy was coming back here and hanging out with my sons?" Jake asked.

Nadia put her hands on her hips. "NO! That stinker never said a word."

Jake looked at his sons. "I guess my sons had a few secrets of their own. The three of them, they have been collaborating all these years. I don't think I need to worry about handing over such a big responsibility. I'm kind of glad now. I feel like I can relax and enjoy getting old with this old gal." Jake pulled his wife close and gave her a big kiss on her cheek.

Oneson and Twoson each gave their mother a kiss

and Nadia did too. Jake led his family party out of the tent to their horses. "Nadia, you want to ride by yourself or with one of us?"

"My own please," Nadia answered. "Come along Tea, go scout the land for us."

Tea changed into a beautiful, long cougar and took off. The four family members took off in a fast trot. Jake called out his shriek that he was leaving the village. Seconds later, Son of Running Deer answered him back. When they reached the portal, it magically opened as always. They left their horses to roam and graze. Tea changed to a small cat and Nadia picked her up. Jake reached for Naidia's free hand and they walked into the wavering portal first and then his sons followed.

***

When they reached Nadia's time, it was turning dark.

"I wish I had left my cell phone in the tree's crevice," Nadia commented.

"Who needs a cell phone?" Jake sarcastically replied. Will, Lacey, Jillie and Miguel should all be able to hear my call when we get into the higher pasture. They are all up I am sure. It's only about eight-thirty."

"Keep forgetting about that Uncle Jake," Nadia answered. "I need to work on my calls. Lacey and Jillie have them down. I'll add that to my list for the summer. And, I can send Tea on ahead too. Tea, go on and get up there for us." Tea vanished.

"We still better go through the tunnels," Jake suggested, "just in case anyone is visiting your cousins."

The four of them hurried through the tunnel and went up into the barn. Jake sounded his arrival call and seconds later Will was bounding into the barn with Wild Wayne at this side. Jake's sons immediately grabbed Wayne and lovingly roughed him up a bit. Wayne loved it and he egged the two on for more.

"Well, we didn't expect to see you all so soon," Will said, as he held out his hand to Jake. Were you homesick little woman?"

Nadia put her hands upon her hips. "I'd stay there if everyone would let me. I love it there."

Jake looked at his young niece and smiled. "I would love to have you there, but we cannot mess with destiny."

"How do you know it's not my destiny to be there?" Nadia demanded.

Jake looked at Will and they both knew exactly what the other was thinking. They had seen Nadia's future and it was here, on this farm, with her own wonderful family.

Jake decided to change the subject. "We have some unbelievable news Will, but maybe we need to tell you all together. Where are Jillie and Miguel?"

"Jillie is at home resting," Will answered. "She has been a bit under the weather ever since she returned. Miguel has Anna Grace with him at the clinic. I left them there about twenty minutes ago."

Jake, Nadia, Oneson and Twoson all knew that Jillie had not shared her news with Lacey and Will. They weren't even sure about Miguel. Jake thought for a moment. "Let's let Jillie rest and we'll tell her later. Let's go get Miguel and head up to find Lacey. She must be busy with that little one."

"She was just putting him to bed when you called out," Will answered, as they all began walking towards the clinic.

Right before they were going to open the clinic door, the door swung out. Miguel, with Anna Grace in his arms, walked outside and jumped a bit. "Wow, you all startled me."

"Sorry there Miguel," Jake replied. "Come join us for a moment at Will's house. I have some news I would like to share with you all."

"Should I go get Jillie?" Miguel questioned. "I need to get Anna Grace home and to bed soon."

"This will only take a few moments," Jake responded. "Nadia, why don't you help him with Anna Grace? Maybe you can sing her to sleep to help your cousin out."

"Would love to," Nadia said, as she held out her arms for the toddler.

Nadia began singing a lullaby she had been taught by her Aunt Beautiful Light. Her cousins joined in singing in soft voices. By the time they reached the back porch, the little girl was out. Her head had fallen onto Nadia's shoulder. "I'll go sit in the family room. Can you all come in there to talk?"

Lacey came from the front of the house and met them in the family room. She saw Nadia gently rocking a sleeping baby girl. "Nadia, don't forget to call your parents when you have free hands."

Nadia smiled and nodded, but she continued to hum the lullaby.

Jake motioned for everyone to come and sit down. "I have a couple of things I want to share with you. I know you're both tired from all the commotion, but I have two important things to tell you three."

Lacey interrupted and asked if Jillie should be there too, but Jake explained they didn't want to bother her if she was coming down with something. He knew that no one seemed to know. If Miguel did, he was not sharing.

Jake cleared his throat. "First thing first; the tribal counsel has decided we want to befriend these three men, offer them ways to contribute to their work, but also benefit our families in all three times. That being said, that leads into my next unbelievable news we came back to share with you all." Jake looked at his sons and then at Nadia.

Lacey moved to the end of the couch. She felt like this news was going to be something major. For a brief second, she thought about Blake and Beautiful Butterfly, but she pushed them out of her mind. "Uncle Jake, spill the beans."

"Someone surprised us last night." Lacey's and Will's eyes locked upon one another. It couldn't be Blake or Beautiful Butterfly. "Running Antelope returned to us last evening. He traveled far and has returned, as Chief of his tribe, from the Appalachian Mountains. Yes, the same wolf tribe that took us in and gave us safety. The same tribe you are from Miguel. The tribe that took in Jillie and taught her the medicines she uses everyday. His wife, Shining Star, is the only child of their chief. The chief is now very ill and he has handed down his succession to our Running Antelope. He has returned to us one last time. He came to see with his own eyes if we still survive and if Sir Edward kept his word. We want to celebrate his return and send him back with our wishes for everlasting peace."

Not one person said a word. Only Nadia's humming continued for another minute. "Well, is no one going to say anything?"

Lacey and Will looked at one another and then at Miguel. Nadia got the message, but she wasn't going to sit there while everyone acted totally ridiculous. "We came back to tell you all and also help everyone come for the celebration."

Lacey squirmed and moved over beside Miguel. "Jillie is pretty sick, huh?"

Miguel looked at her and sighed. "She's not sick, she's expecting and we think its twins."

Lacey jumped up with joy. "Oh Miguel, congratulations! Why didn't you tell us earlier?

"I just found out myself once she returned with Anna Grace. She was exhausted. I demanded she stay in bed."

Will slid over and put his arm around his friend, who was like a brother. "She'll be fine. And you know what I think? I think she should be told about Lope. She'll understand, just as we all have had to understand this destiny." Will's thoughts went to Beautiful Butterfly for one quick second. "I think it may pull her spirits back up."

"I agree Miguel," Lacey added. "She knew a long time ago that Lope wasn't the person she was meant to be with once she met you. She told me so."

Miguel looked at Lacey. "I think you're right. I think she would never forgive any of us if we don't share such wonderful news of Lope's survival and how wonderful his life will end."

"Thank you everyone," Nadia commented. "Let's get this little one over to her bed. Let Jillie sleep a bit longer and everyone get up early."

"We will just stay here and help you get back to the village," Jake began. Let's say we head out by five am. There will be plenty of hands to help with the little ones once we get back to the village. What time do you usually start seeing people arriving for work?"

"It's Monday, the clinic begins seeing patients by nine," Miguel slowly said.

"The students from the colleges come around eight, but they all know where they are working," Lacey added.

"Tom was off this past weekend through today. Nadia, I'll need some help today. Susan won't be here until after lunch."

"Oh, I have some classes scheduled beginning at nine," Nadia said, as she remembered her set schedule. "I'm kind of tired anyway. I was too hyper at the teepee, so I can get some sleep."

Jake and his sons were just as tired. They had been up long into the night from the excitement of Running Antelope's return.

"I was hoping we would hear from Lope," Nadia added. "I may go get him. I want him there with these three strangers."

"No," Jake began, "that would not be a good idea. He's been going back and forth through both portals. I think he knows what he's doing. And, he knows we took those fellows back to the village."

Nadia was too tired to argue. "Where should we sleep Lace?" Nadia got up and handed off Anna Grace to Miguel.

"You can take Wayne's bed and he can stay here in the family room with our cousins."

"Jake, you come with me to my house. If Jillie's up, we'll tell her now," Miguel said, as he repositioned Anna Grace in his arms."

"I'm good with that," Jake said. "See everyone about four or so."

When Miguel and Jake went into the house that he and Jillie now called home, Jillie was sitting at the kitchen table devouring food. When she saw her uncle, she smiled and welcomed him in with her free hand. Her mouth was full.

"It looks like you're feeling better Jillie," Jake said, as he sat down across the table from her and took a quick look around his childhood kitchen.

Jillie nodded, swallowed her food and took a big gulp of milk. "Oh yeah, I just needed some rest. We have some news for you Uncle Jake. I'm expecting again and they are pretty sure its twins."

Miguel smiled at this wife and immediately took their sacked out daughter to her bed. She was definitely out for the night. Miguel walked back into the kitchen and sat down next to Jillie. "Hun, Uncle Jake has some really awesome news to share."

Jillie sat up taller. "Oh yeah; what is it Uncle Jake. Some good news would be great. I need something to take my mind off of this first trimester nausea and exhaustion."

Well, this might just blow you away," Jake replied, as he looked at Miguel.

"OMG Uncle Jake, just spit it out. I'm imagining all kinds of things. What is it?"

Jake took a deep breath. "Lope, Running Antelope that is, showed up last night." Jake didn't say anything else waiting to make sure Jillie didn't faint or get sick.

Tears welled up in Jillie's eyes. She grabbed Miguel's hand and looked at him with a huge smile. "That is some of the best news I have ever received. How is he? Has he returned home to stay?"

Jake smiled and sat back more relaxed. "He's great Jillie. When I say great, I mean he's now a chief."

"Really?" Jillie asked, as she sat back and chuckled. "Our Lope is a chief. That is so awesome Uncle Jake."

Jillie locked eyes with her uncle. "So our Lope is now the chief of the tribe my husband belongs and the one that trained me in my skills. How did he become a chief?"

Jake softly smiled. "The chief of the tribe, Chief Running Wolf has one daughter. Her name is Shining Star. Lope married Shining Star. Chief Running Wolf is very ill and has handed his rule to Lope. Your dear friend is now known as Chief Running Antelope's Wolf."

Jillie didn't say anything for a few seconds. She smiled and thought about her husband, the picture she saw of Nadia and her family on the wall of the farmhouse three hundred years in the future and then of Lope they had all met from the future. "It all makes so much sense. It was Lope's destiny to further our family's survival. Like Will, he is one of the forefathers of this family. I knew there was something about him when we met and became the best of friends. He knows that his tribe has a purpose and that one day I will meet his tribe and now he knows that Miguel is one of his own people. I want to see him. I want my family to see this man who was brave enough to go out on his own. He left his world behind and trusted his guides. I think our guide, God, wrote all this in his plans."

"That was lovely Jillie," Jake said. "We'll leave at five. Try and get some sleep."

"Not sure I'll sleep tonight," Jillie replied. "Miguel, will you help me pack some things for Anna Grace now?"

"I'm glad you thought of that. I sure didn't."

Four o'clock came quickly and everyone was up with the excitement of seeing Running Antelope and the big celebration. At five, everyone gathered inside the old farmhouse. Lacey and Jillie were going over anything else they may need for their two little ones. Wayne was so excited, as his father didn't let him go back as much as he wanted. The back porch door slammed shut and everyone stopped dead in their tracks. Who could be coming into the house at this hour?!

"I saw the lights on up here. Glad I decided to climb up into the barn," Lope said, as he walked towards the kitchen.

"LOPE!" Nadia yelled. "What timing you have. We're just heading back to the village. A huge celebration…"

Jake interrupted Nadia. "We don't have time now. You can tell him everything on our journey to the village. Will, we'll need to take some horses. Four are waiting for us near the cave."

"I'm on it," Will said, as he headed out to the barn. "All men on board," Will called out for help. Miguel, Oneson, Twoson and Lope took off.

Nadia laughed. "We need to think of something to say when we're addressing our Lopes. I think we should call Running Antelope, First Lope. And, we should call Lope from the future, Second Lope."

"Duly noted," Jake commented. "Let's head to the barn. We'll all go through the pastures with the horses."

Tye, Tess, Tea and their mother romped all around them as they made their way to the big oak. From out of the darkness, a black wolf appeared and in seconds Kai was running along his feline best friends.

***

When they arrived three hundred years in the past, the morning light was on its way. The cats turned into the beastly forms. This was a time of unrest in many areas of the United States. Nadia gave the orders. Tess and Tea took off scouting the trail that lay in front of them. Lope and Nadia led the troop and Nadia filled him in on all the excitement of Running Antelope's return. Nadia also called out with cries that sounded just like a tiger, a panther, a cougar and a lion. Within seconds, cries were heard in reply. Lacey and Jillie, who were next in the procession, looked at one another and smiled. It was amazing how their cousin could communicate with animals of all kinds. The toddlers were in the care of their dads, who were behind their wives. Wayne and his two older cousins were behind Will and Miguel and Jake brought up the rear. Tye and Miss Virginia were commanded to stay with the family. They circled all around sniffing the air for any unforeseen trouble. Kai, in his wolf form, ran all around sniffing for danger. Once they reached the edge of the woods that was not far from their village, Jake called out a shriek to alert everyone of their arrival. Son of Running Deer's calls were heard in return. It was safe to continue and they moved at a faster pace.

Many people were waiting to welcome their loved ones. Two older women immediately took the babies from their dads' arms. Lacey and Jillie handed over their diaper bags full of stuff. The women laughed and had a couple of teen girls bring the bags along. Wayne took off when some of his friends his own age came to get him. They had their famous game that all the young boys played way into young adulthood. Beautiful Light came to welcome her nieces again and Jake let her know Jillie had shared her news. Beautiful Light whispered her confirmation to Jillie that she was certain Jillie was going to have twins. Jillie told Miguel and he fell to the ground acting like he had fainted.

As everyone around laughed, the man Jillie had not seen in many years walked through the crowd. He saw Miguel lying on the ground and offered his hand to help him up. He spoke to him in native tongue. Miguel told him of the news of twins. Lope gave Miguel a huge hug and blessed his children. Then, he turned his eyes onto Jillie. He held out his hand to his dear childhood friend. Tears of joy streamed down Jillie's cheeks. Lope pulled her in tight and hugged her. Then he pushed her at arms' length. "Our destinies have brought us wonderful lives that will be intertwined forever."

Jillie nodded and wiped away her tears. "I wish I could have met Shining Star."

Lope smiled, as he thought of his wonderful wife. "Her father is very ill and we are expecting too. We are catching up with you. We are pretty sure we are having three." Lope held up three fingers.

Jillie hugged her Lope one more time and then allowed everyone else to congratulate him. Then, Nadia pulled Second Lope along and brought him in front of Running Antelope.

"Chief Running Antelope's Wolf, I would like to introduce you to Lope. He is one of your very own descendants that traveled six hundred years in the past to meet you and help us with the three strangers that have threatened our land."

Running Antelope stared into the young man's

eyes. He looked at Nadia. "Please tell him that I am proud to meet him."

Lope cleared his throat. He had been taking lessons from Oneson and Twoson. "Dear Great-Grandfather, I am most honored."

Running Antelope smiled and hugged in this young man that was not much younger than him. "I would like to talk with you more." Then, Running Antelope stopped and looked at Lacey, Jillie and Nadia. "One of you will be linked to me?"

Lacey and Jillie held their breaths. They knew it was Nadia, but they didn't want to ruin it for her. They didn't know she had already figured it out, but she didn't know who it was she would marry that would lead to Lope. Miguel Lope Letour was the farthest person from her mind.

"It is me Running Antelope," Nadia replied. "My destiny will be leading me to someone that is your descendant. I'm guessing I will be meeting my dream man in the future."

Lacey looked at Nadia. "Nadia, how do you know that?"

"Lope kind of gave it away once not too long ago. He started to call me grandmother, but I heard it before he caught himself. It's okay. If I have someone like Lope as my descendant, then it means I did something right."

Second Lope hugged Nadia. "That's so sweet Grandmother."

Everyone laughed again.

"Right here, right now, my grandson is older than me!" Nadia commented and the laughter grew even louder.

"Let's plan a celebration!" Jake called out.

The day was busy with cooking, chattering and gaming. And Nadia, she was in the midst of it all. She went around checking to see that everything was just the way it should be for this special occasion.

At four o'clock, the true celebration began with words from Chief Fierce Tiger, Chief Charging Bull, Jake, Sir Edward Miller and then Chief Running Antelope's Wolf. Lacey caught up with her in-laws. Jillie got to share her joy with their village family and enjoy this precious moment with her Lope, a chief. Nadia made her rounds to everyone. Their three new friends, and now second Lope's alliances, took oaths to help Lope establish the most wonderful gift to everyone. They were going to put together the legend of this very land in a documentary that would tell the world how family crossed time to save the land from abuse and destruction. They were going to help mark the entire farm as an historical site. No one could ever sell it off. It would remain in the family and untouched by needless communities. As the celebration came to its sad, but happy end, Nadia asked the chief for permission to speak. He granted it with a huge smile.

"I'm not exactly sure what the future holds for me. But, I want to say how truly blessed I am to be here at such a magical moment in time. A magical moment in time when we have all been brought together that we will never experience again. My life will be dedicated, as my cousins have already dedicated their lives, to keeping this land alive with joy and family." Nadia held her hands up to the sky and raised her left foot to her right knee. "To my family from the past, in my present and way into the future, I ask God to bless the magic and the mystery to never end."

"The Magical Cats"

Written by–
GK (Laura Beth's sister-in-law)

There once were two girls that found a cat.
The cat had two kittens that they found in a house.
The girls loved the cats and name them Tess and Tye.
They seemed to disappear, but where and why?

Chorus:
But, the cats came back. They would not stay away.
They came right back to the house everyday.
The cats came back; they just wanted to play.
They lead the girls to a land far away.

The girls found tunnels under the house.
The mother cat led them as quiet as a mouse.
The tunnels lead them back to a land long ago.
They found a lost uncle they didn't even know.

(Chorus)

The house and the cats are very magical.
Come join the two girls for adventure and fun.
The cats will lead you to a different time and place.
So hurry and come follow them before it's too late.

(Chorus)